PRAISE FOR DOOMSDAY MATCH

"A fast-paced and enthralling thriller that blends ancient history, magic, and action. Once I started this book, I couldn't stop—and loved every single scene. A masterpiece of story and setting. Highly recommend!"

—*New York Times* bestselling author A. R. Torre

"Fans of James Rollins and Dan Brown will love this stunning new thriller from Jeff Wheeler. Doomsday Match is utterly engrossing, a dark and complex tale filled with ancient secrets, adventure, and betrayal. You won't be able to put it down."

—#1 *Wall Street Journal* bestselling author Melinda Leigh

"Jeff Wheeler knocks it out of the park with his supercharged thriller Doomsday Match. From the very first scene, you know you're in for an incredible thrill ride full of constant danger and relentless twists—set against a jaw-dropping conspiracy background. Just when you think you've figured out Wheeler's game, he artfully rips the rug out from under the reader, shaking up the plot. If you're a fan of fast-paced, devious conspiracies with a little more than a touch of magic and mysticism, Doomsday Match is for you!"

—*Wall Street Journal* bestselling author Steven Konkoly

"The sheer readability and suspense works so well that readers will race through those pages to see what will happen next!"

—TJ Mackay, Founder and Publisher of *InD'tale Magazine*

JAGUAR
PROPHECIES

The Kingfountain Series

The Legends of Muirwood Trilogy

The Covenant of Muirwood Trilogy

Whispers from Mirrowen Trilogy

Landmoor Series

Other Works

Your First Million Words

Tales from Kingfountain, Muirwood, and Beyond: The Worlds of Jeff Wheeler

In the Twilight Kingdom: A Legends of Muirwood Tale

JAGUAR PROPHECIES

JEFF WHEELER

Text copyright © 2023 by Jeff Wheeler
All rights reserved.

Published by 47North, Seattle

www.apub.com

Amazon, the Amazon logo, and 47North are trademarks of Amazon.com, Inc., or its affiliates.

ISBN-13: 9781662505560 (paperback)
ISBN-13: 9781662505577 (digital)

Cover design by Shasti O'Leary Soudant
Cover image: © Natural History Archive / Alamy Stock Photo;
© Checubus / Shutterstock; © Prachaya Roekdeethaweesab / Shutterstock

Printed in the United States of America

To Cami

CONTENT NOTE

This novel contains fictionalized violence occurring in a public school after school hours, which some readers may be sensitive to. This type of violence is a reality that unfortunately happens too often in our communities and impacts too many of our children.

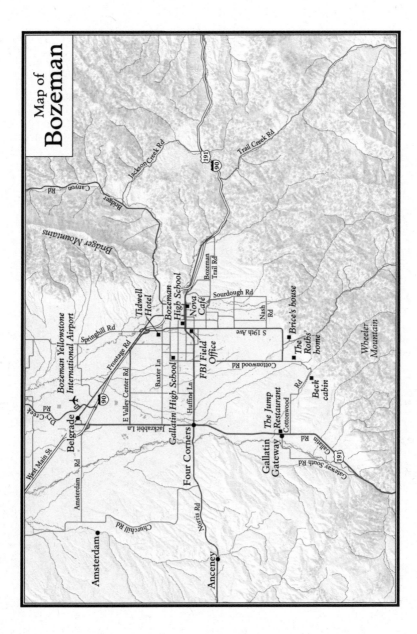

CHAPTER ONE

Villa Sara de Calakmul

Cozumel, Mexico

December 23

There they go to die.

From the glass wall of windows in his office, Jacob Calakmul watched the yacht as it left the resort for a day-long snorkeling trip off the coast of Cozumel. The two families would not be returning. By week's end, if not sooner, one of the families would be dead.

Jacob removed his glasses and rubbed the bridge of his nose. Memories from the previous year recalled themselves. He was not a man often surprised, but last year's contestants in the game *had* surprised him. Shocked him even.

He thought of Mr. Roth often. In fact, the author's new fantasy novel was coming out in early January. Jacob had arranged to have a copy stolen from the author's computer. An underling, a not-so-secret fan of the author's work, had been assigned to read it to make sure nothing incriminating had been added to the book after the Roths' journey to the Yucatán Peninsula.

Nothing.

The book had been finished the year before, and nothing objectionable had been added to it during the editing process.

Nothing revealing the devastation the author had felt after leaving his wife behind in Mexico. She was being held hostage at the hidden Jaguar Temple in the Calakmul reserve to ensure Mr. Roth's silence. Everything Mr. Roth had told the public matched Jacob's orders perfectly. The public story was that Roth's wife, Sarina, was in a diabetic coma in an advanced research facility in Singapore. That's what he'd told her parents. His fans. Angélica had provided him with phony but convincing video footage and photographs of a woman with Sarina's face in a hospital bed with tubes and masks and equipment. And she'd brought Sarina's family on a fake video tour of the facility to make the story more convincing, assuring them in Spanish that everything possible was being done to care for their daughter.

They were watching the author carefully, of course, tuning in to each of his live streams, whether it was him talking or him playing video games online for his fans. Reading his blogs. He'd said that he was taking an indefinite hiatus from writing. The book coming out might be his last. He had not even hinted, in speech or writing, at what had happened to the Roth family during their trip to Mexico.

It was the eve of the one-year anniversary of Sarina's captivity—of Mr. Roth's realization that life was not as he'd always believed it to be and that certain events had been set into motion that would ultimately overthrow the world's political, financial, and social order. So it felt like less of a coincidence that he would be spending this Christmas in Germany, the same country where the Dresden Codex was stored in a museum, available for viewing by the public.

Jacob didn't like coincidences. He didn't much believe in them.

The door to the office opened, and Jacob's personal assistant, Angélica, entered. She offered a confident smile.

"The families are gone?" he asked her.

"Yes. They're heading to the Palancar Reef first," she said, hugging her tablet to her chest. "Two other sites, depending on the crowds, and then they'll anchor off Punta Sur before sunset for ceviche and drinks."

"And they are packed for the overnight trip to Chetumal and the visit to the ancient 'ruins' tomorrow?"

One family knew what the visit truly meant. The other did not. It gave one side the advantage and made them the presumptive winners. The same had been true last year—the Beasleys had known the truth; the Roths had not—only the writer and his family had surprised them all by winning a fight they'd been chosen to lose.

"Yes. They'll be at the Calakmul reserve by tomorrow night."

"Excellent," Jacob said. "And everything is going according to plan?"

She nodded. "Yes. We will take the Pegasus jet to the reserve tomorrow afternoon to meet them. The pilot is rested and ready."

"Good. What news of the Roths? When did they arrive in Germany?"

Angélica lowered her tablet and tapped on the screen. In another day, she would stow away her modern attire and wear a wardrobe more befitting a future queen of the Maya. The makeup and glasses would be gone, replaced by ancient jewelry and the painted symbols of her ancestors. There was little technology in the Calakmul reserve. They had no need for it there, for they had access to something so much more powerful.

"They landed in Frankfurt two days ago. They're staying with Mr. Roth's sister in Wiesbaden."

Jacob frowned. "How far is it from Dresden?"

"Dresden is on the other side of the country. It was part of East Germany before the reunification."

"I know that. How far?"

"Over a five-hour drive, I should think."

Jacob picked up his glasses from the desk and turned to look at the display on the wall. There was a Maya warrior's weapon, a *macuahuitl,* suspended there, along with a rubber ball from the death games and several other relics collected and protected from various dig sites.

"Remind me of his itinerary again," he said.

Angélica was already tapping away at her tablet, having anticipated the question. "They arrived in Germany on Saturday. Over the weekend, they visited some of the tourist places in Wiesbaden, Eisenach, and Erfurt." She tapped again. "Then they went back to Wiesbaden, where he spoke and gave a class at his sister's school this morning at the US Army base there."

"Where else has he been today?"

"Only in Wiesbaden. I think tomorrow they're going south to Karlsruhe to see family."

Jacob nodded. "Erfurt is much closer to Dresden. Could they have made a trip there without us knowing?"

"We have tracking on their phones," Angélica said. "They've followed their itinerary. Trips to old castles, shopping malls, and historical sites. We even hacked his laptop, which he brought on the trip and from which he delivered the presentation at the sister's school."

"Our hacker accessed that network?"

"He used to work for the NSA," Angélica reminded him. "Mr. Roth has been exactly where he's supposed to be. The library where the codex is kept is also closed for the next three days for the Christmas holiday." She paused, then added, "It makes sense that they're spending Christmas away from Bozeman. There'd be a lot of difficult memories for them, with Sarina still away from home. He's done nothing to incur your distrust, Jacob. He wouldn't risk his children's lives."

Jacob believed that was true. Mr. Roth clearly cared for his kids. The family had grown even tighter since last Christmas. Jacob's people monitored the Roths' internet traffic and phone calls. He hadn't gone to the press or law enforcement to report what had happened to them. He'd done exactly as Jacob had insisted. And yet . . .

"I don't like thinking he might have access to the Jaguar Prophecies," he said, giving her a knowing look. "The codex in Dresden is on display to the public."

"There are other Maya codices that were sent by Cortés," she said reasonably. "Not just the one found in Dresden. He can't *read* it. He doesn't know it's important."

"What about his daughter? The magic works for her." Suki had won the death game for her family when she'd tapped into the ancient magic and sent the ball into orbit within the arena. None of the other families who'd been brought to the Jaguar Temple had been able to manage it. She was special, and someday she could be of use. So long as she didn't use her abilities to help her father step out of line.

"She's a teenager at a high school in Bozeman. Not a scholar of ancient hieroglyphics."

Jacob sighed and wiped his mouth. A nagging doubt itched in his mind. One he couldn't scratch. "Before we fly to the Jaguar Temple, have a jaguar priest in Europe go to Dresden. I want that university museum under surveillance until the Roths go back to Montana. I don't trust him."

"The library is *closed*."

Jacob sighed. When he gave orders, he expected obedience.

"He'd be the world's greatest fool if he went up against you," Angélica added, coming closer and stroking his arm.

"Even so, do it. If he comes anywhere near the codex, I want someone there to warn him off."

"Very well. I'll see who is available." She tapped the screen and then nodded. "Anything else?"

He thought about the cruise ship at the harbor at San Miguel. The one with the plague glyph hidden aboard. "When does the *Oasis* leave?"

"Tonight. It's bound for Europe. The plague will start there. The passengers are predominantly from the UK, Spain, and several Nordic countries. The sickness will start spreading in Europe first, but there are also plenty of Asian tourists on board."

Jacob smiled knowingly. The infection would spread to anyone who had not been given the protective glyph. Agents of the jaguar priests had been preparing for this moment, giving protection to the winners of the games and other elite who'd paid for that privilege. But Jacob had deliberately withheld it from the Roths, wanting to see how the author would react after word of the disease had begun to spread. "It will take some time before the World Health Organization can figure out that some are immune."

"And the outbreak in Asia will draw attention away from us," she agreed.

"This is the next step in the fulfillment of the prophecy," Jacob said excitedly. "We will reclaim what is ours through pestilence, drought, and war, which Kukulkán prophesied to our ancestors. The ancient magic of Aztlán shall be ours to command."

She gave him an intrigued smile. "You've never told me where Aztlán is. Will you share that knowledge someday? It's worth more than gold or oil."

"Only after I've made you my queen. My equal. We must fulfill the prophecy first. What was once our people's will be ours again." Their relationship had progressed over the last year. Her value to him as an employee had gotten tangled with his desire for her, setting his sights higher. Maybe he'd always intended for it to end that way.

"How will you start the war?" she asked him.

"The world is in turmoil," he said, pleased she'd asked, even though they'd had this conversation before. She knew how much he enjoyed the recitation of what was to come. "They will turn against each other when people begin to die. And then I will come, just as Cortés did. With a smile on my face, leaving blood and fury in my wake."

CHAPTER TWO

Saxon State and University Library

Dresden, Germany

December 24

"This is the exit," Tawna said, checking both ways to watch for traffic. Driving the autobahn was more intense than Roth had imagined, but his sister was used to it after fifteen years in Germany. As her VW Tiguan took the exit to Dresden, Roth felt more stress bubbling in his chest. This was it. This was the moment that could sink them.

"I think I need to *Ausfahrt* again," Lucas said with mock strain in his voice. A farting noise came from the back seat.

"Dude, if you *really* fart this time, you're riding home in the trunk," Suki said, more than done with her brother's favorite joke.

It had started at the airport, when Tawna had picked them up and Roth had asked where to find the exit. She'd explained the word "exit" in Germany was phonetically related to a certain biological function, and the twins hadn't stopped making jokes about it since.

He turned his head and looked at the back seat. The Tiguan was a little cramped for all five of them, but Roth had the roomy passenger seat and was grateful he wasn't smooshed in the back with the three teenagers, shoulder to shoulder. Suki, the biggest introvert in the family, was leaning against her door and window so hard he wondered if she would have preferred to ride in the trunk. Her hair was cropped in a very short pixie cut, and she'd taken to wearing T-shirts with slogans lately. The one she wore on this trip was black with a gold square and the National Sarcasm Society logo on it with a tongue-in-cheek slogan underneath—"Like we need your support."

"When are we stopping for lunch?" Brillante asked. He was always hungry. Both of the twins were. They'd grown so much over the past year, and Sarina hadn't seen it. She probably never would.

"After the library," he answered, shifting to face the front. He got motion sickness easily and already felt a churning in his stomach from turning in his seat.

"What's the library called again? The Slum?" Lucas asked.

"The SLUB," Suki reminded him. "Kind of like 'slug bug.'"

Roth smiled. The traffic off the exit was pretty heavy, and he helped his sister watch for oncoming cars. It was Christmas Eve, so some of the traffic was probably from people doing last-minute shopping.

Tawna, who had as much interest in accumulating facts as Roth, couldn't miss the opportunity to share her knowledge. "It's short for Sächsische Landesbibliothek—Staats—und Universitätsbibliothek Dresden."

"Why are all German words so long?" Lucas asked.

"It's a very precise language," Tawna said. "What do you want for lunch after we visit the library? Do you want to try the schnitzel from this part of Germany?"

"Schnitzel is awesome," Brillante said, and Roth had to smile. He was probably rubbing his belly as he said it.

"I'd rather have another warm pretzel," Suki said.

"Why not both?" Brillante countered.

The kids had enjoyed the trip so far, although all of them felt the absence of Sarina—it was as if there was always an empty seat. He hated not knowing whether she was alive. Because even though he knew he was being watched, he'd had no communication from Calakmul or his people at all. No photographs of his wife, whom they'd had no choice but to leave behind after she fell into a diabetic coma. No updates on her health. Not even any additional threats.

Over fifty million dollars had been transferred into his bank account after they'd returned home to Bozeman. No audit from the IRS had followed. That money was theirs to spend any way they'd like because they'd defeated another family, the Beasleys, at the death game. But if Jacob Calakmul had believed money and the promise of power would shut him down, then he didn't know who he was dealing with. Roth was bent on unmasking and stopping Calakmul and the massive conspiracy he was leading. If not for Calakmul, Sarina would be with them. She would be well.

And then there was the little girl they'd left behind to die. Not a single night went by when he didn't think of the look on Jane Louise Beasley's face as he walked away from her. Death was the cost of losing the death game, no matter how old or young the player, and the only way he'd been able to protect his own kids was by turning his back on her.

The memories made him grit his teeth and squeeze the armrest. He hadn't told the kids why they were *really* in Germany. Sure, they'd gone sightseeing. His sister, although heavyset like him, was a hiker. They'd climbed up a steep hill to Wartburg Castle near the town of Eisenach just the other day. The Wartburg was famous for many reasons, including that Martin Luther had hidden there to save his life after being excommunicated.

Roth and Tawna both loved history, and while the kids had complained about climbing up and down narrow steps inside the castle, they'd all enjoyed the experience.

But Roth had spent the whole day feeling the weight of what was to come. Of what he had planned for today. Because he had come to Germany specifically for this side trip to Dresden. It was here he hoped to find what he needed to bring down Jacob Calakmul.

Roth had left all their phones and his laptop back at Tawna's place in Wiesbaden so it would *appear* they were still on that side of the country. His burner phone, which he was fairly certain Jacob didn't know about, was nestled in his pocket.

The GPS on Tawna's vehicle continued to guide them down the streets until they arrived at the university. The SLUB was part of Dresden University of Technology.

"Here we are," Tawna said, parking in one of the many open spaces. The school was on break for the holidays, so there weren't many students around.

Roth eased his way out of the car and stretched. They'd been in the car for five hours. In the US, a trip of the same distance would have taken longer, but there was no speed limit on much of the German autobahn, and Tawna was a pretty aggressive driver.

Suki pushed her glasses up her nose and then gave Roth a smile. He felt a stab of pain and regret in his gut. She looked more like Sarina every day. "So what's in this library you wanted to see?" she asked.

"A piece of history," he responded. He'd kept his research private. The kids were all struggling after what had happened in Mexico, even more so because they'd had to leave their mother behind. All of them were seeing the same therapist, a wonderful woman named Creshel. She'd helped all of them process the trauma of what they'd been through. Of course she didn't know what had truly happened in Cozumel. They'd shared the same cover story with her that they'd provided to everyone— they'd been involved in a terrible "accident" that had stranded them in the jungle, and Sarina had become sick after being deprived of insulin for too long. The Beasleys' accident had made the news, but there was no mention of the Roths in any of those stories. Roth suspected that omission had something to do with Jacob Calakmul's long reach.

They walked together across the parking lot and followed the signs toward the SLUB. A few college students were strolling through campus, speaking in German. The atmosphere reminded Roth of his time as an adjunct professor in California, before his books had shot up the *New York Times* bestseller list. Before they'd moved to Bozeman, Montana—a choice he now regretted since it had brought them into contact with the Beasleys, the family that had tricked them into going to Calakmul's resort last year.

The weather was surprisingly mild for December. Tawna had told them before they'd left home that there would only be snow in the high mountains, none where they'd be going. Some days had been overcast, like this one, but it was pleasant.

"When you go to college, can I have your room?" Lucas asked Suki.

"Why do you want my room?" she responded, wrinkling her nose.

"Because I've always had to share with Brillante."

"Where am I going to sleep when I come home?" she asked him. "You really want me out of the house already?"

"No! It's not that. It's just . . . sorry. Now I feel bad."

She tousled his curly hair. "I won't be far away, Little Bro."

"I'm glad you're going to Montana State."

"Me too," she said, reaching over and tousling his curly hair again, just to annoy him, and he swatted her away.

Roth watched the two of them banter and felt another pang of grief. Sarina was missing so much. Their oldest was growing up so fast. Suki was a senior this year, and after graduation, she'd go to MSU and live in an apartment by herself. Being an introvert, she needed her alone time. The twins were already freshmen in high school, which meant they'd move out too in a few years, a thought that absolutely terrified Roth. That was, of course, if the world as they knew it didn't end before then. It was Roth's determination that it wouldn't.

"So where's the SLUB?" Brillante asked with a bored yawn.

"We're almost there," Roth said. After walking through campus awhile, they arrived at a row of old rectangular buildings with lots of windows. Nothing stood out, but Roth had seen images of the SLUB online and knew what they were looking for.

"So this is research for a new series you're writing?" Tawna asked. "I thought you were on hiatus from writing? In that statement you put out, you made it sound like you were quitting forever. But I didn't believe it for a second. And Sarina never would have wanted you to give up telling stories."

"Actually, I've been writing quite a bit," he confided, but he left it at that.

"Your readers will be pleased to hear it. From the way they carried on in the comments, it was as if you didn't have a book coming out next month." She gave him a thoughtful look. "How come it takes so long to publish anyway? I don't think I've ever asked."

"Edits, cover art, audiobook . . . there are a lot of moving pieces," Roth explained with a shrug. "Some writers can put out several books a year, but I can't."

Except for the book he'd written after coming back from Mexico. He'd poured that one out in three months. He'd never written so much so quickly before. The pain, the grief, the anger had gushed from his soul. The kids didn't know about that book. Not even his publisher knew about it. In fact, he knew he was violating his publishing contract by not telling them about it or offering it to them since they had the right of first refusal for his next work.

Partway down the long walkway, another section of the campus opened up, and he recognized it from the pictures online.

"That way," Roth said, pointing.

At the far end of campus was a little greenbelt with some newer buildings. Both were tall rectangular structures made of gray concrete squares that varied slightly in color, making the buildings look like puzzles that hadn't been put together correctly. There were windows on the faces and sides, but not in symmetrical rows—they were vertical slats spaced intermittently in some random scheme. There appeared to be five levels to the building.

"Looks like someone built it using *Minecraft*," Brillante said.

Roth laughed. "You're right."

He knew the building containing the Dresden Codex was the farther one. His stomach was starting to dance with anticipation. For the last year, he'd been meticulous in disguising his internet searches, using public libraries and the local Starbucks instead of his own home. Using devices he'd purchased in cash *after* the trip to the Yucatán, since he believed his home network and computer had already been compromised. He'd been an early investor in Pandora, which was more privacy oriented and harder to track than Bitcoin, and the funds had grown sizably over the years. So he'd tapped into them to purchase the things he needed without creating a trail. Each day he wore a digital mask to hide from the henchmen of Jacob Calakmul, and he'd researched new ways to make himself invisible using the dark web.

The trip he'd planned with Tawna had all been arranged through his home equipment. He suspected that Angélica was fully aware of the itinerary thus far, down to where they'd gone on which days. But he also knew the death game was probably starting at the arena today, meaning Jacob would be cut off from easy communication with his resort on Cozumel.

That's why he'd saved visiting Dresden for Christmas Eve. The timing made him hope Calakmul's attention would be elsewhere.

"Um, Dad, it's closed," Brillante said, pointing. A student was standing at the doors of the weird building, pulling on the handle and looking through the glass. He walked away after unsuccessfully trying to enter.

"Oh, I hadn't thought of that," Tawna said. "The SLUB might be closed today since it's Christmas Eve. I'm sorry, I should have looked that up."

"It's okay," Roth said. "I made arrangements with one of the librarians for a private tour."

Suki gave him a sharp look. Her suspicions were now aroused.

Roth pulled out his burner phone and opened it with a passcode, not facial ID. Only he knew the number. Only he could unlock it. He tapped on the contact and started the call. It rang twice.

"Is that you, Mr. Roth?" answered a voice with a German accent.

"We've arrived," Roth said. "Thanks for doing this for us."

"It's my pleasure, Mr. Roth. It's not every day a world-famous author visits. Welcome to Dresden! I'm glad you finally get to see the codex in person."

"Thanks for all your help with my research, Dominik," Roth said. "See you soon."

He ended the call and took a deep breath.

"Dad?" Suki asked worriedly.

Roth marched toward the front doors of the SLUB. This was where his feelings of anger and revenge had brought him. He hoped he was right. He was *sure* he was right. The prophecy of the jaguar priests was inside this building.

Waiting for him to find it.

CHAPTER THREE

Saxon State and University Library

Dresden, Germany

December 24

The pictures of the SLUB off the internet didn't do it justice. The first floor had been renovated not long ago and had obviously been designed for college students in the modern age. The stacks were built around the perimeter of the floor, and rows of polished-wood study desks had been arranged in the middle, beneath an enormous vaulted ceiling, glowing with light that seemed natural. No students were present, though, and a slightly antiseptic smell from a recent cleaning lingered in the air.

Roth gazed at the beautiful space, mentally comparing it to the staid library at the university where he'd been both a student and a lecturer. There the dusty smell of old books had always permeated the air.

"Have you all enjoyed the trip so far?" asked Dominik Stoltz, who had met them at the doors and unlocked them. He had a strong German accent but was very fluent in English. Roth had been networking with him for nearly a year during his off-the-grid research, using one of several different Gmail accounts he'd created for the purpose. Dominik was probably in his early thirties, with short-cropped hair tinged with green dye. He was one of the staff librarians at the SLUB and incredibly knowledgeable about the history of the codex.

Under normal circumstances, Suki would have been entranced by all the books, but she kept eyeing Dominik and then her dad with narrowed eyes and a frown of concern.

"I liked the castles better," Lucas said, yawning.

"Do you have a favorite?" Dominik inquired.

"The wart one," Lucas said. "Wartburg. It was pretty epic."

"Are there any soccer teams in Dresden?" Brillante asked. The twins' enthusiasm for soccer hadn't waned after the death game last Christmas. If anything, they'd become more focused and driven. More intent on gaining skill.

"We have one team, yes. The Dynamo."

"Can we see a game, Dad?" Brillante asked.

"No," he answered, "we need to head back to Wiesbaden this afternoon."

"Did your father tell you much about the Dresden Codex and how it came to be here?" Dominik asked, glancing at them as he led them into the lobby and shut—and locked—the door behind them.

"Actually, he said nothing about it *at all*," Suki said, giving Roth a probing look and speaking in a tone that implied she thought something was very sus.

"It's a fascinating story, actually." Dominik went on, seemingly oblivious to the suspicion in her voice.

"And the codex is kept downstairs?" Roth asked.

"Yes, this way." Dominik guided them to the staircase leading down. "Only a few codices from the ancient Maya survive to this day. Most were burned by the Spanish. They were made of bark, and while it's more hearty than paper, it's still prone to damage. The Maya codices were written centuries ago. Some before Cortés arrived at the island of Cozumel."

Brillante and Lucas exchanged a look. One of them swallowed. The other began fidgeting.

Dominik noticed. "Have you been?"

"Once," Lucas said, his voice a little shaky.

Suki was glaring at Roth now, silently accusing him of holding out on them. He had. The few times they'd asked him what he intended to do about Jacob Calakmul, he'd been deliberately evasive. He'd told them that he doubted Calakmul could prevail against the power of the US government. What could he do, anyway, as a private citizen? He didn't want them knowing that he *was* doing something about it. Knowing too much could get them hurt or killed too.

Like Sarina.

He clenched his teeth, feeling sweat start to prickle across his back as their host led them down the stairs. "Most of the codices were destroyed, but a few were sent to Europe. There's one in Paris, one in Madrid. One in New York City, the Grolier, until it was confiscated by the Mexican government. And then there's this one in Dresden. It was nearly destroyed during World War II."

"Hitler wanted to burn it too?" Suki asked.

Dominik shook his head as he continued down the stairs. "Not exactly. The city of Dresden was bombed by the Allies. It was in a museum basement, protected in a vault. Nearly every building in the city was destroyed, but the vault was preserved. Unfortunately, the bombs cracked the walls and ground water invaded the chamber." They reached the bottom, and he opened the door, leading them out into a carpeted hall. "The codex was encased in glass to protect it while on display. Many of the artifacts in the vault were irrevocably damaged by the flooding, but the codex was protected by the glass. Mostly. One seam failed, and water got in. That caused the bark to swell."

"But the swelling also prevented more water from seeping in," Roth said. He already knew the story. "They carefully took the Dresden Codex away from the site and brought it to a castle outside of town to dry out. That helped, but the humidity at the time made the wood swell. Some of it pressed so hard against the glass that the chalk coating from the codex adhered to the surface."

"Indeed so," Dominik said. "You can imagine the worry. This all happened in the 1940s. We've kept it protected since. It was moved to this library to be on permanent display. This way, please."

Dominik brought them into a display room, which was solemn and dimly lit. A few books were hung from the walls in display cases, illuminated by little LED lights. But the Dresden Codex, held in an enormous glass display case, eight feet long and three feet wide, was the prominent feature. The codex was laid out before them section by section, the pieces framed by wood and the entirety sheathed in glass. It was arranged in two rows.

"Whoa," Brillante said, coming up to the display case.

He was about to press his hands on the glass, but Dominik took a step toward it, as if to bodily shield the priceless document, and said, "Please don't touch."

"This is cool," Lucas said, approaching next. The brothers stared in wonder at the little hieroglyphs painted into the wooden slats.

Suki stepped closer too, studying the glyphs with a thoughtful expression. "It's more colorful than I would have thought."

"Indeed," replied Dominik. "Black, green, yellow, blue. All very specific colors chosen by the Maya artisans."

The boys were surprisingly quiet, studying several pages before looking at each other and then at Roth. That they'd been stunned speechless said a lot.

"There are seventy-eight pages," Dominik continued. "Both sides, you see. If you look down, you can see the reverse side through the mirror."

"Oh," Suki said, walking down the row. She went to the other side and then suddenly stopped. Her gaze lifted. Her eyes locked with Roth's.

"You said some of the pages were blank," Roth said, shifting his attention back to the librarian. "They're on the bottom?"

"Yes, there were four blank sheafs. One, we presume, was the final page of the codex. We have them spread out, but in their original form they were all folded, you see. So that one you'd expect to be blank. But the other three, curiously, were also blank."

"It's not arranged in the original order of the codex, correct?" Roth said. Suki was staring at him hard now. She looked not just concerned. She looked frightened.

"How did they paint these so small?" Tawna asked, clearly fascinated by the display. Since she hadn't been with them on vacation the previous year, she had no reason for suspicion. "Such detail! This is from the fifteenth century?"

"Older," Dominik said. "It was brought to Europe in the fifteenth century. It's one of the oldest surviving original documents made by the Maya."

"Has anyone translated it?" Tawna asked.

"Oh yes! Well, the scholars have done the best they can. There is still a lot about the language that hasn't been deciphered. But this one is like an almanac. It contains a calendar with future projections."

"How far into the future did it go?" Tawna wanted to know.

"It predicts eclipses into the year AD 2065. Impressive, isn't it?"

Brillante leaned forward, gazing closely at one of the sheets with a glint of speculation in his eyes. "What does this all mean? Does anyone know what it says?"

"Scholars have translated quite a bit of it, actually. Look over here," Dominik said to the boys, pointing to a particular section but keeping his finger well away from the glass. "This rune depicts a solar eclipse. They knew the stars and the planet rotations. They correctly predicted solar and lunar eclipses."

Brillante and Lucas exchanged another look, and Roth felt guilty for making them so nervous. But if he didn't do anything, if he stood by and let Calakmul destroy the world, he'd be an even worse parent.

"How'd they know all that?" Tawna asked, tearing Roth back to the present moment.

"The Maya were astute observers of the universe. They had a calendar system that tracked thousands of years. From the creation of the world, actually."

"You said the calendar went to 2065. Didn't they predict the end of the world would be in 2012?" she asked.

Dominik sighed. "A common misperception."

"The year 2012 marked the end of a long cycle," Roth said to her, "and the beginning of another, but it was *so* long that people figured it meant something bigger. Five thousand years." He looked over at Suki, who was growing very agitated. Her breaths were coming fast, and he could see her trembling. Was she having a panic attack?

Maybe he should have warned her. Maybe—

"You are right, Mr. Roth. It was not the end times as the media portrayed."

Roth walked around to where Suki was standing.

"What's wrong?" he whispered.

"Dad," she whispered back. "The blank ones are *glowing*."

Excitement began to rattle inside his chest. He had learned everything he could about the four codices. He'd read translations of them from various eminent scholars. He'd even used his secret e-mail account to contact some of the professors who'd studied them. Most of the translations were surprisingly bland, legends interwoven with abstract calendar predictions for harvesting crops. Kind of like an almanac, as Dominik had said. But what had intrigued Roth most, something he'd learned from a retired professor from Tulane University, was the existence of those "blank" pages in the Dresden Codex. There was nothing on them. She had theorized they'd been saved for future predictions that hadn't been written down because of the Spanish conquest.

Roth suspected otherwise, and his daughter had just confirmed his suspicion.

Suki had special abilities. While on the run from Jacob Calakmul in the jungle in Cozumel, they'd happened upon an underground cavern, hidden within a pyramid, filled with ancient Maya treasure. Suki had seen something glowing within the treasure—a bracelet that she'd claimed. That bracelet, along with a ring Sarina had given her, a family relic, had helped her access a power that Roth didn't fully understand—a power that Angélica had called the *kem äm*, the Mayan word for "spiderweb." He only knew it had allowed them, against all odds, to win the death game last Christmas. Since Sarina had seen the glow, too, he knew it had to be a hereditary power, something to do with Sarina's Maya background.

He could hear Dominik and Tawna talking in low voices as they discussed different features of the codex as seen from above. But looking at the mirror situated beneath the display case, Roth could see the images on the other side, including the blank surfaces that Suki was standing near.

A chirp from a cell phone interrupted them. It wasn't his burner phone. Dominik pulled out his phone, looked at the screen, and answered the call, walking away from the display case.

"You knew this was here?" Suki demanded of Roth in an intense whisper.

"I knew the codex was here, sure. That much is on Wikipedia."

"When have you—?"

"Shhh," he said, shaking his head. "We'll talk about it later."

She'd clenched her hands into fists. Her breathing was coming faster and faster. Her anxiety was spiraling into a panic attack.

"Breathe," he whispered. "Just breathe."

He was so close to finding what he sought. The anticipation left a coppery taste in his mouth.

"Look, boys, look at that one!" Tawna said. "What a strange little guy!" She'd been observing Roth and Suki and could tell something was wrong, so she was distracting the boys' attention.

"*Ja. Ja. Ich werde.*" Dominik ended the call.

"Just breathe," Roth repeated, putting his arm around Suki.

"I have to go," Dominik said. "There's a man at the library doors, banging on them. Security spoke with him, and he says he left something in here. I have to go check the lost and found. I'll come back soon."

Roth felt a jolt of unease. Was it a student? Was it really?

"We'll be right here," Roth said reassuringly. He'd actually been hoping that Dominik would let them stay down there awhile without interruption. But something nagged at Roth's mind. Jacob's threat to keep secret what had happened to them. He was suspicious by nature, and their trip to Cozumel had only heightened it. It was probably his superpower.

"Try not to touch the glass," Dominik said before hurrying away at a brisk walk.

"What's wrong?" Lucas asked. He was pretty sensitive. He came around the case and touched Suki's arm in a comforting gesture.

Suki was pale. Trembling.

"The blank one. Focus on it," Roth said to Suki. "I think it's trying to reveal something."

"What are you looking at over there?" Tawna asked, but Roth held up his hand.

"I'm scared," Suki whispered.

"I know. But only you can do this. There's something hidden here. I know it. I think the writing is being blocked by the same power we all witnessed in Cozumel." The uncanny golden strands of magic Calakmul had referred to as the *kem äm*, which his daughter had been able to activate despite having no training. "You can do it."

Her lip was quivering. "I don't want to."

He'd wanted to warn her of what he was planning for this trip. He'd almost done so a dozen times. But the power had stopped working for Suki after they left Mexico, as if whatever had enabled her to work the magic or strange technology lay in that continent. Once they were back in Bozeman, the ring and bracelet had acted like nothing but jewelry, although she wore them every day. *She had them on now.* But he suspected her anxiety had played a big role in that. If he was right, she hadn't been able to summon the power again because she was afraid of it.

So he hadn't warned her. He'd brought her here, hoping the surprise would help activate her ability.

They were so close, so close.

Roth knew he couldn't steal the codex, not without causing an international incident, and he'd already told Dominik that he was interested in it as research for a book he was writing. Such a theft could easily be traced back to him. In fact, arranging this private viewing with Dominik had been a huge risk. Despite using an e-mail address he'd crafted for just this purpose, he'd used his real name and profession. He'd created a trail.

"Suki," Roth said. "Just try."

His daughter, still shaking, nodded. She looked down at the mirrored image of the blank codex page. She pressed her hands against the glass, even though the librarian had warned them not to.

Roth held his breath. He believed in her, even if she didn't believe in herself. If there was something there, activated by the magic, she would be able to see it. He hoped she could at least explain to him what she saw so he might be able to recreate it. That might be enough.

The boys had fallen silent, their expressions tense. Tawna looked on in confusion, but she said nothing. It was a quiet moment. A sacred moment. And they all knew it.

As Roth stared at the blank piece of wood in the mirror, it began to shimmer like the ripples of a pond disturbed by a breeze. Her ring and bracelet sprang to life, glowing dimly.

Writing appeared on some of the blank pages.

This was more than Roth had dared hope for. The full image had been revealed, and not just to Suki. He could see it too. Pulling out his phone, he rushed to take a photo of it. There was magic involved, so there was no telling whether it would show up on a photo, but he had to try.

And that's when he saw the text on his burner phone.

GET OUT OF THERE

CHAPTER FOUR

SAXON STATE AND UNIVERSITY LIBRARY

DRESDEN, GERMANY

December 24

A spike of dread pierced Roth's heart upon seeing the words on the screen. His pulse began to race, and the familiar, sickening sensation of fear twisted his stomach into knots. In an instant, he was back in Cozumel, trying to escape from Jacob Calakmul. Trying to protect his family. Watching as strangers armed with sharp weapons or guns threatened them.

"Dad?" Suki asked, her voice quavering. "What's going on?"

He clenched his jaw and summoned his outrage. His wife was either a hostage of Calakmul or already dead. If he didn't fight, millions of other people would die too. Maybe he wouldn't be able to stop that from happening, and his family might pay the price for his efforts, but he had to try. He had to fight.

Ignoring the text, he triggered his phone's camera. Even though his body was trembling from the rush of adrenaline, he steadied himself and focused on the image revealed on the previously blank page of the codex. The angle of the mirror and the lighting was good. The glyphs were probably backward, but that could be easily edited by software. He took several shots of it before moving on to the next page.

Of the four blank pages, there was writing on two and a half. The boys had come around the display case to watch what he was doing. The feelings of dread and urgency intensified. They had to leave. Fast.

He took another picture and then shot the final partial sheet.

These pages, stored on his phone, had never been translated by Western scholars. The Mayan language was so complex that, even after a year of studying glyphs, he knew he'd never be able to translate it himself.

Thankfully, he didn't have to. He had contact with a student whom he'd hired to do so.

"We need to get out of here," Roth said to Tawna. Then, looking at Suki and the boys, he added, "Let's go."

His daughter released her control of the magic, and the pages of glyphs vanished again. Tawna had been across from them on the other side of the display, so she hadn't seen the words appear or disappear. Better if she didn't know his real reason for coming here.

"I saw something glowing on Suki's hand," Tawna said with a wrinkled brow. "What's going on here?"

"We need to get out of here," Roth said, dodging her statement.

"But I thought you wanted to spend a few hours here?" his sister said in confusion.

"I got what I came for."

"And what is that exactly?" she asked, giving him a sharp look, demanding.

"I can't tell you," Roth answered.

"Why not?" Tawna demanded.

"Not now," he said, shaking his head. "Let's go."

He gestured for the kids to follow him and heard Brillante say under his breath, "I told you this trip was sus."

"No doubt," Lucas whispered back as he left the room, closing the door behind him. "I'm starting to think we shouldn't go on any more family vacations."

Their guide still hadn't returned. Nor could he be heard.

Roth climbed the steps two at a time, increasing his pace. Tawna huffed to catch up to him. "What's going on, Jonathon?" she asked in a low voice.

"Dad's been obsessed with this stuff since our trip," Suki said. "He's bought all these old books. They're stacked up in his closet."

So she'd noticed. He'd tried to be careful, knowing there was likely some sort of surveillance equipment in the house, but some of the books he'd needed were only available in print.

"Is this for the new series you're going to write?" Tawna asked.

Roth didn't want to talk. He was keenly aware of his surroundings. Of the mystery of what had become of Dominik. Of the warning that sat on his burner phone. "We need to get back to the car. Now. Come on, boys, faster."

The twins were still whispering to each other behind him. When they all got back to the main floor, Roth's heart started thumping faster when he heard a raised voice shouting in German.

Instead of crossing the study area they'd come in through, he motioned for the kids to follow him and Tawna into the maze of book-shelves. Nervous energy thrummed through him as he tried to move quickly but quietly. His vision was sharp, his breathing fast. All effects of adrenaline. He'd been dealing with PTSD symptoms since their trip. His therapist had told him this was how the brain reacted to trauma and stress.

He caught sight of an emergency exit door straight ahead.

Then he heard a sound that stopped him in his tracks—a fist strik-ing flesh. Grunts of pain. He held up his hands and stopped everyone. Tawna looked bewildered, but she knew better than to say anything.

They all did, even though the boys were pale with fear and Suki looked both angry and frightened.

Silence stretched through the library. The sick feeling in Roth's stomach expanded. There was no longer any room for doubt: someone who worked for Jacob Calakmul was inside this library. Despite his efforts to conceal his true purpose, Roth had been outsmarted. He'd been found out. They had to get back to the car, return to the army base. He would feel more secure there, and Tawna would be safe there too.

He put his finger to his mouth and then began walking quietly toward the emergency exit. The sound of footsteps on the carpet made him halt again.

He gestured for the twins to slip into one row of bookshelves, and he brought Suki and Tawna with him into another. When he reached the edge, he looked back the way they'd come. Lucas was peering around the corner of his row too, and Roth held up both hands and directed him to back up.

Turning back, Roth peered into the dim light of the empty library. The sound of footfalls was moving away. Then he saw a man, half-shadowed, pass the aisle, moving toward the stairs going down. Relief surged in Roth's chest.

As soon as the man was out of sight, Roth motioned for them all to follow him toward the exit at a run. He kept glancing back, worried that their pursuer would come charging after them. It wouldn't take long for him to notice no one was in the display room . . .

When he reached the doors, he saw the warning sign—the stick figure of someone running and the word *"Notausgang."*

"The door's alarmed," Tawna said, pointing at the placard.

"Good," Roth said, coming up and shoving the handle. A strobing light began to flash. That would alert the campus security team. With any luck, they'd apprehend the man who'd followed them inside. Or at least alarm him enough that he ran.

Either way, Roth and his family would be gone before they got there.

Once they were outside, he felt the cool December breeze on his face. They were on the short end of the building. The door was made of the same stone as the siding, so it had blended in at first glance. After exiting, he started to walk briskly.

"Let's get back to the car," he said. Once they were away from the building, he shifted into a run.

"Dad!" Brillante called.

"We've got to hurry!" he said. "Let's talk in the car!"

"You're going the wrong way!" Suki shouted. He turned and saw her pointing in the other direction. The two SLUB buildings mirrored each other. In the confusion of the moment, he'd become disoriented and starting racing in the wrong direction.

"Are you sure?" he asked, looking at the open yard, feeling certain he'd been going in the right direction.

"Yes!" Suki said in exasperation.

"She's right," Tawna said, her cheeks pink with cold. "The VW is that way."

They rushed away from the sculpted lawns and went back down the main path by the older-looking buildings. He knocked aside the worry of being spotted by police or campus security. There was someone in that building who was after them—someone who now knew that they'd just left it.

Roth kept glancing behind him, checking to see if they were being followed. If the man from the library had left the building, there was no sign of him. There were just a few students milling about, looking toward the sound of the alarm. Then he saw some campus cops come rushing toward him on their bicycles, pedaling hard.

"Out of the way," Roth said, directing the kids to get to one side of the path. About six bicycles rushed past, the riders wearing uniforms.

They had silver bike helmets and yellow jackets with *"Polizei"* written across the backs in reflective lettering.

He hoped the intruder was caught. Interrogated. Taken out of action. He also hoped Dominik was okay. He knew Calakmul's people would kill someone without compunction. But would they want to expose themselves so blatantly? Jacob was much more subtle than that, and Dresden wasn't his home turf.

They were all breathing hard when they reached the VW Tiguan. Tawna was sweating and panting as she clicked the key fob to unlock the door. "I don't understand what's going on," she said, wiping sweat from her brow.

"Can't explain now. Get back on the autobahn," Roth said. He quickly got inside and buckled up. The kids climbed in the back and did the same. Tawna climbed in behind the wheel, moving more slowly, still eyeing him.

He looked out the window, back toward the SLUB. The engine fired up. He thought he saw someone standing by a tree at the edge of the parking lot.

"Go!" he shouted.

Tawna's hands were shaking, but she put the VW in reverse and backed up, then switched gears and accelerated out of the parking lot. The sound of police sirens started up, growing louder. Maybe Dominik was hurt? Guilt prickled beneath Roth's skin.

As they pulled out of the university parking lot, Roth turned around and saw flashing blue lights. Several police vehicles were rushing to the university. His heart skittered, but he was relieved they'd made it out of the parking lot. He hoped the librarian was all right.

His own hands were shaking as he pulled out his burner phone. He replied to the warning text with a brief response. *We're out.*

Then he tapped on the photos icon. Relief unfurled inside him because he hadn't been certain that the images would photograph. They had. He zoomed in, checking out the details of the glyphs. The image was crystal clear, and he couldn't stop himself from grinning.

He forwarded the images to one of the few contacts saved to that burner phone, Illari Chaska, with the message *Need you to start translating these now.* He pressed send. Illari was an activist-student in Los Angeles. She was someone he'd met on the dark web who knew how to translate Mayan.

He felt the Tiguan accelerate, and soon they were back on the autobahn.

"That was really, really weird, Jonathon," Tawna said. "Even for you."

He gripped the grab handle above his head. His stomach was already churning from texting while she was driving, his motion sickness always quick to ignite.

"The whole thing was pretty sus, Dad," Brillante said. "Was that . . . did we go there on purpose?"

"Of course we went there on purpose," Suki said angrily. "What's going on? I thought this was a vacation so we *wouldn't* have nightmares this Christmas."

"I'm sorry I kept the truth from you guys," Roth said.

"What are you keeping from us?" Tawna said. She'd accelerated significantly, and they were now racing down the autobahn.

Roth felt increasingly queasy as she dodged around cars, but he wasn't about to tell her to slow down. "I'll make it crisp, Tawna. I didn't want you getting involved."

"Too late," Tawna said, swerving around another car.

She had a point. And if Calakmul knew why he was in Germany, then he also knew all about Tawna. She deserved to know a bit about him too.

"Last year, when Sarina got sick, we were taken hostage in Cozumel."

"By the cartels?" Tawna asked in shock, her mouth falling open.

"Worse," Suki said. "A ruthless billionaire who can turn into a jaguar."

"Let me tell her, Suki," Roth said with a sigh. "You're already making it sound weird."

"It was weird! I haven't told any of my friends, not even Brice, what really happened!" Suki said furiously. "I really wanted to, but you wouldn't allow it! 'It's just us,' you said. 'We're the only ones who can know.' Or did you lie about that too? Have you told people?"

"Yeah," Roth said.

"Who?"

"About a thousand people so far," he said.

"What the actual heck, Dad!" Suki shouted.

"No way!" Lucas exclaimed.

"Dude." Brillante chuckled.

"If you'd just shut up a minute back there, I'll explain." He felt like groaning. He was going to vomit if Tawna didn't slow down, but they needed to get as far away from the SLUB as possible. The kids fell quiet. "Thank you." He sighed and shifted in his seat. He looked down at his phone. No further texts.

"I wrote a book about what happened to us in Mexico. I didn't use our names. I published it under a fake name from a fake KDP account."

"What's a KDP account?"

"It's . . . um . . . a self-publishing platform. A ton of indie writers use it. I've had to learn about formatting e-books, hiring cover artists, and all of that. But none of the people I dealt with know who I am. I'm using an alias. The book is about us getting kidnapped in Mexico. It's about the Calakmul family and their thirst for revenge."

"Dad," Suki groaned.

"I didn't use his name. Well, I tweaked the spelling. None of our names are in the story, actually, and I had to tweak the locations and what the death games are called too. But it's all there, concealed beneath different words. I can easily update it with the real names. Places. Words. About a thousand people have downloaded the e-book version already. I'm going to start paying for ads on the platform to boost sales to a much larger audience after we get back. But I'm not doing this to sell more books. I control the manuscript. I'm going to change the names and republish it under my own name when I'm ready to go after Jacob."

"He's going to kill Mom!" Suki warned. "Then he'll come after us!"

"I have plans in case he comes after us," Roth said. "And Mom would want us to fight him with everything we have."

"So this *is* about a book," Tawna said with confusion.

"Except this one's a *true* story," Suki said angrily.

"Which no one will believe," Roth added. "But I'm laying out all the evidence. There are chat groups on the dark web talking about the book. People trying to find out who I am. I mean . . . who the author is. There are a lot of conspiracy theories circulating in the world right now. Some people have said they had a rich neighbor who disappeared after going to Mexico. Whole family . . . dead. We weren't the only ones this happened to. Right now, I have the evidence concealed with fake names. But anyone can download and read the e-book. People all over the world have already read it."

"And what are we going to do when those murderers decide to pay a visit to Bozeman?" Suki wanted to know.

"This is why we have that prepper cabin." He'd rented one in the mountains, accessible only by ATVs or snowmobiles. "We'll be prepared if something like that happens. Besides, I was careful to cover my tracks with the book. I even wrote the whole thing at Starbucks. Not the same one. I went to all of them."

"Are we in trouble?" Lucas asked.

"This is insane, Dad," Suki muttered. "Insane. Someone needs to stop this guy, but why should it be you? You're an author, not some kind of secret agent. And he has Mom. The risk is too great."

Roth squeezed the grip even harder. "We've discussed this, kids." He turned and looked back, even though it made his stomach queasy. "There's a reason they haven't put us in touch with Mom. We have to accept that she's probably dead."

"I thought she was at a treatment facility in Singapore?" Tawna said, aghast. He felt a swell of sympathy for her. It wasn't fair of him to have involved her, and if he could have avoided it, he would have. But he'd needed the excuse to visit Germany. "What on earth is going on here?"

"That was a cover for us coming home without her. Tawna, we knew something screwy was going on at the resort. We tried to escape, but Sarina's insulin pump was damaged. The rest is just like we told you, only we weren't just lost in the jungle. They were hunting us. We found refuge in a little Christian orphanage in Cozumel, but they weren't able to help Sarina. She'd gone too long without insulin. And then Calakmul caught up to us—"

The pain in his heart hadn't faded. He could still see her lying on that dingy little couch as she kissed him goodbye. Tears of anguish pricked his eyes. That was the last time they'd spoken. Calakmul had claimed his magic could keep her alive but not cure her.

His voice felt strangled as he spoke. "We were all taken to a remote location in Mexico. The ancient Mesoamericans played this ball game where the losers were put to death. The Maya were exceptionally good at it. This group . . . Calakmul's people . . . they'd started up the games again. We had to compete with another family from Bozeman. The Beasleys."

A gasp escaped Tawna. "The family that invited you to go down and have Christmas with them?"

"They set us up," Brillante said. "Jerks."

"We won the game, though, and they were killed," Roth continued. "Calakmul's people made it look like an accident in the news, but we know what really happened." He thought again about little Jane Louise. She was the one who'd warned them about the games. He felt again the inadequacy of not having been able to save her.

"I can't believe this," Tawna said. "This is . . ."

"Crazy," Roth answered. "I know. And it's true. They're part of a vast conspiracy, Tawna. They want to take over the world, and they have abilities that defy understanding. They're also working with powerful people." He remembered again the faces he'd seen at the game, some of them prominent people. Important people. The kind who could help Calakmul's crazy plan become a horrific reality.

"I hate remembering," Suki said, her voice thick with tears. "I've tried to forget. But sometimes I wake up in the middle of the night, and it's so dark . . . and then I remember everything."

"That's why you sleep with the lamp on now?" Lucas asked in a quiet voice.

"Yeah. Guess so."

"Sometimes it feels like Mom's still at the house," Roth said, his voice trembling. "I don't know if it's her ghost or a space-time continuum thing. This last year, I've done a lot of research into stories about the magic of the Maya. I've discovered some pretty crazy theories. Like this French scholar from the early 1800s, Constantine Rafinesque. He believed the Mayan glyphs had traces of ancient Libyan or Coptic . . . um, Egyptian hieroglyphics. He thought there was a *connection* between Africa and Mesoamerica."

"Didn't the pharaohs believe in a weird afterlife?" Suki asked. "I learned about that in elementary school."

"The Egyptians were obsessed with life and death. And so were the Maya. The Maya knew more about planetary orbits than Copernicus or Galileo. They had an uncanny knowledge of the world, but their records were all destroyed, except for four. The Dresden Codex, the one we just saw, was made *before* the Spanish came."

"So it can't have been written in reaction to them," Tawna said slowly.

"You think what I saw in the museum can help bring Mom back?" Suki asked, her voice shaking with hope.

Roth could feel his sister watching him, probably full of disbelief. His kids, full of longing. Clenching his free hand into a fist, he swallowed to keep from bursting into tears. "I don't know, honey. I don't know. But I do think it can bring down Jacob Calakmul."

CHAPTER FIVE

Jaguar Temple

Calakmul Biosphere Reserve

December 24

Every stela, every carved wall, every statue within the temple complex shimmered with golden light, illuminating the darkness of the jungle. The jungle was a savage place, teeming with predators—serpents, jaguars, spiders, and other nocturnal hunters. It was not safe to leave the perimeter marked by the glowing lights, which offered a shield against the denizens of the jungle.

The two families who would be competing in the death game had already arrived and were being prepared for their duty. Hundreds had gathered from all over the Yucatán Peninsula to view the game. Hundreds more had flocked to the reserve from other locales. Bankers, politicians, actors, and executives had all come to witness the games again and celebrate the coming triumph.

All who came knew that the prophecy would be fulfilled, and it would be fulfilled soon.

The planets were coming into alignment on schedule.

"Great One, the games are ready," said Uacmitun, the warrior chieftain who guarded the ancient city. His hunters also patrolled the surrounding jungle and killed anyone who ventured near it. Uacmitun was wearing the ceremonial armor and garb of the ancient Maya. Jacob had not yet changed from his Western clothing but felt the urge to do so. He could feel the humidity in the air, the deep warmth that had seeped into his pores.

"Excellent. Any troubles in the jungle?"

"None, Great One. We caught a small group of treasure hunters a month ago, skulking around the ruins outside Xmejía. We abducted them, brought them here, and sacrificed them on the altar."

"Where were they from?" Jacob asked.

"Belize," he answered with a sneer of disdain. "Would you like us to punish their families?"

Jacob didn't care about Belize. "No need."

He heard the sound of someone approaching and halted, turning his head. Angélica was striding toward him fast, her throat glistening with sweat. Her eyes had a feverish and worried intensity. Uacmitun leered at her.

"What is it?" Jacob asked, concerned by the agitation evident on her face and infuriated that Uacmitun would dare to covet a woman he had claimed as his own. If the man had been less loyal or less important to his plans, Jacob might have succumbed to his surge of wrath and shown his claws.

"The pilot got a transmission," she said, out of breath. "You need to come back to the Pegasus with me."

"Can't this wait?" Jacob said with a scowl, still seething from the disrespect shown by his subordinate.

She shook her head. "It's about Mr. Roth."

Uacmitun's nostrils flared with anger. The previous year, one of his hunters had nearly decapitated one of the twins for climbing up on the roof of the temple. Angélica had interceded to spare the boy's life, something that had ignited the warrior chieftain's animosity. He was obviously still disgruntled over the incident but wouldn't accost her directly, not when he knew she was Jacob's potential consort. Or his future queen.

Jacob nodded to Angélica and followed her swiftly through the yard of the acropolis, back to where the jet had landed. It was still mostly dark, the canopy of the jungle blotting out the early-morning sky. There were no hangars in the primitive jungle, so the pilot usually took the jet to Chetumal after dropping them off. It was highly unusual for him to still be around this long after they'd disembarked.

"What do you know already?" Jacob asked her as they hurried.

"Roth is in Dresden."

Jacob felt a surge of rage. Hadn't he foreseen this possibility? How could the American have been so reckless? Hadn't he been warned?

"And?"

"He went to the museum where they keep the codex on display."

"So he's decided to play the part of the spider, has he?" Jacob said, trying to contain his fury and failing. "Did he go alone?"

"The children are with him. So is his sister. She's the one who drove them."

"I want her dead," Jacob snarled.

"She lives at the army base. The security is strict there."

"Of course. That's why he's risked it," Jacob retorted, livid. "I can't believe he's endangering his wife's life like this. I want Sarina brought to one of my resorts. Not the one on Cozumel, but another. I want him to *see* what happens when someone crosses me."

"Of course," Angélica said briskly. "I'll have her sent to Sian Ka'an."

They reached the main courtyard, where the Pegasus jet awaited them. It looked like a military-grade craft, but it was outfitted with high-end luxuries for wealthy travelers. The wings were embedded with propellers so that the plane could take off vertically, like a helicopter.

As Jacob and Angélica approached the aircraft, the pilot noticed them from the cockpit and quickly opened the flight-deck door.

"Boss, I have Victor on comms," said the pilot. "Come up to the cockpit."

Jacob climbed inside and sat in the copilot seat. Angélica came too but waited at the door since the space was cramped. The pilot sat down and picked the radio up off the cradle.

"Victor, he's here, over." The pilot handed the radio to Jacob while he put his headset back on.

"So Mr. Roth is causing trouble?" Jacob asked, then released the talk button.

"Yes, sir. He went to the museum in Dresden. I had someone on campus as directed. The museum was closed for the holiday, but an employee was waiting at the door to let the Roths in."

Jacob scowled. "You had one man?" he asked.

"Yes. Just the one. After they went inside, he started banging on the door. That roused security. When someone opened the door to talk to him, he incapacitated the man and went after the Roths. But they were gone."

Jacob was getting angrier and angrier.

"Gone?"

"They left through an emergency exit. It triggered the security alarms, and soon the local police came."

"Surely a jaguar priest can handle the local police. Don't tell me he was caught."

"No, *jefe*. He's trailing them on the freeway. Seems like they're heading back to the sister's place. It's a several-hour drive."

Jacob pressed the radio against the bridge of his nose.

One man. They'd sent one man. What an absolute disaster. Although a single jaguar priest should easily be able to subdue an overweight American untrained in battle, Roth was different. He was wily, unpredictable. And then there was his daughter . . .

"Sir?" Victor asked. "Do you want me to fly to Germany? I can get them out."

"Hold a moment," Jacob said. He left the line open and looked at the pilot. "How long to fly to Germany?"

The pilot shrugged. "Commercial travel? On Christmas Eve?"

"No! Now. The Pegasus."

"A dozen hours? It's halfway around the world. We'll need to refuel."

Something Mr. Roth had been counting on, no doubt. In fact, if the pilot hadn't still been at the Jaguar Temple, waiting for the next window when satellites weren't overhead, then the news would have come in too late for them to act on it.

"Do we have anyone else nearby?"

This is where Angélica's prodigious memory would prove helpful. They had no internet on the jet. Her tablet would be useless.

She frowned, thinking. "Luxembourg. It's closer to Frankfurt. We could extract them from there."

Jacob felt a surge of relief. The Germans were allied too closely with Washington, and they couldn't risk coming on the radar of Interpol. But Luxembourg? They could work with Luxembourg.

"I want a van and driver to head from Luxembourg immediately. The priest needs to keep tailing the Roths. Once the van gets there, have him crash into their vehicle. We'll put everyone in the van and cross the border to Luxembourg. Start preparing your flight plan. We're leaving."

"Now?" the pilot asked worriedly.

"Now!" Jacob insisted.

"What about the game?" Angélica asked.

"It will happen on schedule," Jacob said. He lifted the radio. "Victor, meet us at the airport in Cozumel with an extraction team. We're on our way. Over."

"Roger that. Over."

Jacob handed the radio back to the pilot, who looked fearful. "But the satellites. We'll be detected."

"It's a risk, I know," Jacob said. "But I have to take it. Roth has been scheming. He knows too much for that." He looked at Angélica, whose tech abilities and multitasking were as prodigious as her memory. "Get strapped in."

She nodded and got settled in her usual seat, across from his.

Jacob went to the door and leaned out, finding Uacmitun standing at the base of the Pegasus.

"Change of plans," he said to the warrior chief. "We're leaving. You will act for me and run the game." Jacob summoned the power of the Maya ring he wore. A swarm of golden motes of dust gathered around the warrior. Jacob felt the power thrum inside him, accompanied by the usual reckless energy and exhilaration. There were glyphs carved into Uacmitun's armor. Glyphs that lent him strength, agility, and uncanny senses in the dark.

But the power that Jacob possessed went far beyond that. He had the power to *transform*. It was a secret, one of the greatest secrets of the jaguar priesthood. But the greatest secret of all lay in Aztlán. Jacob had only been to that sacred place once. The memory of his father's face flashed in his mind.

When the spell had finished, Uacmitun had been altered to look like Jacob Calakmul—an illusion similar to the magic that protected the important parts of the Dresden Codex and made the writing on some pages appear invisible. Blank.

Had Roth figured it out? Was that why he'd taken his children to Germany, after all? His daughter had the magic of the ancient Maya in her blood. She, perhaps, could see the truth beneath the deception.

Jacob had underestimated Mr. Roth before. He didn't intend to again.

"We'll be back," Jacob said to the illusion of himself. "And this time, I'll cut out Roth's heart myself."

"Yes, Great One," Uacmitun answered eagerly. He was clearly thrilled by the task. For the opportunity to *be* the head of the jaguar priests instead of serving him. At least for a while. Uacmitun and his family had been loyal to the Calakmuls for centuries, since before Cortés had come.

He knew the penalty of disloyalty.

It was time for Roth to learn the same.

CHAPTER SIX

A5—The Autobahn

Near Alsfeld, Germany

December 24

The burner phone vibrated in Roth's pocket. He was still clutching the grab handle near his ear, watching his sister maneuver through traffic at high speed. His pulse had slowed as she put more distance between them and Dresden, which was now several hours behind them. He'd answered his kids' questions. He'd told Tawna everything that had happened to them in Mexico. Talking about it had brought the old feelings raging to the surface. Along with his bone-deep determination to bring down Jacob Calakmul. Although she'd had dozens of questions, Tawna shared his imagination and had, moreover, *seen* the glowing bracelet and ring. She'd accepted his story without hesitation. Her loyalty and belief had comforted him. So had her assurances that she'd be careful.

He pulled out his phone, recognizing the number on caller ID. It was Dominik from the SLUB.

"Dominik?" he said, lifting the phone to his ear after accepting the call.

"Mr. Roth! Are you all right? Where are you?"

"We're fine. Everything's fine."

"Where are you now, Mr. Roth?"

"On the autobahn," he said carefully, frowning.

"Mr. Roth, there was an intruder at the SLUB today. I was knocked unconscious. I'm at the hospital. I've been worried about you and your family."

"We're safe, Dominik. We got out."

"Thank God. The police would like to speak with you. Where are you?"

Roth watched the countryside fly by outside his window. "We're heading back to Frankfurt."

"Frankfurt? Is that where your sister lives?"

Roth hadn't offered up that information, nor would he. "No. Nearby."

"Mr. Roth, the man who attacked us has not been found. He's still . . . how do you say . . . at large. The police would like to speak with you. I have Officer Schauermann with me now."

Roth did not want to get involved with the authorities. The fewer people who knew about his visit to the SLUB, the better. "We are fine, Dominik. I don't know what the police officer would want to say."

"Please, Mr. Roth. This is important. Here he is."

Roth frowned and sighed. When they got back to Wiesbaden, he'd try booking them early plane tickets back to the US. If Jacob's henchmen were coming after them, they needed to get to their hideout.

"Mr. Roth? This is Officer Schauermann."

"Guten Tag," Roth said tightly.

"Ah yes, *guten Tag*. We reviewed the security footage from the SLUB, Mr. Roth. You and your family went out the emergency doors on the north side of the building. That triggered the alarm, which allowed the police to arrive swiftly. Thank you."

"You're welcome. We just . . . wanted to get out of there. We heard the intruder hitting Dominik."

"Yes. I'm sure you did." He paused, then added, "The cameras in the vault with the codex. They showed you taking pictures with a camera phone. Just before the incident."

Roth felt his stomach clench again. "Yes?"

"Why did you come to the SLUB today, Mr. Roth?"

"To see the codex."

"But why today, Mr. Roth? Why did you want to come when the SLUB was closed?"

He could tell him what he'd told Dominik, that he was researching for a book, but something about the officer's line of questioning told him the man had already connected the random attack in the library with his visit. He obviously couldn't have guessed the rest, of course, so Roth didn't know what to say. Should he just hang up? They didn't know where he was staying. If they searched the flight registers, they'd realize he'd come in through Frankfurt . . .

Another car smashed into theirs.

The phone flew out of Roth's hand as he struck the side door. He saw the car hurtling toward the guardrail on the right-hand side just before the Tiguan struck it. Sparks flew against the window. The kids began screaming.

Tawna corrected, and they were back on the highway again. Adrenaline raced through Roth. He grabbed the hand grip again, planting his foot against the dash. What the . . . ?

They'd been struck from the left. Another car was driving next to them, its right side dented. The driver had dark hair and bronze skin. Glowing eyes.

His heartbeat stuttered as he watched the BMW come at them again.

"I'm getting out of here," Tawna said. "Something's not right."

"Yes!" Roth screamed in panic.

The BMW hit them again, this time near the rear, sending them into a spin. He heard the shriek of brakes and felt his stomach groan from the sudden whip of momentum. He clenched his teeth and braced for the car to strike the barrier, but they missed it, coming around in a full circle.

Tawna was yanking on the steering wheel, her face a grimace of fear. She slammed on the brakes, but another vehicle struck them from the front. Roth looked out the windshield and saw a white Mercedes van.

They'd stopped.

"Reverse! Reverse!" Roth shouted. He pulled the gear shift for her. "Go! Go! It's them! They're after us."

"Dad!" Lucas wailed, sobbing.

Tawna slammed on the accelerator, and the VW squealed as it backed up. The van's engine roared.

A little tinny voice came from the floor of the car. "Mr. Roth! Mr. Roth!" The burner phone was still on, though little good it would do them.

As Tawna drove backward, Roth looked back at the chaos of the highway as the other cars swerved to avoid them while traveling at high speeds. He didn't see the BMW, but it was probably behind them. The van advanced and struck their hood again.

"Turn hard!" Roth said. He wished he were driving.

When Tawna didn't react, he yanked on the steering wheel. The VW spun around in a circle, and then he changed the gear to drive again. The engine shrieked from the abuse.

He saw the BMW coming at them.

"Punch it!"

Tawna jammed her foot on the accelerator again and swerved toward the strip of grass separating the lanes, heading right into oncoming traffic. Horns blared at them. Cars swerved. Roth nearly threw up.

The VW bucked a bit, but she brought it back onto the correct side of the freeway, now totally devoid of cars. The BMW and the Mercedes van were behind them.

"Officer!" Roth yelled, hoping it would be picked up by the phone's receiver. "We're on the A5, just past . . . where? What town did we just pass?"

"We just passed Alsfeld!" Tawna shouted.

He repeated the information. "Our car was struck by a gray BMW and a white Mercedes van . . . like the Sprinter kind. They're trying to kill us!"

"Mr. Roth! Mr. Roth!" the tinny voice said. "Can you hear me?"

"Officer! We need help!" He looked down to see if he could find the burner phone, but he couldn't see it.

"Dude!" Brillante shouted fearfully. "They're coming up on us from behind."

"Faster!" Roth said to Tawna, twisting around to get a view of the pursuing vehicles.

She gripped the steering wheel, her mouth twisted with determination. He felt the momentum as the speedometer needle arced around swiftly.

"Dad, look!" Suki shouted.

He turned and saw a circular weave of golden netting coalesce on the freeway ahead of them. They'd seen this same magic in the arena in the death game. It had repulsed the balls and sent them flying back into the court. This net stretched the width of the highway. If they struck it at this speed, their car would flip.

"What is that?" Tawna yelled.

"Suki, get rid of it!" Roth said.

His daughter closed her eyes, opening her hand and spreading her fingers. His heart raced as he waited to see if the magic would work, but Suki always did best in a crisis, and this was no exception. The ring and bracelet began to glow, motes of golden dust scattered as they reached them, and their VW rushed past safely.

"What was that thing?" Tawna said with wonder.

"I'll explain later. We've got to outrun them."

"I can't outrun a BMW, Jonathon," she said. There was steam rising from the hood. The car was already redlining. Ahead, he saw the huge rectangular blue signs displaying the next major towns: "Hannover, Kassel, Dortmund, Westkreuz Frankfurt."

"How long before the police respond to calls about an accident?" Roth asked her.

"I don't know. It depends. But the Beamer is gaining on us!"

Roth turned around and saw she was right. It was bearing down on them from behind, the van farther back. The bend in the road had hidden the wall of cars behind their pursuers. His heart was racing. There were no exits to take. Just hills and trees. Even though it was winter, there wasn't any snow.

"We could pull over and run for it. We just need some time for the police to get here."

"Mr. Roth! Mr. Roth!" cried the disembodied voice on the other end of the phone.

Where was it?

"I can't see the phone. Can any of you?" Roth asked.

"It's back here," Lucas said, sniffling.

"Can you reach it?"

"I'll try."

He could hear Lucas straining for it, could even see him in his peripheral vision.

"I'm going about as fast as I dare," Tawna said. "I'm going over 210 kilometers an hour."

"How fast is that?" Roth asked.

"One hundred thirty miles per hour, I think. I can't control the car very well."

She was right. She was weaving between all three lanes, taking each curve in the road so quickly it made his stomach sink. This was crazy. And still the BMW was gaining.

"Got it!" Lucas said triumphantly. He handed the phone up to Roth.

"I've got the phone back!" Roth said into the receiver.

"Mr. Roth! Is anyone injured?"

"Not yet. They tried ramming us off the road. We're being chased by a . . . by a gray BMW and a white Mercedes."

"I know. You said that. Where are you now?"

"Still on the A5."

"We're setting up a roadblock at Reiskirchen, Mr. Roth. Can you make it there?"

"I don't know. We can't outrun the BMW. My sister's driving as fast as she safely can, but it's still closing in on us."

"All right. We'll send some patrol cars your way. When you see them, immediately pull over."

"Thank you," Roth said. *"Thank you."*

A bullet went through the back window.

"Everyone down!" Roth said, panicking.

"Mr. Roth! Mr. Roth!"

"They're shooting at us!" He leaned over as far as he could. Then he saw the BMW coming up on their right. He couldn't see the van, so it had to be farther back. The driver's-side window was down, and he saw a handgun.

"Brake! Brake!" Roth shouted.

Tawna slammed on the brakes and the car began to swerve uncontrollably. They went into a spin, and the guardrail filled Roth's vision as they hurtled toward it.

"Hold on!" he shouted.

They struck it once, then again. The hood was a rumpled mess. The airbags deployed. Steam obscured Roth's vision, and the smell of metal stung his nose. Roth tried to free himself from the seat belt, but it was locked. His neck and back ached. He looked around wildly to see if anyone was injured. Thankfully, the safety features in the vehicle had protected his family.

"We've got to get out of here," Roth said. He finally released the belt and yanked on the door handle. The door groaned but opened. He came out, dizzy. The BMW was backing up toward them. Roth rushed to the back door and opened it. Brillante came out first, then Lucas, then Suki. Tawna was still struggling to get her belt loose.

The white van rolled to a stop behind them.

The BMW stopped, and a man in a silk suit got out, holding the pistol with the barrel aimed at Roth's face.

"Mr. Calakmul would like to see you," the man said with a menacing frown. Roth caught a glimpse of tattoos beneath the collar of his shirt. "Get in the van. All of you."

Tawna freed herself at last and came out of the Tiguan, her hands up.

"Just let us go," she begged.

The man looked at her, smirked. He shifted the Glock to her.

"No!" Roth shouted as the gun fired.

The man with the gun went down, a mark of red against his silk shirt.

The shot had been fired from behind them. Roth turned in shock in time to see a second shot taken. *Relief. Recognition.* A man in a dark suit and an open-collared shirt stood beside the van, his gun aimed at the van's driver and still smoking.

It was Steve Lund.

Finally.

CHAPTER SEVEN

BND Branch Office

Frankfurt, Germany

December 24

The EMT flashed a light in Roth's eyes, making him squint. His entire body was sore, but they'd given him some ibuprofen for the pain. The flashlight clicked off.

"Any ringing in the ears, Mr. Roth?" the EMT asked with a heavy German accent.

"No more than usual. My neck is a little sore." Roth massaged it.

"Your kids are in good health. Your sister, too, but she'll need to see her chiropractor. She lives in Wiesbaden, *ja*?"

"Yes," Roth said. He was just grateful they were all alive after the nightmare on the autobahn. It had been close, much too close, and he knew he'd be thinking about that awful moment when the man had aimed his gun at Tawna. He'd thought they were lost. He'd been sure of it.

The door clicked open, and a member of the BND entered. The Bundesnachrichtendienst was the German intelligence service, similar to the CIA in America. After the car chase on the highway, they'd taken jurisdiction and brought Roth and his family to their branch office in Frankfurt. The building was marked "Deutsche Telekom."

Steve Lund had advised Roth not to reveal anything, insisting he'd do the talking to the BND officers. Hiring him and his company as private bodyguards had been a good call. Lund was a pro, had global connections, and was level-headed and strategic. All he knew about the Calakmul problem was that Roth and his family had been targeted by a "cartel leader" during their vacation in Mexico. If he sensed there was more to it, he didn't prod. It was Lund's job to protect them, not to analyze why they'd found themselves in trouble in the first place. Since he'd spent his earlier career in the FBI, Lund had the skills for situational awareness and strategies and the funds to make things happen off the grid. He was also adept at blending in and looking like an ordinary guy.

The new arrival asked a question in German, and the EMT nodded and began to put away his gear.

"If you'll come with me, Mr. Roth," said the officer, gesturing for him to rise from the metal chair where he'd been sitting.

Roth stood and felt an immediate ache in one of his back muscles. "Where are my children?" he asked.

"They're in a room watching TV," said the officer. "My name is Hobrecht. We'd like to ask you a few questions."

"Where is Steve?" Roth asked.

"He's waiting in the room with field ops. This shouldn't take long, Mr. Roth."

"Thank you. It's Christmas Eve. We're anxious to leave. After what just happened, I want to get my kids back home." Especially knowing that Calakmul would already be preparing to come after him. At home, he had contingency plans. Here, he had nothing.

"I understand. We have families too, Mr. Roth. I'm sure you're anticipating a visit from Santa tonight."

"Instead, we got Krampus," Roth joked. He knew the German legends about Sankt Nikolaus's devilish companion. "I swear my kids were being good this year."

Hobrecht chuckled. "You know of Krampus?"

"My grandparents emigrated from Germany. So yes . . . I know the legend."

"Something you've used in your books, no doubt?"

It was a subtle acknowledgment that this intelligence officer *knew* who Roth was.

Roth shrugged noncommittally, and then they reached the room. When Hobrecht opened the door, Roth was relieved to see Lund already there.

Looking at the man, you'd have suspected him to be a retired elementary school principal or a softball coach. He was nearly bald, except for a light fuzz of gray hair around the back and near his ears. He wore glasses, a tweed jacket, and a button-down dress shirt and had a very unassuming smile. In fact, Lund *was* retired—from the FBI—and ran his own private-security firm, protecting those who could afford his services.

When Roth entered, Lund gave him a genial smile, a subtle nod. He was standing against a wall with a whiteboard. Several other officers were in the room, two female and one male. Several open laptops sat on the table. One of the screens showed the passport of the man from the van who'd nearly shot Tawna.

Hobrecht gestured toward a seat at the table, and Roth sat down. He felt nervous about being there, worried he might let too much slip.

"Mr. Roth, you chose well in your selection of bodyguards," Hobrecht said, giving Lund a deferential nod. "Mr. Lund has a strong reputation in the private-security business. I've spoken to the chancellor's office and informed them that it's my opinion that shooting the men who attacked your family was well within his professional rights, and that your family might have been harmed if he had not done so."

Roth breathed out in relief. "That's putting it mildly."

"Mr. Lund feels that these men were opportunistically trying to kidnap you and hold you for ransom due to your wealth and prestige. There are any number of ways they could have discovered your intention to travel to Germany for Christmas, although as I understand it, not even the director general of the library knew a famous author was coming. Mr. Lund tells me you'd like to cut your trip short and return to Montana?"

"Absolutely," Roth said, leaning forward. "We're all pretty shaken up, and my sister's car is totaled."

"There's a flight this evening from Frankfurt, which would get you back home for Christmas. We can escort your sister back to the army base in Wiesbaden and have your luggage brought to the airport. Would that be acceptable?"

"Yes, and appreciated," Roth said. He felt his tension ebbing.

"However, there is one part of the story that I'm confused about, Mr. Roth. I've spoken to Dominik Stoltz at the SLUB in Dresden. He said you were fascinated by the codex on display at the museum library."

"Yes?" Roth said.

"He said you were doing research for a new book, but your itinerary made visiting Dresden difficult during normal hours."

"Yes, the museum was closed."

"Can you explain to me, Mr. Roth, why an author of fantasy novels would be so interested in seeing such a relic? Neither Mr. Stoltz nor Mr. Lund offered much of a reason for your interest in it."

Roth looked at Lund, who had a very stoic and guarded expression. He'd clearly done the best he could to throw the BND off the scent. Now it was Roth's turn. The question had been asked very casually, but he suspected the interest behind it was anything but casual—and the wrong answer might delay their return to Montana.

That would not work with Roth's plans.

"I'm fascinated by Mesoamerican history."

Hobrecht frowned. "I'm not familiar with that term. Meso—?"

"Mesoamerica is the homeland of the ancient Aztecs and Maya. It's part of Mexico, Guatemala, Belize, and Peru. The Indigenous cultures from there. The Dresden Codex is one of a few primary sources relating to the ancient Maya."

"And its images are available for free on the internet, Mr. Roth. Why travel all this way?"

"Actually, it was our trip to Mexico last Christmas that inspired both the trip and my research," Roth said. "I have a new book I've been working on. Travel inspires my imagination more than desk research."

"I see," said Hobrecht. The look he gave Roth was inscrutable. "Is it a coincidence, then, that these two men who were shot and are now in the hospital undergoing surgery were also from . . . how did you say it . . . Mesoamerica?"

"In all fairness," Lund said with his subdued, almost bored manner of speaking, "I think it's *your* job to figure out who they are and why they tried to abduct Mr. Roth and his family. My job is to get the Roths safely home."

"I'm just trying to make sense of the clues, Mr. Lund," Hobrecht said defensively.

"You have the facts before you," Lund said with a shrug. "I flew to Frankfurt ahead of the Roths so I could be waiting at the airport. I've followed them on their sightseeing trips. Everything went perfectly well until Dresden when I saw that man banging on the door. I texted Mr. Roth that I thought there was trouble. He and his sister promptly evacuated the building with the kids, and campus police were called in. The Roths left in his sister's vehicle, and I followed. When the BMW crashed into them, I called a BND field agent I know, and you all responded with alacrity. I feared a homicide was likely and imminent, so I took down the two men with nonfatal gunshot wounds. You can interrogate them and find out who they're working for, but it's likely a Mexican cartel. I don't see any reason why we should remain in Germany while all of that happens."

He'd made his points succinctly, offering no more information than was necessary. Of course, he didn't have much more information than what he'd given them.

Hobrecht sighed. "I know these things, Mr. Lund. I know that both men came from outside Germany. Are they connected with a cartel?"

"I have no way of knowing," Lund said with a shrug. "Your job. Not mine. There's an FBI field office in Bozeman, Montana. Once you learn the truth, notify them, and they'll get the information to me. You have my cell number, so you can also call me directly. Right now, I think it's in the best interest of the family to return home for Christmas."

Hobrecht held up his hands. "I have no grounds to keep you detained. The men who broke the law are already in custody. It'll be hours before they're out of surgery and conscious again."

Hobrecht's phone rang, and he looked at the screen. "Chancellor's office," he grunted. He took the call and began speaking swiftly in German. After a few minutes, he ended it.

"Your contact in the State Department works holidays, Mr. Lund?" Hobrecht asked, bemused.

Lund shrugged. *"Stille Nacht, heilige Nacht."*

Turning to Roth, Hobrecht said, "You're free to go. We'll escort your family to the airport, bypass the security checkpoint, and then you can make your evening flight."

"Thank you," Roth said, relieved. He'd been squeezing the armrests, but he relaxed his grip. Lund had contacts everywhere. His employees had all previously worked for intelligence agencies around the world. One of his best men was from the Mossad in Israel. Lund never used his name.

In all, the protection service cost $1.5 million per year, paid in cryptocurrency. It was Lund who'd suggested the burner phone, and he contacted Roth only via the phone Calakmul didn't know about.

"Shall we?" Hobrecht asked.

Roth stood, and they brought him to the room where his kids were being kept. When he entered the room, Lucas jumped to his feet and rushed over to give him a big hug.

"How's everyone feeling?" Roth asked. He held out his palm to Suki, and she placed hers against it so they could wrap their thumbs against each other's hands. An introvert's hug.

"A little sore. Wish I had a cup of *xocolatl*," Lucas said. That was the drink they'd been given down at the Jaguar Temple hidden in the jungles of the Yucatán. It was some sort of spicy chocolate confection that also removed aches and pains and accelerated healing.

Brillante was watching a soccer match on the TV. It had the logo of the Premier League on the screen. "Can we finish the game first?"

"Dude!" Lucas said. "We're going home!"

"*Are* we going home?" Suki asked urgently.

"Yeah. We're heading to the airport now."

"Is Aunt Tawna coming?" Lucas asked.

"No. She has a lot of insurance paperwork to fill out. But she'll be okay." He hoped it was true. He'd figured even Calakmul wasn't bold enough to attack her on a US military base, but now he felt more worry twining through his chest.

"I'm coming to the airport with you guys," Tawna said, appearing in the doorway. "They'll drop me off at the base afterward. Want to see you little munchkins for as long as I can!"

Brillante turned off the TV. Lucas came and hugged her.

She wrapped her arms around him, but addressed Roth over his head. "You owe me a phone call, Jonny."

The endearment made his heart ache. It was the same pet name Sarina used for him.

———

The departure gate at the Frankfurt airport was unremarkable. There were big glass windows looking out at the planes and a waiting area full of uncomfortable seating, interspersed with huge pillars. The crowd at the airport was pretty sparse that night, but there were other passengers lingering in the area, and he could see the gate agents were getting ready to announce boarding.

Roth checked his burner phone for a reply from Illari Chaska, to whom he'd sent the images from the Dresden Codex. Nothing yet. Then he checked his regular phone, which had 80 percent battery. The only message was from Tawna, confirming that she'd made it back to the army base. They'd gone back there with her before coming to the airport, needing to gather their things. It was only a thirty-minute drive from Wiesbaden to the airport, so Tawna had come back with them and then taken a taxi home again.

Roth was grateful for his sister. He was also worried about her. But she lived most of her life within the confines of the army base and only ventured out for sightseeing trips, which she couldn't do until her car was replaced. And now that she knew what was going on, she would be especially careful.

He texted her back to let her know they were at their gate with the boarding passes.

"So that *guy* over there," Suki said in a low voice, a subtle nod toward Lund. "I've seen him at Gallatin High before. I thought he was part of the administration."

"He sort of is," Roth explained. "I hired him to keep an eye on you guys. He's private security. You know those panic buttons I had installed? He's behind that."

"Weird flex, but okay," Suki said, looking impressed.

"'Weird flex'?" Roth asked in confusion, rubbing his forehead. He couldn't keep up with all the teenager slang.

"Yeah, weird flex. 'Flexing' means *showing* . . . I don't know . . . like *showing more force than the situation requires*. I don't think any of the other rich kids at school have private security."

"I'll bet none of the other kids were kidnapped by were-jaguars and forced to play the death games," Roth pointed out. "I wanted to give you guys a safety net without stressing you out too much. Being watched over isn't great. But maybe I made a mistake in not telling you. We're being watched by people who want to destroy the world, so it's kind of nice to know we have tough guys on our side too."

"True dat," Brillante added, not even glancing up from the game he was playing on his phone.

Roth continued. "All three of you go to the same school. He's been working with the principal to improve security at Gallatin."

"Really? What's his name?"

"Just call him Uncle Steve."

She made a face. "Awkward."

"I know. But I sleep better at night knowing he's watching over you guys. You'd rather not home school, right?"

Tilting her head, she studied him. "It can't be cheap having someone like him around."

"He's not around all the time himself. There are others who are part of the security detail assigned to our family. He offered to come on this trip personally to make sure we made it back safely."

"So he's our guardian angel."

"I thought Grandma Suki was our guardian angel?" Lucas said, leaning over from the other side.

"Guess we have two," Suki said. "Now stop butting in on our conversation."

"Sor-*ry*," Lucas said in an exaggerated way. "Didn't realize it was invitation only." He pulled out his phone and started playing a game on it.

"Dad, this trip to Dresden is why Jacob Calakmul is coming after us again," Suki said, her voice even lower. "What do you think is going to happen once he finds out about the book?"

"It's okay. It'll all be okay."

She shook her head slightly. "I'm ashamed of myself for actually believing your lame story when you said we were coming here to see Aunt Tawna. I guess I wanted to believe it."

He shrugged. "That was part of it. I hadn't seen her since that quick visit she made to Bozeman after we moved."

"I remember. She always brings us treats you can't buy in the US."

Tawna had never married, and she liked to travel and see her siblings as often as she could. She'd always made her nieces and nephews feel important. And Roth had a sinking feeling in his gut because he knew he had put her life at risk. He'd told himself she'd be safe at the military base, and he still wanted to believe that, but was he fooling himself?

There was quiet for a while as an announcement was made in English and German over the loudspeaker. When it finished, Suki sighed.

"Dad, the school play is right after Christmas break. I've been looking forward to it all year. We've worked so hard."

"I was looking forward to the play too," Roth said. "But now . . . I don't know what's going to happen. We're going to have to wait and see."

"This isn't fair. The play is important to me." The theater department was putting on a production of the Broadway play *A Gentleman's Guide to Love and Murder*. Suki was the stage manager, a role she'd worked hard for. There was one scene where she was onstage—well, her *arm* was onstage, handing an axe through the curtain to the main character, Monty Navarro. Roth hadn't seen the play, but Suki had reported that the rehearsals were going well. She'd said she was excited for him and the boys to see it—and sad that Sarina wasn't going to be able to.

"I'll talk to Uncle Steve about it. Right now, I can't make any promises."

Suki looked furious, arms folded, lips curled down. She glanced away from him. He knew she wasn't just upset about potentially missing the play. She was worried he'd endangered Sarina with his actions.

And he also knew her enough to know she was also furious with Jacob Calakmul, the man who'd taken so much away from them and now might be taking away the play too.

Another announcement came over the intercom. "Welcome to United flight 927. We'll begin boarding soon, starting with our first-class customers."

"That's us!" Lucas chimed in. "First class! *Awe*-some!"

"Dude, did you see the goal I just kicked in?" Brillante asked, holding the screen out so his brother could see the replay.

Suki was still fuming.

Roth's cell phone began to ring. Not the burner, his regular phone. He looked at the screen, and his stomach dropped. Sweat began to itch across his entire body.

Cozumel, Mexico.

No caller ID.

CHAPTER EIGHT

BOZEMAN YELLOWSTONE INTERNATIONAL AIRPORT

BOZEMAN, MONTANA

December 25

The Roth family had been traveling nearly all of Christmas Day. Their fancy dinner had been lunch at a restaurant at Denver International Airport, and the only presents exchanged had been from the gift shops there. He'd originally promised the kids they'd do their regular Christmas traditions after getting back from Germany, and none of them had actually expected to be back home that day, so there was no tree waiting for them with wrapped presents beneath it.

Roth's entire body was sore from the incident on the autobahn. He'd purchased pain meds at the airport in Germany and was ready for more as he and the kids shuffled from the terminal, dragging their suitcases behind them. Reaching into his pocket, he pulled out his phone and checked the screen. No further missed calls. He hadn't answered the call from Cozumel, and no voice mail had been left. He'd shown the number to Lund, who had tried to figure out whose number it was, but there were still no answers.

A text alert sounded from the burner phone in his pocket. He switched to the other device and saw the text from Lund.

Jordan is waiting at the house. All clear.

Roth sighed with relief and stuffed the phone back into his pocket. Jordan was a young guy, twenty-five, who'd entered the private-security field after he was discharged from the army. He'd served in Arlington in the Old Guard as well as the 82nd Airborne and had done a deployment on the border in Texas to try to stop human traffickers and cartels. He was an expert marksman, one of Lund's requirements for his field guys, and was one of the regulars who rotated at Gallatin High School to protect the kids.

Jordan was thorough and trustworthy, so if he'd cleared the house, that meant no surprises would be waiting for them back home.

"Dad, can we stop by Chick-fil-A on the way home?" Lucas asked. "I'm in desperate need of a cookies-and-cream milkshake."

"I'm sleeping in tomorrow," Brillante said, rubbing his eyes.

"They're closed on Christmas, I think," Roth said. "Sorry. Any other place you miss?"

They were walking past the luggage carousels on the way to the parking garage affixed to the airport.

"We can grab some food on the way out. What do you want, Suki?"

She was looking down at her phone. "Brice is here."

"What?" Roth asked, alarmed.

"He's parked outside right now."

"Brice is here?" Brillante asked enthusiastically.

Both of the twins liked Suki's boyfriend, whom she'd gotten to know through the theater arts department at school. Brice was one of the most popular kids in their class, very outgoing and extroverted, which was a profound contrast to Suki's introversion. When they were together, though, her eyes lit up and she was more animated—if no less sarcastic than usual.

"What's he doing here?" Roth asked.

"I don't know," Suki said. "He wanted to know what time our plane was landing, but I didn't tell him to come."

When they reached the sliding doors, they slid open and revealed Brice. He was a big kid, tall and large, due to a thyroid condition, and he had thick, wavy dark hair that he wore long.

"Merry Christmas, my poggers friends!" he shouted boisterously, waving to them as he stepped inside. He had a Wendy's bag in his hand and a Frosty, both of which he immediately offered to Suki. Roth caught the smell of fries coming from the bag.

"Awww," she said, taking it. "What are you doing here?"

"I was so bummed we wouldn't see each other at Christmas, and then you said you were coming home early, and I said I had to see you, and you said maybe . . . Hello, Mr. Roth . . . can I take Suki home with me?"

"It's good to see you, Brice," Roth said.

Suki gave him a pleading look. She wanted to go with Brice.

"Maybe you could hang out tomorrow?" Roth suggested.

"I wanted to show her a Studio Ghibli film she hasn't seen yet. It's perfect. It's about cats. Have you seen *The Cat Returns?*" he asked, directing the question at Suki. "You'll love it!"

She looked at Roth again, her eyes saying, *Please?*

Roth rubbed his face and scratched the beard at his neck. He just wanted everyone to be safely gathered at home. Especially since it was Christmas. But his daughter didn't ask for a lot, and he hated to deny her, particularly since he knew that Brice lived near them, both houses in the Sourdough area of Bozeman.

"I promise on my grandmother's urn that I'll have her home before midnight," Brice said, pressing his palms together. His gaze shifted to Suki. "I can't wait for you to see your Christmas present. I've been dying to show it to you."

"Are your parents home?" Roth asked.

"Oh yeah. My brothers are in town too. But I got dibs on the movie room. My mom's making us a batch of caramel Bugles for the movie."

"I'll bring some home for you, Dad?" Suki asked, her eyes digging into Roth's pleadingly.

He *did* love caramel Bugles. "Okay. But please be back before midnight. Turn in your phone before you go to bed."

"I promise," Suki said. She opened the food bag, pulled out a waffle fry, and ate it.

"Dude, share!" Brillante held out his hand, and Suki gave him one.

"Can we go too?" Lucas asked.

"No," Roth said, "but you can hang out with them tomorrow if they're cool with it."

"That would be awesome," Brice said. "I'm stressing about the play."

In *Gentleman's Guide*, he was playing nine different roles. Suki had helped him come up with different personas for each, along with little ways of acting them to help differentiate them all. Brice was just the kind of person who could pull off such a challenging role.

"Before midnight," Roth reminded them. "And text me when you get there."

"Later, derps," Suki said, giving her brothers quick high fives. She offered her suitcase to her dad, but Brillante grabbed it first and offered to take it back home.

Roth watched the two of them as they walked outside first, Brice's hands moving expressively as he talked. Roth turned around and looked for Lund.

Another text chirped on the burner.

I'll make sure they get there.

"Who's that from?" Lucas asked, looking at the text.

"Uncle Steve. It's all good. So . . . some food before we get home?"

"You know it!" Lucas said, giving him two thumbs up.

———

The neighborhood was dark by the time they'd gotten the Denali from the parking garage, stopped downtown for food, and then driven to the edge of the mountains on the south side of town. The streets of Bozeman hadn't been plowed that day, and the foothills were a little slushy. The Denali was four-wheel drive, thankfully, so they easily climbed the mountain and entered the exclusive neighborhood.

"Whoa, deer!" Lucas said.

Roth slowed down and watched the two does cross the bend in the road ahead of him. The properties in the area were a mix of farmhouses, larger homes, and even mansions—all respectfully separated and giving each other plenty of room. When they'd visited Bozeman on a house-hunting trip, Roth had been amazed by the amount of space, considering their tiny lot in Fremont had been so small and was worth about $1.2 million compared to homes five times larger going for $2 million in this neighborhood. With his earnings as a *New York Times* bestselling author, he'd paid cash for their place. One of the reasons they'd chosen Bozeman were the many hiking trails in the mountains. It was beautiful country, with old cottonwood trees that bloomed green in the spring and blew fluff like snow. During the winter months, the mountains were excellent for snowmobiling.

As they passed the road leading to the Beasleys' mansion, Roth felt his chest clench with dread. The six-million-dollar property had been empty for a year. The deed of the house was in a family trust, which Roth now owned without anyone's knowledge. He couldn't rent it out to just anyone, not a mansion of that size. And selling it felt . . . wrong too. Every time Roth drove past it, he felt a sense of deep guilt. If only he could have saved little Jane Louise, but it hadn't been in his power to protect her, no more than it was in his power to help whoever was in Cozumel even now, in Jacob Calakmul's clutches.

He took the final turn onto the street. A text arrived on his burner phone. He glanced at it.

"Don't text and drive, Dad," Lucas said.

"Yeah, stop setting a bad example for your kids," Brillante teased.

It was from Suki. She'd made it to Brice's house safely, and she thanked him for being flexible and letting her go.

"I won't respond. Just wanted to make sure she was safe."

The street they lived on climbed steeply. The Denali's engine growled as it went up. There were pine trees laden with snow surrounding each property on the drive, adding to the sense of privacy. The rooftops were all white as well. At the top of the street, the road ended in a cul-de-sac. The Roths' home was the second to the last, and he turned up the driveway, noticing a set of tire tracks in the fresh snow. When he pulled up to the house, he saw a Jeep parked out front to one side. The car door opened once their headlights hit it, and Jordan stepped out of the vehicle and gave him a wave.

Roth pushed the button to open the garage door, and the garage lights turned on as it opened. He slowed and then stopped the Denali as Jordan approached the driver's-side window.

When he lowered the window, Jordan looked into the vehicle. "Welcome home, family. So now you know about us, right? We're the bodyguards you never knew existed. The ghost squadron. My name is Jordan Scott. I take it Suki's at her boyfriend's house?"

Lucas made kissing noises as affirmation.

"Dude, don't be gross," Brillante said.

Roth felt a wave of weariness press into him. "Boys."

"Heard you all had an exciting trip," Jordan said, leaning on the frame. "Wish I'd been there. Now, I've been inside, checked every room, every closed door. Even saw the dirty laundry under one of the twins' beds. Tsk. Tsk. Do your laundry!"

"It was Bryant's! Totally Bryant's!" Lucas cackled.

"Whatever." Jordan slapped the rim. "I'm just teasing. Have a good night." He dropped his voice lower. "Steve asked me to stick around until Suki gets home. Want me to scare her boyfriend off? I could take him into the woods, zip-tie him to a tree?"

His expression said he was still teasing. At least Roth hoped so.

"Don't you dare!" Lucas said, laughing.

Jordan grinned.

"Better not," Roth said. "Thanks, Jordan. I'm glad everything's been quiet. I'm expecting a visit from some pretty bad guys. The next few days could get tense. I told Lund as much at the airport."

Jordan nodded. "You're in good hands. Lund has plans after plans after *plans*. He's consulted in security for some pretty big companies."

Roth already knew as much, but he suspected Jordan had said it to comfort the twins—and appreciated the effort.

"Like who?" Brillante asked.

"Like Intel, among others. They make computer chips. Some ninjas tried to steal a shipment in Malaysia. *Hee-waaaa!*" He made a sound that reminded Roth of the cry Bruce Lee had made in his movies while delivering a well-placed chop or kick. "After they implemented Lund's ideas, stolen shipments were almost totally eliminated. Those ninjas didn't stand a chance."

"Dude . . . ninjas? Seriously?" Brillante asked skeptically.

"The real deal," Jordan said, slapping the car again. "Welcome back from Germany. Merry Christmas!"

"Thanks, Jordan," Roth said and raised the window. He pulled the Denali into the garage and shut the door. After bringing their luggage in, Roth and the boys sat around the dining room table and ate the fast-food dinner. The hardwood floor was still clean from before the trip since no one had been there for days. The lack of Christmas decorations hit Roth hard. Sarina had always been big on decorating for the holidays, and it was a stark reminder that she still wasn't with them. Since they'd intended to spend Christmas with Tawna, no one had bothered to do anything.

The dining table was in the corner of the kitchen area, near an island counter with three stools by the sink. Sarina had always loved this space since it was so full of light, with five windows in one of the walls, three in another, and a large plate-glass door leading to the back patio. The lights out there were off, so the door only showed a reflection of the kitchen, something that unsettled Roth since he couldn't see what was outside.

That's why you have Jordan and Steve, he reminded himself. *That's why they're here.*

After dinner, the boys turned on the TV and started playing the Nintendo Switch together. Roth went to his den and turned on the laptop. He'd checked his e-mail remotely from the airports, looking for anything that would cause alarm. He dreaded getting a message from Jacob. Would he answer the cell if it rang again? Or was it best to ignore the calls?

He sat back in the easy chair and pulled out his phone to text Suki, asking how the movie was.

Haven't started it yet. Just talking.

Roth rubbed his forehead.

No messages about the translation of the pages. A quick check of his regular phone revealed he'd received no messages from his publisher either, which was to be expected since it was Christmas. He felt his eyelids start to droop. He should go sit with the boys and fall asleep on the couch by them. But getting out of the chair felt like too much.

The sound of a slamming door startled him awake. He could hear the television on in the other room. His heart began to pound. He got up quickly and left the den.

"Boys?" he called out.

Jordan stepped into the kitchen from the garage, gun drawn.

"Three SUVs are coming up the drive," he said, his voice worried. "I've triggered the security alarm to notify the team. Where are the twins?"

Headlights could be seen from the windows in the front door and the windows on either side of the great room. There was so much glass. It felt like a fishbowl. He looked at his watch. It was 11:03 p.m.

"Brillante! Lucas!" Roth shouted.

No answer.

CHAPTER NINE

Aspling Residence

Bozeman, Montana

December 25

In the Sourdough district of Bozeman, the term "neighbor" was used pretty loosely. The Roths and the Asplings lived too far apart for the houses to be considered walkable distance, but they lived on the same ridge south of the city that bordered the mountains. Brice's house was by itself at the end of Canyon Meadow Road, the turn-off for which was easy to miss for people who hadn't been there before.

"Was that from your dad?" Brice asked.

They were in the game room, which had a huge L-shaped fabric couch and several gaming chairs pulled close to the large-screen TV. The carpet was totally weird—it had cartoon images of old movie reels and popcorn on it. If you dropped something on it, you had to get on your hands and knees to feel for it, because everything blended in with the design.

"Yeah," Suki answered. There was an electric fireplace with a fake fire pretending to burn in the cabinet below the television. Even with that, it was still chilly. A *Beatles: Rock Band* gaming set for the Wii was stuffed in the corner, and movie posters decorated the walls—*The Princess Bride, Toy Story, Star Wars,* along with several others. Brice's family were all movie nuts.

Brice sighed. "I have to take you home?"

She shook her head. "I said we hadn't started the movie yet. We should probably start it, though. My body is still on Germany time."

"I like talking to you." He reached for his drink and took a sip. "Empty. I'm going to get another. Do you want a soda?"

"A root beer would be nice," Suki said.

Brice rose from the couch, stretched, and left the game room, passing by the Ping-Pong table on the way out.

She hadn't told him the real reason she'd come home early from Germany. Not the high-speed chase in Germany on the autobahn. Not the codex they'd seen at the library in Dresden or the pages that had glowed with glyphs when she unleashed power from her bracelet and ring. Not the fear that Jacob Calakmul would keep coming after them, again and again, because her father had decided to try for revenge.

Brice shared everything with her. There was no holding back. But she had so many secrets from him, and they were starting to eat her up inside.

Suki shook her head. She'd stopped seeing the family therapist after a few weeks. It hadn't helped. Instead, she talked to her dad about her feelings. And she and Brice had become so close over the last year. College was around the corner. Real life. But what did "real life" even mean when she knew people could turn into jaguars? When she herself could make objects levitate with her mind? Well, not her mind *exactly*—she didn't really understand what the *kem äm* was. The fabric of space-time?

She stared at the copper bowl half-filled with microwave popcorn, sitting on the square coffee table. Closing her eyes, she thought about the magic. It had worked in Dresden. The urgency of the moment had overridden her anxiety, just like it had in the death game.

The power coursing through her veins was an ancestral gift from the relatives who'd emigrated from the Yucatán Peninsula. It terrified her. After all, it meant she had the same abilities as some truly frightening people, and she didn't want to be like them. But if it could help protect her family, and not just reveal words in an ancient record, maybe she should start trusting it more.

In her mind, she envisioned the webbing of *kem äm* cradling the popcorn bowl. She felt the prickly tingles shoot down her arms, spreading gooseflesh across her skin. When she opened her eyes, the copper bowl was hovering over the table, supported by a circular disk of woven specks of golden light. Then she heard Brice coming.

She blinked, and the webbing disappeared, and the copper bowl landed with a loud thud on the wooden tabletop and spilled over. Some of the popcorn dropped to the floor, blending in with the fake popcorn on the carpet.

Suki swore under her breath and hurriedly began scooping the snack back into the bowl.

Brice came in with two sodas and looked at her picking up the mess.

"I'm such a klutz," she said.

"I once spilled a whole box of Legos in here," he said with a smile as he scooted around the bend in the couch and joined her. "I tried picking up all the pieces, but for weeks no one would walk in this room without shoes. It was painful."

Suki grinned. "I think I stepped on one two weeks ago."

"You probably did." He handed her the soda. "You're going to love this movie. Seriously. If I could be a talking cat, I totally would."

"I just wish I *had* a cat," Suki said. "My dad's allergic to them."

When they'd lived in Fremont in that tiny house on its crowded street, Suki used to coax the neighbor's cat to come into their yard so she could pet it.

Brice turned on the TV and used the remote to find the movie. Suki finished picking up the popcorn pieces and stared at the bowl.

What if he'd seen her levitating it? Maybe she'd wanted him to. Maybe she'd wanted him to know. Should she just tell him?

"It's a little weird," he said by way of introduction, "but aren't all of their movies strange? *Howl's Moving Castle. Spirited Away. Kiki's Delivery Service.* But this one is probably my favorite. You don't think it's too late to start it, do you?"

"I think we're good," Suki said hesitantly.

He eyed her quizzically. "What's wrong? Do you want me to take you home?"

"No. It's not that."

"What aren't you telling me?"

"Just start the movie."

He shook his head no and stuffed the remote into his pocket. She hated awkward tension, and this conversation was quickly going south. But what could she tell him? She was afraid if she opened up, even a little bit, the whole story would all come spilling out. She actually wanted to tell him the whole story—she thought he'd believe her—but he'd almost certainly want to tell his parents. The Asplings were nice, but a story about the ancient Maya death games would probably freak them out. Knowing about it would also put them in danger.

"I tell you everything," Brice said. He pulled a face. "You didn't like the Christmas present I got you?"

"No," she said.

"You didn't like it?"

"It's not that. Actually, it's not about you at all. Can we just watch the movie?"

"Not until you tell me why you're so upset. Are you stressed about the future still? About college?"

"Yes, I'm always stressed about that, but this is different." She paused, her heart beating fast. Her breaths coming quickly. "Something happened on our trip to Germany."

"Don't tell me you fell in love with a dude in lederhosen," he said, aghast—but joking.

She forced laughter, her heart still pounding fast. "We weren't just in a car accident." A feeling of warning pulsed in her chest. She wanted to shove it away. It persisted.

> *Dangerous. Don't tell him.*
> *But I want to tell him!*

> *It'll be weird if you do. You'll have to show him the*
> *magic. He'll freak out.*
> *He won't freak out.*

> *He will.*

A car accident was the reason she'd given him for getting home early. He'd taken it at face value, but the secrets she'd been hiding were struggling to break free.

He sat down on the couch and held her hand. "Whatever it is, Suki, it doesn't matter," he said, looking into her eyes. "Just . . . I wish you trusted me."

"Way to go for the kill shot."

He smiled. "We don't have to watch the movie. I think we should keep talking."

"Nah, I want to see what's impressed you so much. Turn it on."

He did, but there was a tension between them now. The movie was everything he'd promised, though, and they slowly relaxed toward each other as it played, both of them enjoying the experience of watching it. Things finally felt normal again, or as normal as they got lately, when her phone buzzed in her pocket. Was her dad changing his mind about how late she could stay out? She pulled it out to check.

The text made her chest lurch. It was from her dad.

Don't come home.

CHAPTER TEN

ROTH RESIDENCE

BOZEMAN, MONTANA

December 25

Adrenaline surged through Roth's veins. He raced across the kitchen to the family room, where he found the boys. Relief cascaded through him when he saw that Brillante had fallen asleep on the couch. Lucas had headphones on and was playing a game on his phone. But the relief was short-lived. They were under attack. There were three cars outside and only one guard inside.

Roth maneuvered around the stuffed leather couch and quickly roused Brillante by shaking his shoulder.

"Whaa—?"

"Wake up. We have to go," Roth said firmly.

Lucas looked worried and pulled the headphones off. "Dad?"

"They're coming!" Jordan warned. He'd positioned himself at the edge of the living room with a view of the front door. "Two, three, four . . . six . . ." He brought up his pistol and held it trained on the door, ready to fire.

Roth could feel his pulse thundering in his ears. Brillante rushed away to the master bedroom. Roth pulled out his phone and quickly texted Suki: *Don't come home.*

"We going to the panic room?" Lucas asked tremulously. Roth had had one installed in the basement after they'd returned from Mexico the previous year. It was a hardened structure, meant for withstanding natural disasters or home invasions.

"We might have to," Roth said, perspiration dripping down his back.

A loud knock thumped at the door.

That surprised him. In fact, he would have expected Calakmul's goons to try sneaking in.

Another loud knock landed on the door.

Brillante came sprinting back, phone in hand.

"Can you see them?" Roth asked Jordan.

"The headlights from the SUVs make it—wait. There's a woman standing at the window."

"A woman?"

"She's in an FBI jacket," Jordan said, but he hadn't lowered his pistol.

Roth approached Jordan and peered over his shoulder. He saw a woman with dark hair at the door, turned around as if talking to someone behind her. Sure enough, she wore a dark windbreaker with the recognizable big yellow letters on the back.

"I'm going to answer the door," Roth said.

"Not sure that's a good idea," Jordan said. "Could be an act."

The woman turned back and peered through the glass. She saw Jordan holding a pistol and quickly drew hers, aiming it at them. "FBI!" she shouted.

Roth stepped away from Jordan and held up his hands. "Put it down, man. Calakmul's people wouldn't come knocking. And they wouldn't bother with the pretense of being FBI." Whether or not that was true, Roth didn't want a shoot-out in his living room.

Jordan frowned but holstered his weapon.

"Mr. Roth?" the woman asked through the glass.

He nodded and then slowly approached the door.

"Stop," she ordered. "Is the door locked?"

He nodded again. "I've got a security system. I can unlock it with my phone."

"Keep your hands in the air. Both of you. Are your children home, Mr. Roth?"

"Yes," he said, grateful he'd already texted Suki to stay at Brice's house.

The woman still had her gun pointed at him through the window. "Open the door with your phone. No funny business. I have a warrant."

Roth's pulse throbbed, but he did as she said and slowly pulled out his phone and entered the passcode to unlock it. The deadbolt clicked as it released, and then the door opened and two other agents entered, weapons drawn.

"Dad?" Lucas asked worriedly.

"My sons are in the other room," Roth said firmly. "Please lower your weapons."

The woman entered next, her weapon already stowed away, and held up a badge. "I'm Special Agent Monica Sanchez, Bozeman resident agency. I'm sorry to come in like that, but I saw that man with a Glock."

"This is Jordan Scott from my private-security team," Roth explained. "He's one of our bodyguards. We weren't expecting anyone, especially this late. We just got back from Germany earlier today."

"You have ID on you?" Agent Sanchez asked Jordan.

"It's in my back left pocket," Jordan said, his hands still up. He looked and sounded edgy.

Roth's burner phone began to buzz in his pocket. His heart rate was beginning to ease, but he couldn't ignore the possibility that Agent

Sanchez was a plant. He knew the Calakmul family had a long reach. There'd been prominent people at the death games, famous people, so it was no stretch to imagine he had employees embedded in the FBI as well.

"Can you tell me what this is all about, Agent Sanchez?" he asked.

"Search him," she said.

"Do you have a warrant?" Jordan asked.

"I had to wake up a judge on Christmas night," Agent Sanchez answered tightly. "But, yes, we do."

One of the other agents approached them. He took Jordan's weapon, then quickly searched him while another agent held a gun on him. The guy doing the search took Jordan's wallet out of his back pocket and opened it.

"Jordan Scott, works for Lund Security Ops," the agent said. "You're one of Steve's boys?"

"Yup," Jordan said. "My arms are getting tired. Can I lower them?"

"Yes," Agent Sanchez said. "At first we thought we'd arrived at a hostage situation. You can understand why we'd be careful." She grabbed the radio from her pocket. "Perimeter secure?"

There was a knock on the glass of the back door, and they all looked out and saw an agent standing there with a flashlight, snow covering his shoes. He held up a radio receiver, and his voice echoed from the one Agent Sanchez held.

"Roger."

"What's going on, Agent Sanchez?" Roth asked, feeling anxiety well inside him again.

"Those your sons?" she asked, looking around him at the twins.

"That's Lucas, and that's Brillante," he said.

"Where's your daughter? The report from Salt Lake said you had three children."

"She's at a friend's house tonight. Why don't you tell me what's going on? It's cold out there. Can we shut the door?"

Roth wasn't sure what to believe. These people seemed like FBI agents. They had the clothes. The gear. But he couldn't shake the suspicion that something wasn't right. Was this all a ruse?

Agent Sanchez waved another man in from the porch. "Keep the engines running," she told him. "We'll be leaving soon."

"I'm not going anywhere," Roth insisted.

She waited for the agent she'd spoken with to leave and then turned and gave Roth an impatient frown. "I know it's late, Mr. Roth. I know it's Christmas. But your family is in danger. Can we discuss this in the dining room? Unlock the back door as well, please."

Roth obeyed and used his phone to disarm the back door. After that, she waved for the man at the back door to enter. The man who'd been outside stomped his shoes on the small rug at the door, the snow sloughing off.

"Sure, we can talk," Roth said, both because he wanted to hear what she had to say and he couldn't see a way out of it. "Jordan, can you confirm their warrant, please?"

Agent Sanchez reached into her jacket pocket and withdrew a folded piece of paper, which she handed to Jordan. Roth, who was standing nearby, saw him unfold it and noticed the official-looking letterhead: "United States District Court." There was a bunch of typed text, some filled-in blanks, and a magistrate judge's signature at the bottom.

"It's legit," Jordan said, handing the warrant back.

"Can we sit down?" Agent Sanchez asked.

As they went and sat around the dining table, which was still littered with the remnants of Wendy's, Roth's burner phone went off again. He looked at the caller ID and saw Lund's number on the screen.

"I need to take this," he said.

"Is it your daughter?" Agent Sanchez asked. "She's in danger too."

"It's Steve Lund," Roth said, then answered the call. "I'm in the kitchen with Special Agent Monica Sanchez from the FBI."

"I'm on my way over," Steve replied. "The security system is going crazy."

"Could you swing by and pick up Suki first?" Roth asked. "She's still at her friend's house. I'll text her to let her know you're coming."

"Sure. Have they told you why they're there?" Lund asked.

"Not yet. About to find out. Call me before you come, okay?"

"Roger that."

"Where's your daughter?" Agent Sanchez asked as he hung up the call.

"A friend's house," Roth answered. "What's going on?"

"We received intelligence that your family has been targeted by the gang MS-13. Do you know who they are?"

Roth did. "It's a Latin American gang, the Mara Salvatrucha, that branched out to LA in the eighties."

"You know your history, Mr. Roth," Agent Sanchez commented.

"I'm from California, and that gang operates in the Bay Area," he said. His stomach had tightened into a knot. Calakmul had made it clear that he had plenty of foot soldiers already in the US, and it seemed likely that MS-13 was another strand in his web. "What do they want?"

"To kidnap you and your kids. The intelligence arrived at the Salt Lake City field office, which covers Utah, Idaho, and satellite offices in Montana. I believe you have a friend who works in law enforcement in Utah?"

"Will Moretti," Roth said.

Agent Sanchez looked at one of the other agents. "Yes. That's the man. He's on an antidrug task force down there. Once he heard your name was involved, he insisted we escalate our response."

Roth smiled and thought inwardly, *Thanks, man.* Will Moretti had been his close friend since childhood. Along with their third best friend, Westfall, they'd been the Three Musketeers, and they'd all called one another by their last names. Life had led the friends down different paths since high school, but they'd kept in touch. Westfall had died last year, so Roth and Moretti were the only two left. Moretti was also the only other person who knew anything about Roth's troubles.

"I put together a team to protect your family." She scrutinized him closely. "It is highly unusual for MS-13 to target a man like you, Mr. Roth. We have a drug-sniffing dog outside. I'm going to conduct a search of the premises, but let's get you and your family out of here first. Where is your daughter?"

Suspicion tightened in Roth's gut. She'd asked about Suki several times. Did that signal she was working with Jacob? He'd had a special interest in Suki after seeing her use the *kem äm*. He'd even allowed her to keep the bracelet and ring she wore, encouraging her to practice her abilities.

"There aren't any drugs here," Roth said. "That's not why they're after us."

"Please allow me to be skeptical of your claim, Mr. Roth," she said, propping a hand on her hip. "We both know the rich indulge in drugs too. They're just less likely to get caught. You, with your connections to an officer on an antidrug task force, are even less likely to get caught. But I can't think of many other reasons why the MS-13 gang would take an interest in you."

Roth pinched the bridge of his nose. "Is it in the warrant to search the place?" he asked Jordan.

"Yup," he responded tonelessly.

"I mean it," Roth said, eyeing her warily. "They're not after us because of some drug deal gone bad or whatever. This has nothing to do with drugs."

"So you tell me what it's about." She gave him a pointed look. "You said you were attacked in Germany?"

"We returned from our trip this afternoon," Roth said. "Haven't even unpacked our suitcases yet."

Their going to see the Dresden Codex had triggered Calakmul obviously, leading to this rapidly escalating chain of events. But Roth's work had begun long before the trip to the SLUB. He'd made the necessary arrangements to ensure his plan to expose and stop Jacob Calakmul would move forward even if he were killed. But he was missing the key piece of the puzzle—the prophecy in the codex.

Someone else had it, though. Jacob Calakmul, who had a vested interest in keeping its contents secret.

"Why did you go to Germany, Mr. Roth?" Agent Sanchez asked pointedly.

"To spend Christmas with my sister," he answered, glancing over at the boys. They were unusually quiet yet again. Fear shone in their eyes.

"Yet here you are on Christmas Day. Let's leave my team to execute the search warrant and go to the field office in Bozeman where we can talk further and keep you safe. Just bring your bags. The ones you haven't unpacked."

Roth sat up straighter. Something told him that if he left with them, he wouldn't be coming back. "We're going to stay here until Lund gets here with my daughter."

"I have probable cause to search your home for narcotics, Mr. Roth. So let's level with each other. What are you taking, pain pills? Something stronger? I know how it goes: you get the pills for a surgery, and then it becomes a problem. You wouldn't be the first."

"Sorry to disappoint," Roth said, leaning back. "You won't find anything stronger than Diet Coke in the house. But we're not going *anywhere* until Lund gets here. He used to work—"

"I know who he is," she said. "If we find evidence, I can arrest you and bring you to the agency."

"So go ahead and search while we wait. I have nothing to hide." Which didn't mean they wouldn't find anything. If they were part of Jacob's operation, he had no doubt they'd find a pouch of cocaine or something "conveniently" in his bedroom . . . giving them authority to arrest him and take him and his kids away. She'd mentioned Moretti, though, so maybe they were the good guys.

Or maybe a Pegasus jet had already landed at Bozeman Yellowstone International Airport.

Agent Sanchez rose from the chair, giving him a cynical look. "Bring in Hazel," she told one of her guys. "Top to bottom. Let's move."

Drumming his fingers on the table, Roth glanced over at Jordan. "Sorry you have to stay a bit longer."

Jordan looked concerned. "The paperwork's there, but I'm not sure this is legit," he said under his breath. "The timing is suspicious."

The front door opened, and a huge German shepherd came in, straining against the leash, tail wagging vigorously.

CHAPTER ELEVEN

Fox Harb'r Resort

Nova Scotia, Canada

December 26

The smell of coffee in the common area, the low murmur of voices, and the dim lights revealed the late hour. Jacob Calakmul looked up from the day-old newspaper in his hands, watching the few remaining ultra-rich having drinks in the lobby. Some had carried in skis or snowboards, brand-new and unwrapped on Christmas the previous day. In the hours they'd spent in Nova Scotia, he had recognized many nationalities and heard a variety of languages—Russian, German, French, English. This particular resort catered to the wealthy and elite. The couches were all chic and low-backed. The walls were lined with windows overlooking the picturesque snowbound landscape and the waters. These were a contrast to the flat jungles of the Yucatán, which were vibrant and green year-round. And hot.

A hotel staff member approached with a coffeepot.

"Would you like more *xocolatl*?" she asked.

Jacob nodded, watched her refill his empty cup, then lifted it and took a sip. He felt the restorative powers of the drink energize him, countering the fatigue of air travel. They'd needed to refuel in Nova Scotia on the way to Europe, and upon learning of the Roths' escape on the autobahn, plans had changed as well. He glanced at his watch, an F.P. Journe Swiss make worth several hundred thousand euros. A symbol of prestige that few could afford. Well, few had as much *gold* as the Calakmul family controlled.

It was after two in the morning in eastern Canada, which made it before midnight still in Bozeman, Montana.

He was waiting for a call.

Angélica approached, wearing snowpants that fit her snugly, along with a coat—a Fjällräven women's coat that would have been impractical in the jungles of Mexico but suited the conditions of their new climate.

She held a smartphone to her ear, listening as she approached, and sat down in the chair adjacent to the couch where Jacob sat.

She spoke in Mayan to prevent eavesdroppers from understanding the call—whether they be eavesdroppers from the hotel or any telecom company or intelligence agency listening in. Mayan wasn't a language the international community had bothered to learn. Of course, he understood her every word.

"Understood. Well done. Thank you." Angélica ended the call and stuffed her phone into her jacket pocket.

"Well?" Jacob asked.

"Still recovering in post-op from the surgery. Handcuffed to the gurney. But the wound wasn't fatal. He's still unconscious. The accomplice, the one from the van, isn't talking."

"Of course he won't speak," Jacob said. To become a jaguar priest or to work directly with one required the strictest of oaths, those made with magic. They would divulge nothing or risk losing their lives in a gruesome manner.

"The German authorities are still trying to trace their identities. They haven't appeared in any criminal databases they have access to, nor will they. They're finding lawyers for them at the moment."

"I'm confident Xavier can break them out once he's recovered," Jacob said. "Walls cannot restrain a jaguar priest. Have the Roths arrived home?"

"Yes. And the FBI is there now."

"Good," he said with a slight smile. "I hope the Roths feel safe. Is the MS-13 gang in position as agreed?"

"Nearly. They had trouble getting a vehicle, but that problem is solved. The daughter isn't there. Suki."

Jacob tilted his head. "Why isn't she with the family?"

"She went to see her boyfriend. He showed up at the airport and picked her up," Angélica said.

"Where does he live?"

"Don't know yet. We should have a lock on her phone soon and be able to trace her location."

"I want the whole family brought to the Jaguar Temple by this evening," Jacob said, feeling his anger flare. "This is beginning to feel like what happened in Cozumel last year. No more mistakes."

"We have their phones monitored. They're at the house. But someone else is involved. The person who shot our men in Germany. I have no phone records of this man, who he is, or how Roth hired him. Clearly Roth has been acting without our knowledge and using a burner phone. His actions at the library make that obvious."

Jacob frowned and rubbed his chin. "Clever man. Always has been."

"His laptop is still being monitored, and the cameras we installed in the house are operational. We know they're home. The FBI is there. There's also a security guard with them."

"How do we get the number for the burner phone?"

"We don't. That's the purpose of a burner. He can throw it away and get another one."

"Have you identified the security guard?"

"No. Young man, early twenties."

"So not the one from Germany."

"No, this fellow came to the Roths' home before they arrived. Searched it too. We think he's working for the other man."

"I want to know who it is, and I want him brought to the Jaguar Temple as well."

"Of course."

Her phone rang. Angélica pulled it from her pocket and answered it immediately. "Yes?"

They were sitting close enough that Jacob could hear the other voice on the line.

"The MS-13 gang has left the rental facility. They're heading to Roth's neighborhood."

"Excellent," Angélica said. "What of the jaguar priest who went with them?"

"K'oxol ghostwalked to the residence ahead of them so he can prepare. Apparently the family won't leave the house. The FBI has begun searching and brought a narco dog so he can't get too close yet."

Jacob shot a worried look at Angélica. "The surveillance equipment."

"They might find it if they start looking in vents."

He shook his head in annoyance. "Take the family as soon as the gang is in position. Kill the agents—except for ours."

"Did you hear the orders?" Angélica asked into the phone, her voice shaking.

"Yes. It will be done."

The call ended.

Jacob pursed his lips angrily. "I shouldn't have let them go last year," he whispered, gazing at the window, which reflected the lobby lighting and furniture. It was too dark outside to see anything but snow.

"You warned him."

"And I don't make idle threats. The end is coming soon. He would have been made a ruler in the new order. The seed of Jacob. How short-sighted of him to throw that away."

"He loved his wife. Maybe he seeks revenge because you kidnapped her?"

"Revenge, inflamed, is dangerous," Jacob said flatly. "It must be studied, controlled, and planned. As Aristotle said in *Nicomachean Ethics*, men regard it as their right to return evil for evil—and, if they cannot, they feel they have lost their liberty. The time to seek revenge against the Spaniards was not while the pox was raging. It was after it subsided."

He thought on the situation with Mr. Roth. It was more difficult to extract someone from the United States. The government was tied down in knots of regulations and protocols, and the officers who administered those protocols were not always susceptible to bribes. Of course, some of them would take bribes, provided they were high enough and there was enough time to leverage someone's loyalty. That was why Jacob Calakmul didn't trust anyone else picking up the family. That was why he'd decided to go himself in the Pegasus to Bozeman.

Soon the family would be under his power again. And this time, their ending would be different.

"Should I wake the pilot to ready the jet?" Angélica asked.

Jacob looked at his watch again. "Soon. We need to leave within the hour." He lowered his wrist and stroked the edge of the couch. "I thought the daughter had some promise," he mused aloud. "Socorro. Her grandmother's name. It's a good thing she's not there to help them tonight."

Angélica's brow wrinkled. "What do you mean?"

"She can control the *kem äm*. It would make K'oxol vulnerable to their bullets."

"*Oh,*" Angélica said. "Of course."

The *kem äm* was part of the magic of the ancient Maya. When the death games were being played, webs of it were used to block off each end of the court, preventing any corporeal object from leaving. A ball that struck the web was immediately repelled back into the game.

The same applied to bullets.

With a jaguar priest on the scene, the MS-13 would easily come out ahead. When the FBI agents tried to kill them, they would only kill themselves.

CHAPTER TWELVE

ROTH RESIDENCE

BOZEMAN, MONTANA

December 26

"Mr. Roth, why hasn't your daughter returned home yet?" asked Agent Sanchez as she approached the kitchen table. "It was over thirty minutes ago that you made that call."

Even though it was the middle of the night, the lights in the house were all on, and FBI agents were coming in and out of the kitchen. Roth, weary from the long day, was sitting at the table, struggling to think with a tired brain.

"Because I've told Lund to keep her away for now," he replied to Agent Sanchez. She'd heard the phone call but hadn't seen the follow-up text he'd sent.

"I thought Mr. Lund was picking her up?"

"He did. They're in downtown Bozeman now."

"What? Where exactly?"

"I actually don't know," Roth said with a stifled yawn. "He didn't say."

Agent Sanchez sighed. The dog handler came up from the basement. The German shepherd's tail was wagging so powerfully it thumped against the china cabinet and nearly upended a dish.

The agent maneuvered the dog into the kitchen. "Clean," he said curtly.

Agent Sanchez frowned. "Take him back to the van."

"You look surprised not to have found any drugs," Roth said. Actually, *he* was surprised that no one had planted any. "Am I under arrest?"

"Agent Sanchez? Can you come over here?" beckoned another agent. The dog handler went to the door and stepped outside.

As soon as Agent Sanchez had walked off, the twins approached Roth. "How long are they staying?" Brillante asked in a low voice.

"I don't know," Roth confessed.

"They were looking for stuff everywhere," Lucas said. "Where's Suki?"

"She's downtown with Uncle Steve. I told him to keep moving her from place to place and wait for our call. If I don't know where she is, I won't have to lie about it." He dropped his voice. "I'm not sure they all can be trusted."

"Is it sus that they're searching our house?" Lucas asked. "Are they the good guys or not?"

"I don't know for sure," Roth said in an undertone. "But we haven't done anything wrong."

"Is this about the codex in Germany?"

"That's not why the FBI came. They came—" He stopped abruptly when he heard footsteps approaching.

Agent Sanchez came striding into the kitchen again. When she reached the table, she put her hand on her hip again in an authoritative pose. "Mr. Roth, were you aware that there's surveillance equipment in your den? Are you being investigated by another government agency?"

"What are you talking about?" he asked. He'd suspected that Jacob Calakmul was monitoring his house from the inside. He'd assumed his cell phone and computer were compromised and that they were possibly being watched in other ways. But he'd never inspected his house for the devices because he didn't want Calakmul to suspect he knew he was being watched.

"The duct vent has a microcamera installed. Agent Spencer just found it. It's tapped into the house power and is transmitting a signal. You didn't know?"

Roth shook his head. "Isn't that . . . illegal?"

"It is," she agreed. "When I applied for a warrant, there was no record of a previous order authorizing such a thing. Only the FBI has jurisdiction on American citizens."

"Can you find out who did it?" Roth asked.

Another agent came in. "The Wi-Fi router is compromised as well," he said.

"You mean all my internet traffic is being monitored?" Roth said. He tried to sound surprised but wasn't sure he pulled it off. He'd expected as much, of course. Which was why he'd been working on his secret project on a different laptop and using his burner phone as a hotspot for data.

"What kind?" Agent Sanchez asked. Outside, the German shepherd began barking. She glanced toward the front door in apparent annoyance.

"The kind the NSA uses," said the agent. "This is unusual." She looked at Jordan, who was slouching in a chair, eating a microwaved burrito. "Did your company install these?"

Jordan shook his head. "We use Vivint high-end systems," he replied. "We alarm windows and doors and install motion sensors. Nothing in the vents. We don't do that kind of thing. It's *illegal*, as you said, to spy on our customers."

"Then I think we've said enough about it," Agent Sanchez said, giving the other FBI agent a pointed look.

The dog's barking intensified. Agent Sanchez's lips pursed as she glanced at the door again. "He'll wake up the neighborhood."

"Dogs don't bark without a reason," Jordan said, getting up from the chair. His posture indicated that *he* was taking the threat seriously, and Roth felt his heart speed up.

She held out her palm. "Hold there, soldier. I'll send one of my agents."

A handgun went off, three rapid bursts like loud claps, startling everyone.

Agent Sanchez grabbed her radio. "What's going on out there?"

"Agent down! Agent down!" crackled a voice through the receiver.

Roth's stomach plunged. He checked on the boys—near the table, frightened—then looked to Jordan, who was on his feet but still didn't have his gun.

"Who's down?" Agent Sanchez shouted into the radio.

The dog was barking in a frenzy, adding to the confusion, then it yelped in pain and fell quiet.

"I need eyes, who's out there?" Agent Sanchez demanded.

"This is Garcia," said another voice. "I'm coming around from the back."

"Be careful!" she said.

"Rutgers is down. Repeat, Rutgers is down. He's been shot."

The other agents in the house had all drawn their firearms, and two were heading to the front door. A bullet cracked through the window and hit one of them in the shoulder. The moment was surreal and horrifying. All year, Roth had been preparing for another battle with Calakmul, but he couldn't have prepared himself for this—for violence in his home.

"I need my gun back," Jordan said angrily to Agent Sanchez. When the FBI had confiscated his weapon, they'd given it to her. She returned it to him.

"Roths, under the table!" Jordan roared. He grabbed Lucas and pulled him down. Brillante went under next, and Roth scrambled down himself. He knew when a situation was beyond his control, and this certainly qualified. It was why he'd hired Lund and his people to protect him and the kids. But Jordan was one man, and it was obvious they were facing many. He had to get his kids out of there. Soon.

Jordan crouched low, aiming his weapon at the front door.

"I can't see a thing out there!" another agent shouted. "We're in a fishbowl!"

Agent Sanchez stayed near Roth and his family. She crouched on the opposite side of the table, radio in one hand, pistol in the other. Fear wrinkled her brow, but she stared at the front door with a look of intensity.

"We need backup!" she shouted into the radio. "Man down. Multiple targets."

"It's MS-13," someone said.

"Clear the way to the SUV," Agent Sanchez shouted across the room when another agent entered the room with his service weapon out and ready.

"Roger that!" he called back. He stalked toward the door, moving past the injured man who'd been shot through the shoulder.

The door opened, and the agent aimed his weapon into the night air. They waited a few seconds, no shots were fired, and then Spencer went out. The SUVs' engines were still running, headlights shining into the house, further obscuring the surrounding darkness.

From under the table, Roth watched through the open door as the agent hurried toward the closest SUV. Something caught his attention. He turned, fired, and instantly went down as if he'd shot himself.

"Spencer is down!" Garcia shouted from the radio.

"Shut the door," Agent Sanchez shouted. A nearby agent darted forward and shut it. "Garcia—who else is outside?"

Silence.

"Garcia?"

No answer.

Roth looked at Jordan, who nodded at him. "The safe house."

"You mean the panic room in the basement?" Agent Sanchez said.

"That's just a decoy," Roth said. "We have a real safe house. A cabin. We're getting out of here."

"Where is the other half of the detail?" Sanchez asked. Some of the agents were crouching behind furniture, weapons at the ready.

"Man down!" cried a voice on the radio.

"They're picking us off, one by one," Agent Sanchez said angrily. "They might have a sniper. I would not advise going outside. The panic room in the basement will buy us time for backup to arrive. They're probably watching the street. This is a dead end, so there's only one way out."

"That's exactly what they're planning on," Roth said. "We have snowmobiles in the garage."

More gunshots sounded, and then bullets pierced the front door. The sound of a body slumping away from it could be heard as another agent went down.

Jordan aimed for the door, but Roth put a hand on his arm. "Guns aren't going to help right now. Let's go. Boys, follow me. Stay low."

"Mr. Roth, it is my duty to protect your family," Agent Sanchez said, blocking their path. "Going outside will get you killed."

"And staying here will get us kidnapped," Roth shot back. Was she working for Calakmul? She seemed sincere. Her confusion and concern for her colleagues was evident—and so was her fear. If this was acting, she was good at it.

More gunshots sounded.

"I need backup!" Agent Sanchez shouted again into the radio. "Agents down. We're outnumbered!"

The line crackled in response.

Roth pulled out his burner phone and texted Steve. *Under attack. Going to cabin.*

"Let's go!" Jordan said. Using his body as a shield, he crouched low and directed them to follow him toward the garage. Roth fell in behind him, his heart hammering as he stuffed the burner phone into his pocket. They crawled through the kitchen entry, and as soon as they were past the counter, they rose and began to run. Jordan kept his pistol aimed around the corner, and then he darted to the garage door and opened it, sweeping it with his weapon. The fluorescent lights were still on from when they'd arrived earlier. Roth usually left them on to avoid stumbling in the garage when going out to the spare fridge for a soda. He'd also formed a healthy dislike of dark spaces after hiking through the jungle—and inside pyramids—in the dark last winter.

"Snowsuits," Roth said, pointing to the body suits hanging from hooks in the wall organizer. The boys hurriedly put on the pants and jackets, and Roth did the same. So did Jordan. They each pulled on a balaclava, snow boots, and gloves.

Agent Sanchez came into the garage. "I'm coming with you."

That was suspicious. It was precisely what someone who wanted to kidnap them would insist on doing. But he wasn't sure leaving her behind to die was a better choice. He hated not knowing. "You can go to the panic room and lock yourself in," he suggested.

She shook her head. "I'm protecting your family, Mr. Roth. That's my job."

"That's *my* job," Jordan insisted.

There were four snowmobiles, one for each member of the family. Brillante and Lucas looked fearful but eager as they straddled their snowmobiles, ready to ride.

The garage had two automatic doors. One facing the driveway, the other facing the backyard.

"I don't know how to ride one of these," Agent Sanchez said. She grabbed the last jacket, Sarina's, and tugged it on.

Roth nodded for her to climb on the back of his snowmobile, which was a two-seater. Once they were all settled, ready to take off, Roth said, "I'm leading. Boys, follow me. Jordan, take the rear."

They all nodded their agreement, and Jordan went to the garage door console and hit the button. As the door began to lift, everyone hit the ignitions on their snowmobiles, which fired on instantly. Then he remembered his regular cell phone. He pulled it out of his pocket and saw three missed calls from Suki before he tossed it onto an Igloo cooler. He didn't want to show Calakmul the way to the safe house.

As soon as the door was open halfway, Roth gunned the engine. The sled lurched through the opening, running across the concrete until it hit snow and began to grab traction. The headlights illuminated the path ahead. He heard the sound of the other sleds and quickly turned his head. He saw Agent Sanchez, grabbing onto the side handles and pressing herself against the back seat, and the boys, following his tracks in the snow. A gun fired behind them. Roth didn't know who was being aimed at, but he felt the adrenaline spike. They had to get out *now*, before one of the boys got hit.

The sled accelerated as he cleared through the back ring of trees. The bitter cold wind against his face was exhilarating. The snow churned up in waves behind him, the motor bellowing noisily, the stink of the exhaust filling his nose. He glanced in the mirrors, seeing the headlights coming up behind him.

The mountains south of Bozeman weren't passable by truck, even with four-wheel drive. They'd taken all the snowmobiles, so the people who'd ambushed them at the house could not follow them. On foot, it would take hours to travel the distance a sled could travel in minutes.

Roth might not be good with directions, but he knew the way to the cabin. He'd practiced enough that he could probably find his way there blindfolded. And he'd taken the boys and Suki there on four-wheelers several times so they knew the way too.

He called it the safe house. A cabin in the mountains only accessible by off-road gear. It had food storage. Weapons. It operated off solar panels, a gas line deep into the earth, and enough wood to survive multiple winters in Montana. There was cell phone service for his burner phone but no internet.

Roth had been preparing for this moment for the last year. The moment when he faced Jacob Calakmul on different terms.

He and his family would not be hostages this time.

It was time to turn the tables.

Especially if Agent Monica Sanchez wasn't who she claimed to be.

CHAPTER THIRTEEN

Beck Cabin

Bozeman, Montana

December 26

Roth gunned the sled's engine to get up the last hill to the cabin, which occupied the high ground in a densely wooded slope at the base of the canyon heading up to Wheeler Mountain.

He parked his sled beside stacks of wood covered in gray tarps and then killed the engine. His forearms, wrists, and hands were sore from the cold and the bumpy ride up into the mountains. Brillante and Lucas came up and parked their snowmobiles next to his. Lucas pulled down his balaclava and blew out a steam of air. Agent Sanchez was staring at the cabin in surprise, her breath coming out of her mouth like fog.

"It's going to be c-cold in there!" Lucas said, teeth chattering.

Roth climbed off the sled. The boys cut their motors as well. No sign of Jordan, but Roth could hear the noise of his snowmobile in the distance.

Agent Sanchez was still staring at the cabin with a strange expression. "Where are we?"

"Off the grid," Roth answered.

He pulled off his gloves and then went to the cabin door. It had a touch pad. After he put in the code, it clicked open and revealed a key. He took the key and then unlocked the door. There were flashlights and headlamps stored in a bin just inside the door. Roth grabbed a headlamp, strapped it on his forehead, and clicked it on. He headed down to the basement to turn on the generator. It was a one-touch system, fueled by propane because propane wouldn't freeze.

The system kicked on quickly, and the cabin lights illuminated.

Down in the basement were racks of weapons—shotguns and AR15s. Lund had helped Roth acquire all the weapons legally. There were enough bunks in the cabin to quarter about thirty people and food storage and MREs to last several years. There was a well and pump to provide unlimited water.

There was also another panic room down there. Top of the line. The entire cabin had been constructed by an old gentleman preparing for the apocalypse, but he'd died of natural causes, and his posterity hadn't wanted the place. Lund had acquired it as a safe house for the Roth family, since it was close to their residence, so it was added as part of the security lease Roth had paid for with cryptocurrency.

Roth climbed back to the main level. It was a tight space, but all the cooking implements were compact designs.

"Can one of you light a fire in the woodstove?" he asked the boys. The boys loved building fires, and they quickly went to work.

Agent Sanchez was looking around, her breath visible in the cold space. She was shivering.

"I imagine you didn't grow up in Bozeman," Roth said to her. He needed to know more about her, to determine if she had any links to the Calakmuls.

"Wichita Falls, Texas," she answered.

"Where's that?"

"North of Dallas. My dad was in the air force, and he was stationed at Sheppard for a while when I was a kid."

Texas. That was a border state with Mexico. Of course, there were also twenty-seven million people in Texas, and most of them had nothing to do with Jacob Calakmul.

"Dude, those are too big." Brillante chuffed. "Smaller pieces first."

Agent Sanchez's phone began to buzz. She unzipped the overcoat she'd put on and retrieved the phone from her jacket pocket.

"Sanchez," she answered.

Roth felt his stomach twinge. He didn't want her revealing where they'd gone. It defeated the whole purpose of having a safe house if their enemies discovered its location.

The sound of the last snowmobile's engine got louder, signaling its approach to the cabin. Roth went to the door and opened it again. Jordan killed the engine and stepped off, kicking snow off his boots.

"You get lost?" Roth asked. Then he nodded toward Agent Sanchez and her cell phone and shot Jordan a worried look.

The bodyguard gave a slight inclination of his head to communicate he understood Roth's concern. "Made some false trails. In the daylight, it'll be easy to follow the trail up here." He didn't make a move on Sanchez's phone, though, and neither did Roth. He figured they were both thinking the same thing. Going for her phone now would be like declaring war. Better not to go there quite yet, especially with the boys around.

"Good thinking," Roth answered. "The wind blows pretty hard up here. The drifts will bury the tracks too."

"Didn't think of that. Good. Got a fire going yet?" he asked the boys and joined them.

"Working on it," Brillante said, trying to add smaller chips as kindling.

"Add some lighter fluid."

"They learned the old-fashioned way," Roth interjected. "Armory is downstairs."

"Thanks. Let me get some ready. Make sure they'll work."

Roth shut and locked the door, and Jordan headed down to the basement.

". . . in the mountains somewhere," Agent Sanchez was saying. "Everyone is here except for the daughter. What happened down there? Did you call in local law enforcement? The Bozeman PD Special Response Team?"

Roth saw flames crackling inside the woodstove. Lucas was blowing on the burning newspaper, but it was already well on its way to keeping them warm. The stove could heat up the entire cabin once it got going, and there was enough wood to keep it fed for a year or two.

Brillante yawned. "Bruh, I'm so tired. Can we crash?"

"Let's talk about what happened a minute first," Roth said.

"Do we have to?" Lucas asked. "We're really tired."

"I know. But what happened at home . . . that was pretty scary. I just want you to talk about it if you feel like it."

"Maybe tomorrow," Brillante said. "I'm wiped. This has been . . . a lot."

"Me too," Lucas said. "We need some time to think about it. Do you know what's going to happen next, Dad? What we're doing tomorrow?"

"I wish I did. Get some rest," Roth said. "Use the sleeping bags. They'll hold your body warmth. I'll heat up some water in a Nalgene bottle for you both."

"Awesome! Thanks, Dad!" Lucas said.

Roth checked his watch as they left. It was 1:30 a.m.

He thought of the three missed calls from Suki. He hesitated and then used his burner phone to call Lund.

"You made it to the Beck cabin?" Lund asked.

"We did. Suki tried calling me on my normal phone, but I had to leave it behind. Can I talk to her?"

"You bet. I've got an extra burner. She'll use that from now on. Here you go."

Suki's voice was breathless. "Dad! Why haven't you called me back? I've been freaking out!"

"We're all okay. We just made it to the cabin. You still safe?"

"We're downtown," she answered breathlessly. "A whole bunch of police cars took off an hour or so ago. Was that for you?"

"Yup," Roth answered, smiling. "Let me talk to Lund real quick. Glad you're okay."

"Brice is worried about us, Dad. I haven't told him about what happened to us in Mexico, but I'd like to."

"Not yet. Let me talk to Lund."

"Okay. Here he is."

He heard a crackling of static as she handed the phone over, then Steve Lund's voice came over the receiver. "Busy evening, Mr. Roth."

"I'd say."

"Is Jordan still with you?"

"Yeah, he's down in the basement checking out the weapons cache. What have you heard so far?"

"The field office in Salt Lake called in the Special Response Team. And more agents and gear from Salt Lake are heading your way."

"Is that like a SWAT team? I didn't know they had one in Bozeman."

"It's similar. A joint op between the county sheriff and city police. I'm going to keep moving so as not to draw attention, but I'll rent a snowmobile in the morning so I can get her back to you. Then we'll make plans. In the meantime, you should probably get some sleep, Mr. Roth."

"I'll try. Keep in touch. Stay out of sight."

"Roger that." The call ended.

The fire the boys had made was going strong now. Roth went to the woodstove and added a log, leaving the door ajar so the fire would suck in more oxygen, making it burn hotter and faster. Then he went into the miniature kitchen and added water to a kettle, which he put on the flat top of the stove.

"All of them?" Agent Sanchez asked into her phone, her voice devastated. "That's . . . that's horrible. Yeah. Yeah. Will do. I'm glad we made it out when we did. Okay. Bye."

Her face was pale as she hung up the call. Her expression haunted. It was exactly the reaction he would have expected of someone in her position, but had she been trained to deceive?

"They're all dead," Agent Sanchez said. "They must have used armor-piercing bullets. Went straight through their Kevlar vests." He watched the tendons in her hand tighten as she squeezed her phone. Her eyes narrowed accusingly at him. "We should have gone to the satellite office, Mr. Roth."

Her colleagues had been slaughtered, but he suspected it wasn't because of armor-piercing bullets. Something told him the magic of the Maya had played a part.

He scratched his chin. "Yeah, if we *had*, then my family would probably have been kidnapped already."

"You know more than you've told me," Agent Sanchez demanded.

"I think you do too," Roth replied, studying her. She still looked genuine to him, but he couldn't let that sway him.

Jordan came back upstairs holding one of the AR15s.

Agent Sanchez's eyes swayed to him, widening as she lifted her palms to face him. "I'm a federal agent. Put that weapon down."

"I'd like to ask you a few questions, Agent Sanchez," Roth said. "You're the only agent who made it out of my house alive tonight."

"I was *trying* to protect your family!" she shouted at him, her eyes darting from him to Jordan and back.

"We'll see. Tell me what you know of *Jacob Calakmul*."

He was watching her for a reaction. For a flare of recognition.

He imagined she was trained to pass a polygraph test, but even so, some initial reaction might pass through—a widening of the eyes, a constriction of the nostrils. Something.

"Who?" she asked with a confused look.

"Jacob Calakmul from Mexico."

"MS-13 isn't a Mexican gang," Agent Sanchez said, her gaze back on the AR. "It's Salvadoran."

"I know," Roth said. "So you haven't heard that name before?"

"No," she answered. "I know all of the major cartels in Latin America, and there's no Calakmul in any of them. There are a lot of wealthy people living in Bozeman, Mr. Roth." Her gaze swung back to them. "They get their drugs from mules. Is that what this is about? Do you have the drugs hidden in this cabin?"

"Not even close," Roth said. "It's about the death games. Down in the Yucatán Peninsula. They started again in 2012. You didn't know?"

Roth was tired of playing so cautiously. All the federal agents who had come with her had already been killed. Calakmul was ruthless. If she wasn't involved with Calakmul, she might as well learn what she was up against. They were all in too deep now.

"I'm from *Texas*," she said in exasperation. "I've never even been to Mexico."

So far, her answers had all implied she was ignorant of the situation. Of course, she could also be a good liar. Jacob Calakmul had bragged about his people, their reach.

"Have you been to Honduras? Belize?"

"No. Not Guatemala either. Too dangerous for a federal agent to be a tourist in any of those places. Your questions make no sense. Do you know why MS-13 was sent to kidnap you?"

"I do," Roth said. "Calakmul sent people after us in Germany too. And I guess the question is whether I believe *you* are working for him too."

Roth felt in his pocket for his burner phone. He had Moretti's contact info on the phone. It was possible his buddy wouldn't answer a call from an unknown number, but maybe he should give it a shot. Agent Sanchez had said he was worried about the situation with MS-13. It was possible he'd be able to do something to help. Maybe he even knew whether Roth could trust Agent Sanchez.

After they'd escaped Calakmul's resort on Cozumel, Roth had called Moretti to let him know they were in trouble. His friend had looked Jacob Calakmul up in a criminal database, but there wasn't anything on him. Which was no surprise now. He'd also given Roth a few numbers and other assistance, which Roth hadn't been able to put to use because he'd been recaptured by Calakmul. He'd seen Moretti at Westfall's funeral, and his friend had, very understandably, asked him what had happened. Not wanting to put any more of his friends in danger, Roth had shared no more than what he'd told Lund. Moretti didn't know about the death games. He didn't know about the jaguar priests. And he definitely didn't know they were bent on taking over the world as part of a twisted revenge scheme. It was safer that way. He'd tried to follow up once or twice since then, but Roth had always asked him to drop it.

"Moretti," came the answer immediately.

"You're awake."

"Roth?" his friend said in a tone of wonder. "Is that you?"

"Yeah. Yeah, it's me. Good to hear your voice."

"Are you okay, bud?"

"Yeah, we're all fine. Thanks for lighting the fire under the FBI."

"I'm not supposed to say this, but I'm on my way up to Bozeman. Now. Was asked to bring some cavalry up there. I've got my guys. So I guess the FBI has already contacted you?"

"I'm with Agent Sanchez right now," Roth said.

"You at the satellite office? I was so worried about MS-13 coming after you." He paused. "This isn't your phone number. Where are you calling from?"

"This is my burner phone. I left mine at the house so they couldn't follow me. Some of the FBI agents have been killed. We're . . . at a safe place. I've got the boys with me."

"Then where's Suki?"

"She's downtown with my security guard. We'll get together in the morning. I'm glad to hear you're coming up. We need to talk."

"Yes, we do. I shouldn't be talking to you about official stuff, but this directly involves you guys . . . The trouble you're in relates to whatever you got wrapped up in last year in Mexico, doesn't it? The Calakmul mess?"

"Afraid so."

"I'll call you when I get up there. See you in a few hours."

"Definitely. Thanks."

He ended the call.

"Who was that?" Agent Sanchez asked.

"My friend. Will Moretti, the guy you mentioned earlier. I trust him."

"Mr. Roth," she said, looking him in the eyes. "You need to understand that I did everything I could to protect your family. That's still my job. That's why I'm here."

Roth was still holding his phone when he saw the text arrive from Moretti.

Don't trust her.

CHAPTER FOURTEEN

Main Street / US Highway 191

Bozeman, Montana

December 26

Suki and Brice had been texting since Lund had given her a burner phone, and that was the only thing that had kept her from totally freaking out. Mr. Lund had shown up suddenly and whisked her away to downtown Bozeman after removing the SIM card from her normal phone. His car had that weird new-car smell, even though it wasn't new. It was clean, thank goodness, but sitting in the passenger seat, listening to an almost-stranger breathe, had gotten old fast. She was also grateful that he at least wasn't one of those adults who tried to strike up awkward conversations with teenagers who really didn't want to talk to them. He was quiet. Introverted. And so far he had kept them safe. Those were all good things.

Brice didn't know what was going on, of course, but she'd explained that she had to leave because the FBI had shown up at her house to ask questions about their trip to Germany. He'd tried to pry more information from her. She'd wanted to tell him more—to tell him everything—but it was possible her phone would be taken from her, so she needed to be careful not to reveal anything that might be damaging to her family. So they started texting about their college plans. Suki was planning on MSU, and Brice was thinking about BYU-Idaho because of its theater program.

You know that little theater in West Yellowstone?

She did. *Yas.*

One of the professors owns it and they audition students to perform there every summer. Its dope.

She did know the theater and had gone there with her family several times. The actors served food during intermissions, and it was always a good show. She could see Brice performing on that stage, although she secretly hoped he'd make it to Broadway someday.

You'd be sick.

They were parked in a tiny lot behind some shops on Main Street in Bozeman, tucked away. Since it was the night after Christmas, there were few cars on the road, which made theirs stand out every time they changed locations. Main Street had been totally empty when they'd driven down it to park behind Nova Café, which was Mr. Lund's favorite breakfast place. It wouldn't be opening for several more hours, but Mr. Lund had said he was a regular there. The owner knew him and would allow them to eat in a private booth.

They're so good tho. I'd suck compared.

Brice was extremely talented, but he lacked confidence in himself and needed regular doses of validation. Not many realized this, because he came across so extroverted and confident and hilarious.

You'd smash the place. You'd crush it.

BYU-Idaho was in Rexburg, about a three-hour drive from Bozeman. If she went to MSU, then they wouldn't see each other as much as they had this year. Her stomach sank at the thought. He'd helped her get through the worst year of her life, and she didn't want to be without him.

Mr. Lund turned on the ignition, and the heaters began to roar. He put the car in gear and pulled out of the empty parking lot.

"Where next?" she asked him, still staring at the glowing screen.

"McDonald's for coffee. The Starbucks isn't open yet. There's one on Main Street."

"Just past the high school," she said, nodding. She knew exactly where it was. Same parking lot as the Hobby Lobby and Safeway.

It was still the middle of the night, and her body clock was totally confused because of Germany. Her back ached from sitting in the seat for so long, but at least they were warm. It was freezing outside, and the sidewalks were lined with snow. The streetlights were on, the road unplowed with a thin glaze of snow and ice. No other cars were on the street.

She texted back: *Maybe? Let's get thru the play first. You ready for that one high note?*

Brice was an excellent singer, part of the school choir, but the challenging role he played really tested his vocal range.

I can't do it! Not reliably. Help me!!!!

Suki was smiling when another car came into view on Main Street, heading toward them. It felt strange to see someone else on the empty street, and the headlights made her wince. She wanted to put down the sun visor, but figured it would be stupid since they'd be passing it in a few seconds.

It was a large SUV, a Yukon or Suburban, white. It was surprisingly clean, with barely any spattering of slush and dirt on the sides. That worried feeling she'd had all night began to throb to life. She knew in a flash that the vehicle was dangerous and the occupants were looking for her. She also knew this was no ordinary hunch—it was one of the warnings she occasionally got, the kind that always turned out to be true. Although she had no way of knowing where they came from, she thought they were from her namesake, from Grandma Suki.

Mr. Lund sucked in his breath.

"What?" Suki asked nervously.

Then she saw what had set him off. The driver had tattoos all across his face and bald head. His eyes were cruel, and he had a thin goatee. A vaping stick rested between his lips, and a curl of smoke jetted from his mouth. He turned and looked at them as their cars passed.

"Um, get out of here," Suki whispered, her stomach clenching into knots. She gripped the armrest and put her phone down.

Mr. Lund began to accelerate.

Suki heard the squeal of tires from behind them. She twisted in her seat and saw the SUV do a 180 in the middle of Main Street. Terror filled her.

"Go!" she pleaded.

Mr. Lund glanced in the rearview and pressed hard on the gas. Their car lurched forward.

"Their engine is bigger. Can't outrun them," he said curtly, no emotion in his voice.

"We can *try*!" Suki insisted, panicking.

They raced down Main Street, past the Starbucks that still hadn't opened, still accelerating. She saw Bozeman High School on the right, and they raced past it. Suddenly Lund swerved right on Fifteenth Avenue, right before the McDonald's. The car began to slide in the slush.

Lund gunned the engine, correcting for the snow as the car fishtailed and then rocketed down Fifteenth past the fast-food restaurant. Suki looked back and saw the SUV coming around the corner after them, sliding across the opposite lane before it straightened out again and lunged for them.

"Your seat belt better be on," Lund said curtly.

Suki had unfastened it when they were parked, so she clicked it back on again as he took another hard corner past the Hobby Lobby, going left.

"Where are we going?" she asked.

"Losing them first," Lund said. They were now on a residential street. When they reached the end, he blew past a stop sign. There were no cars, but Suki winced and looked away. He made a left turn, immediately followed by a hard right, their car sliding sideways. Suki couldn't help but gasp in surprise, grateful they didn't crash into any of the curbs.

Lund straightened out and accelerated again. A side street came up halfway down the block.

"That way!" Suki suggested, pointing.

"Good call."

Lund made the turn, but when she looked back, the SUV was still coming after them.

Suki didn't know the side streets, but she anticipated they'd get off on Nineteenth, which was a major road where they could go faster. The street ended in a split. Lund took the left one, and suddenly they were at a cul-de-sac.

"Dead end!" Suki cried out.

Lund hit the brakes, torquing the steering wheel, and the car did a complete 360. She felt the pull against the car door and nearly smacked her face into it. Stomping on the gas pedal again, Lund turned around in the cul-de-sac and started the other way just as the SUV neared the intersection. They rushed past, the other car's headlights blinding her, but she still saw the tattooed driver, his chilling eyes and frown radiating an evil energy she could feel deep inside.

Their vehicle rushed down the street, gaining speed, but this one also ended in a cul-de-sac. The SUV was charging hard after them.

"What do we do? What do we do?" Suki shouted.

There were two houses on each side of the cul-de-sac and some greenbelt beyond, now covered in snow. Her heart hammered a crazy beat. Going off road in a sedan wasn't going to work. The SUV had the advantage of height.

Lund accelerated into the driveway of one of the houses. Suki's heart hammered harder, but then she saw it—a parking lot just past the house, beyond the neighborhood. They were off road for only a few seconds before they hit the curb, which rattled the whole vehicle, and slid into the parking lot of a small apartment complex. Lund was swerving hard to get control of the car again, fishtailing around, and then they were going hard again. The parking lot had been recently plowed. She saw a major street up ahead.

"That's Nineteenth!" she said, pointing.

Lund swerved onto it, going right again, sliding across multiple lanes. He didn't hit anything because there were still no cars out. Steam was wafting from the hood.

Then they were swerving again, going down another street into another residential neighborhood.

Suki turned back and saw the SUV coming onto Nineteenth. They were still visible to it, but Lund made some more hard turns, going through the neighborhood, taking a turn at every intersection so that their vehicle would soon be out of sight. They were going fifty to sixty miles per hour in the residential neighborhood, undoubtedly waking people up.

The smoke from the hood was getting heavier.

"Need a place to hide," Lund said tightly. "This car can't take much more of this abuse."

"What about my high school?" Suki suggested. "You have the keys to get inside, right?"

"Actually, I do," Lund said. "It's on the west edge of town."

"With the way you're driving, it's only five minutes from here. It'll be closed, so we wouldn't be putting anyone in danger."

"We can ditch the car and hide at the school. Pretend someone wanted to murder you: Where would you hide in there?"

"Why aren't we calling the cops right now?"

"I don't think it's a good idea," he said flatly.

"But why?" Her mind churned up an answer she didn't like. "You're worried they've been hacked, aren't you?"

115

"Afraid so. I'll call them if we can't shake these guys, but it shouldn't be our first move. Just in case. So . . . answer my question. Where would you hide?"

Suki knew the answer instantly. "The lighting room in the theater. There's only a narrow stairway leading up there. We could barricade the door easily."

"Can you find it in the dark?"

"I can find it blindfolded," she said with a grin.

CHAPTER FIFTEEN

BECK CABIN

BOZEMAN, MONTANA

December 26

Moretti's text put a sour taste in Roth's mouth. He'd just started to think Agent Sanchez might be okay, that she might be on their side. After a moment of staring at the screen, he tucked the phone back into his pocket.

Jordan was giving him a quizzical look.

"What was the message?" Agent Sanchez asked, her tone suspicious.

Roth walked over to Jordan and brought up the text thread. He showed it to him.

The FBI agent reached for her sidearm. Jordan was faster. In an instant, he had his Glock up to her temple. Agent Sanchez froze, then raised her hands.

"Turn around," Jordan ordered.

"I'm a federal agent, and you're going to prison if you do this," she said, her voice shaking.

"We'll lawyer up," Jordan quipped. "Come on. Turn around." He wagged the gun to reinforce his command. "Let's play nice."

"Mr. Roth, I'd advise you to call off your guard dog before you *both* end up in prison."

"I'll take my chances," Roth said, grateful that Jordan was there. He couldn't have handled the agent himself.

Agent Sanchez turned around, hands still up.

"You know the drill. Behind your head, on your knees. I don't want to shoot you, Agent Sanchez. But I will if you try any of that Quantico stuff on me."

"What Quantico stuff?" Roth asked.

"FBI agents are trained to disarm someone even if they've been hit with pepper spray. She's already preparing to fight me for control of my weapon. That's why we'll do this my way."

Roth saw the agent's lips purse with anger. It was obvious that was exactly what she'd planned to do.

"I was trying to *help* this family!" she insisted. "If I don't call in—"

Jordan snorted. "Your team is dead, Agent Sanchez. Convenient. No witnesses. Now, get down before I stop being nice."

Hands still up, she lowered herself onto her knees.

"Sit on the chair, please," he said next, pointing to one of the hard-backed chairs. He kept his weapon trained on the back of her head and stepped closer cautiously.

Agent Sanchez eased onto the chair he'd indicated, fingers interlocking behind her neck.

"Thank you. You know how to do this." Jordan bent down and drew her sidearm with one hand and gave it to Roth, who had taken some gun-safety classes at a local firing range after getting back from Mexico. He knew how to check, load, fire, and clear pistols and rifles. But he wasn't a soldier, and he knew his limitations.

"Left hand first," Jordan said. He withdrew some zip-tie cuffs from his jacket and then bound her wrists to the armrests on her chair. He also zip-tied her ankles together. Once she was disarmed and subdued, he relaxed.

"I want you to call the Bozeman office and tell them where I am," she said firmly.

Roth shook his head. He reached into her pocket and withdrew her cell phone. It had facial recognition, so he held it to her face and unlocked it.

"Another felony," she snarled.

It was an iPhone, so he knew the layout and quickly went to contacts. No one from Mexico was listed. Not surprising. He scrolled through her texts from the last forty-eight hours to see if there was any information that would be helpful.

The phone buzzed in his hand, signaling another call was coming in. He rejected it and kept looking. Other than FBI lingo and a few personal texts from family members, he didn't see anything incriminating.

"Do you have a burner phone?" he asked.

"No," she said flatly.

"Check her, please," Roth told Jordan.

The search was done quickly, but there were no more electronics other than her FBI radio, which was now well out of range since they were in the mountains. Roth was tired. He was *exhausted*. Waves of heat were coming from the woodstove now. He pocketed her phone and set her weapon down on the counter as he heard the whistle from the kettle beginning to hiss. As he'd promised his boys, he filled up two Nalgene bottles from a cupboard and tightly screwed on the caps. There were some old wool socks on the shelf too, and he slid the bottles into the socks.

"What are you doing?" Agent Sanchez asked.

"Learned this trick in Boy Scouts, actually," he said. "The wool provides insulation so the bottles stay warm. Slip one in your sleeping bag and snooze away. Did this winter camping many times up in the Sierras."

"California?" she asked.

He nodded. "Let me go tuck in the boys. I'll be right back." He climbed upstairs and found that both of his sons had passed out in their sleeping bags on the little bunk beds in one of the upper rooms. He slid the sock-covered bottles into their bags.

Brillante stirred. "Thanks," he grunted.

Roth kissed his curly hair and then repeated it for Lucas, who stayed asleep.

They'd had a whirlwind trip to Germany, and ever since their visit to the SLUB, they'd been in nonstop danger. He needed to rest as much as the boys did. But what to do with Agent Sanchez? She was right. They would all be in serious trouble for imprisoning a federal agent.

He sighed. Maybe some federal scrutiny wasn't a bad thing?

No, it was definitely a bad thing.

Roth went back to the kitchen and found Jordan sipping from a mug. A canister of hot chocolate powder sat open on the counter.

"Tired from Germany?"

"Not anymore," Roth said. "Germany is eight hours ahead, so now it feels like the day is ready to start."

"If you're alert, then I'm going to crash for a little bit," Jordan said. "She's not going anywhere. I've got her gun." He patted his pocket. "We can switch off in a few hours, okay?"

Roth nodded in agreement and then pulled up a chair across from her, straddling it backward. He took out her phone again and unlocked it while she glared at him.

"What's this all about, Mr. Roth?"

"We're about to talk about it," he said. He pulled up the voice-recording app on her phone, showed it to her, and pressed the red button to start recording.

"You realize you have the right to an attorney," she said, obviously referring to his Miranda rights.

"So do you," he shot back. He set her phone on the table next to them, then crossed his arms on the backrest of the chair and leaned forward. "I'm also betting that your phone is backed up on the cloud, so a copy of this recording will be available electronically."

"It will. For the record, I've been strapped to a chair with zip ties, and I'm being held against my will."

"Noted. Now, let's get down to the heart of the matter. A year ago, my family went down to Mexico for Christmas vacation. We were lured there by some of our neighbors, Eric and Kendall Beasley."

"The family that died in the boating accident on Christmas Day." Her tone was inscrutable.

"You heard about it?"

"It was in the local news, Mr. Roth. I live in Bozeman too."

"Well, they didn't die in a boating accident. They were murdered by a man named Jacob Calakmul. He owns resorts in the Yucatán Peninsula and probably elsewhere. We were going to stay at the one on Cozumel, but my wife and I learned that it was all a scam."

"Like a Ponzi scheme?"

"No. You know the Maya used to play a ball game. With hoops on the walls of the court?"

She shrugged. "Did they? I'm from Texas. I learned Spanish in high school."

"They call the game many things. In Nahuatl, it's called *ōllamalīztli*. The Maya called it *tlachtli*. Or *Pokolpok*. That one sounds like 'apocalypse.' In 2012, the end of their doomsday calendar, Calakmul and his ilk started the games up again. The losers are sacrificed. The winners are promised special status after our civilization collapses."

Her nostrils flared, and her eyebrows quirked in a look of total incredulity.

"Were you involved in a crime, Mr. Roth?"

"We were held against our will. We were forced to participate in the games last Christmas. And strangely, we *won*. I watched Jacob

Calakmul, who calls himself a jaguar priest, transform into a jaguar and kill Eric."

She licked her lips. There was no look of recognition at all in her expression. She was reacting to his revelation as if *he* were a conspiracy theorist. "Why didn't you report this to the authorities when you returned?"

"While we were down there, my wife's insulin pump was damaged, and she went into a diabetic coma. She's still down there, Agent Sanchez. They said if I revealed any of this, then her life was forfeit. They assured me that law enforcement in the United States wouldn't believe my story. Neither do I expect you to believe me. Without proof."

That last bit caught her interest. "And?"

"I'm getting to that part. I came home without my wife. I don't think she's still alive. I can't know for sure, but I've researched diabetic comas. I've spoken to ER doctors and done my homework. They don't last a year. So I think she died, and they didn't want to tell me because they were afraid of what I might do." Dark anger roiled inside of him, a force he'd been struggling to tame since he'd persuaded himself that Sarina was gone. Permanently. If she had survived and woken up, it made sense that Jacob would have told him as much in order to strengthen their hold on him and his family.

"Did you abduct me because I'm Hispanic?" Agent Sanchez asked, fear flashing in her eyes.

He shook his head. "No, because I think you're *working* for him."

She blinked, her expression dumbfounded.

"I don't know whether I can trust you, Agent Sanchez. Calakmul had a personal assistant of sorts named Angélica who graduated from Stanford. I've done some research and found her records at the school. But she's a nobody compared to others who were there. Celebrities. Someone from Congress. Business elites. I saw people I've only seen on TV there."

Agent Sanchez shrugged. "And will you name these individuals to verify your claims?"

"I'm spelling this out because it's being recorded. I'm assuming someone in the Federal Bureau of *Investigation* might take this seriously and research families who have traveled to Latin America during the holidays and died under mysterious circumstances, only for their wealth and assets to be mysteriously shuttled to someone else. I'm the legal owner of the Beasley mansion here in the Sourdough area. And I can't sell it because I don't feel like I really *do* own it." Roth sighed. "Because I don't want it."

"How can you own a house you didn't purchase? There are deeds, contracts."

"I know. And the deed is now in the name of a trust that I own. All of the Beasleys' financial assets are also mine."

"And you're telling me that a man turned into a *jaguar* and killed him? Is this some sort of metaphor, Mr. Roth?"

"*I* didn't kill him. We won the game, so we were permitted to leave. We tried to save his youngest, his little girl . . ." Roth felt his throat clench, the same way it did every time he thought about leaving her behind.

"The children were killed too?"

"I was there when Beasley was murdered. The rest of the family was supposed to be sacrificed to the Maya gods later that day. They planned to rip their hearts out."

"That's gruesome, Mr. Roth."

"Yes. Calakmul and his jaguar cult have been preparing for this since Cortés invaded Mexico in the 1500s. There is a prophecy they think they're fulfilling. That's why my family went to Germany for Christmas."

"Wait . . . what?" She looked confused.

"The ancient Maya wrote their records on a sheaf of bark called a codex. After the conquistadors conquered the Aztecs and Maya, those codices were systematically collected and burned. Only a few of them remain. And one is in Dresden, Germany. I've been gathering evidence for the last year, Agent Sanchez, because I knew people like you would either be in on the scheme or wouldn't believe me."

"You must admit that this seems rather far-fetched."

"It does. Truth is stranger than fiction. I saw what I saw with my own eyes."

She regarded him with obvious doubt. "Certain narcotics can produce realistic hallucinations."

"Indeed. You've named one of a hundred reasons why I didn't come forward. If my wife is dead, then by default, I'm the prime suspect. I get that. I have a vibrant imagination, so I understand how this looks. And why you brought a drug-sniffing dog to my house when you got a tip that MS-13 was interested in me. But I'll happily submit to a blood test that will prove I'm clean of all substances except highly caffeinated beverages and Ghirardelli brownie mix."

That little joke at the end made her smile reflexively. Her reactions had all been very human, very reasonable. His gut told him that she wasn't part of the cabal. That Moretti, perhaps, was wrong or overcautious in thinking otherwise.

"There were others there at the game," Roth continued. "Business leaders. Some politicians. Actors."

"Will you name them?"

"I'm prepared to, yes. I can testify about what I saw. You can imagine that I've been very reluctant to share what I know, considering how deep this plot goes. I don't know you. I don't know if I can or should trust you."

"How about your friend Moretti?"

"He's on his way here to help."

"That doesn't answer my question," she said firmly.

Roth shook his head no but then realized the recording wouldn't capture that. "No . . . for the record. Well, I mentioned Calakmul's name to him, but I didn't give him any more details. I knew anyone I told would be put in danger. Not even Steve Lund knows the whole story. He believes a cartel is after me."

"So you've put me at risk by telling me," she asked, still dubious.

He shrugged. "Either you're working for Calakmul or now you've seen the video tape."

"What?"

"The movie, *The Ring*. You've seen the videotape. You will die in seven days. You haven't seen it?"

She shook her head no, looking even more concerned.

Roth shook his head. "Bad analogy, then. Sorry. It's just a movie. Look, Agent Sanchez. My wife is probably dead. They were going to kill my children, who mean the absolute world to me. That's why I hired protection. That's why I snagged this prepper cabin in the middle of nowhere. Calakmul intends to take down the US government. He wants to reestablish the Aztec and Maya empires as the ultimate rulers of the world."

Her brow furrowed again. "With blowguns and spears? I did see *Apocalypto* on Amazon Prime Video when it was free."

"They have Mexican special forces working for them. And the cartels. But their plans are bigger than that. They've been quietly encouraging the drug crisis in America. The obesity epidemic. School shootings. But the scariest crap is their magic."

"Magic? Seriously?"

"If my daughter, Suki, were here, she could *show* you. It's real. I'm not talking card tricks or sleight of hand. It's called the *kem äm*. And it can do some pretty crazy stuff."

"Crazy like how?"

"In the arena, if the game ball hit the magic netting protecting the court, it would shoot right back . . . at the one . . . who . . . kicked . . ."

He stopped, realizing what had probably happened to the FBI agents earlier. A person shielded in *kem äm* would be invulnerable to bullets. But not those closest to them.

She looked at him in confusion as he made a face.

"Or turn a bullet back on the shooter. The agents who died tonight might have killed *themselves*."

Her look was astonished but also incredulous. She was trained in law enforcement. All of this would sound crazy to her. Of course it would. But it made sense. An agent would shoot if threatened. The magic of the Maya held a strange twist on physics. Roth realized he needed to warn Lund of this possibility. He'd shot one of Calakmul's guys in Germany, but it might have been a lucky break—one he might not get again. He pulled out his burner phone and quickly texted Lund to be careful, saying that Calakmul's people seemed to have some form of bullet-deflecting technology.

Just as he clicked send, a text arrived. The text was from Illari, the researcher he'd hired.

Where did you find these? There's a curse on it.

"Oh crap," Roth said. He reached over and stopped Agent Sanchez's phone recording.

CHAPTER SIXTEEN

BECK CABIN

BOZEMAN, MONTANA

December 26

"Why did you stop the recording?" Agent Sanchez said. "That's a burner phone, right?"

"It is," Roth answered, staring at the screen, seeing the indicator that Illari was still typing another message. "And I promised this person they wouldn't get involved."

"Have you heard of the QAnon conspiracy, Mr. Roth?" she asked.

"Who hasn't *heard* of it? They said an anonymous government employee was posting secrets about child-trafficking in Washington, DC."

"Are you part of that movement, Mr. Roth?"

"Me? No!" he chuckled. "I've had fans ask me that before, but I was a history professor before I ever became an author. There's no evidence to support any of it."

"You do realize that everything you've told me sounds more radical than the QAnon conspiracy?"

Roth frowned. "The difference is that I've *been* to Cozumel. We *were* kidnapped, taken to the ruins of a Maya temple, and we *watched* a neighbor die. We watched him be ripped apart. I think that's a little more compelling than a few rumors gone wild on the internet."

"I saw my friends get shot tonight. I don't believe that some ancient *magic* killed them. It was MS-13."

Roth shrugged. "They were probably part of it, but I'm guessing most of the shoot-outs you've been in or heard about aren't that fatal. Should be easy enough to prove what happened."

"How so?"

"Forensics."

"If you're wrong, are you willing to accept that you might be a man distraught at losing his wife and have conjured this . . . story in order to cope with your grief?"

"I have a feeling you were a psychology undergrad."

"I was," she said, angling her head to study him. "Profiling criminals is part of the job."

Another text arrived. *This stuff is bad news. Call me when you wake up.*

Roth typed back. *I'm awake. Will call soon.*

"Who is that?" Agent Sanchez asked.

"Another piece of the puzzle," Roth replied. "Do you want some hot chocolate? Coffee would take longer."

"Hot chocolate is fine," she said. "But . . . can't drink it." She jiggled her wrists in the zip ties.

Roth went to the kettle and poured another steaming mug. He added several scoops of powder, stirred it with a spoon, and brought it back to the table.

Roth knew there was a utility knife in the counter drawer and got it. "I'll cut one hand loose. I'm going to be over there, watching you while I talk on the phone. Don't try anything foolish, Agent Sanchez."

"I'm not the one racking up felonies, Mr. Roth."

"True," he said. He sliced the zip tie on her left wrist, then set the mug down in front of her. He was ready in case she tried to grab him, but even he was more capable than someone tied to a chair.

He put the knife back in the drawer and then walked through the kitchen toward the back door of the cabin. Making sure to keep the agent within his line of sight, he tapped on Illari's name.

She picked up instantly. "Where did you find these glyphs?" she demanded in her slightly accented voice. He didn't know what she looked like, but they'd spoken before since he'd used her to translate ancient Mayan a few times over the past year. She was a college grad student who didn't have great job prospects because of her beliefs in the Mexica ideology. She thought all Europeans should voluntarily abandon the United States and give the country back to Indigenous peoples. When he'd questioned her on how far she would go to fulfill that aim, she'd made it very clear she was a pacifist. If it weren't done through diplomatic means, then any gains would also be losses. She wasn't out to exterminate anybody. She was, in a word, idealistic. That conversation and others had helped him trust that she wasn't part of Calakmul's conspiracy. Of course, he'd still had Lund do a background check.

"They're part of the Dresden Codex," Roth answered.

"That's impossible. I've *read* the Dresden Codex."

"This was writing from the blank pages."

"Are you messing with me?"

"I just got back from Germany, Illari. I took photos of it with this phone."

"But they're blank. I've seen the photos online."

"I can explain it later, but I promise you. These are from the blank pages. I was there. Now, what does it say? What's this curse you mentioned?" He glanced at Agent Sanchez and saw her sipping from the mug.

"In K'iche', these people are called the 'Kowinem.' A word that means *power* and *ability*. That was what they sought. Power, wealth, prestige. They committed any number of heinous crimes to get what they wanted. These people were the shadow government. They put up kings and took them down. They had blood oaths and curses and secret crap like that."

Sounds like Jacob Calakmul, Roth thought to himself. "Okay, so what's the translation? Don't tell me it's another description of the rising and setting of Venus."

"It isn't. The pages are marked on all four corners with the jaguar rune, and under each one is a threat of death for revealing what's on the page." She paused. "No, actually. I put that wrong. Each threatens a different way that the person will be *killed.* It says the meaning can only be revealed to someone who shows the proper sign."

"What?" Roth asked, confused.

"The Kowinem used hand signals, gestures, to distinguish each other from the main populace. They were a secret society. Very few of them knew each other's identities. So if someone was caught, they couldn't reveal the others."

"Like drug lords today," Roth said.

"Exactly. They'd wear masks to their meetings." Another pause. "I've seen all the photos of the Dresden Codex. This is nothing like them. This *can't* be from the one in Germany."

"But you told me that the codex wasn't arranged in any particular order. Or, if it was, that the original order is unknown. These were the blank pages, set facing down."

"I get that, but seriously. How did you read a blank page? Tons of scholars have gone over and examined the codex. You just happened to find something no one else has seen in centuries?"

"I said I'd explain later. I can't right now. But it's something like hidden ink. Okay?"

"If you say so, but I'm . . . just seeing these threats is giving me really bad vibes."

"It sounds like the curse that's at the end of the Bible. You know, the one that says if anyone adds to the Bible, then God will curse them with the plagues from Egypt. An empty threat. So did you translate it or not?"

Illari paused. She sounded troubled. "Oh, I did. But I don't think you're going to want to publish this in your book. There's some stuff you're just not supposed to talk about. Someone might try to kill you if they think you're betraying the Kowinem's secrets."

"So you believe the Kowinem still exist?" Roth asked her quietly, feeling a chill course down his spine.

"Yeah. I heard stories about my uncle. They tried to recruit him."

"No way."

"Yeah. They don't let just anyone in. In order to join, the person has to kill someone, a close family member. Like one of those gang initiations." Silence hung over the line for a second, and she added, "I don't want anyone knowing I was the one who sent this to you."

"Okay. If you don't want recognition, that's all right. Can you send me the translation from an account that can't be traced back to you?"

"Super easy. But I want to see that donation first. The one you promised."

"Deal," Roth agreed.

"Okay, then I'm going to create a rando e-mail account from the library and send the translation to you. I meant it, though, don't tell anyone I did this. Don't tell anyone you *know* me."

"Can you send it to me today?"

"Sure, but the libraries don't open until later. I need some sleep."

"That's fine. But I need it today."

"Send me the money first."

"I will." He considered what she'd told him. "This is something no scholar has ever seen before, right? I don't even think the Spanish realized what they had."

Or maybe they had known. Prior to making the trip to Germany, Roth had done his research. The codex had been in Dresden since it was acquired by a librarian in 1739 from a private collector from Vienna,

Austria. It had survived two world wars and the Allied bombing of Germany in the 1940s. But no one knew who'd been in possession of it prior to 1739. During Cortés's time in the Yucatán, however, many artifacts from the ancient Maya had been sent to the Holy Roman emperor, Charles V, who had been king of Spain before becoming the Holy Roman emperor. It was conjectured that the codex had been sent to him in Vienna in 1519. There was a discrepancy of nearly two hundred years during which the possession of the codex was unknown.

Maybe the information had been known, only to be forgotten—lost over centuries.

"You got that right," Illari said. "This is groundbreaking. It's a prophecy about the future."

Roth swallowed. "Thank you. This is so helpful."

"I'll text you after I've sent it from the spoof account."

"Got it. Bye." Roth ended the call. He switched the app to his bank account and forwarded the agreed-upon donation to the nonprofit he'd been supporting in order to get Illari's help. He sent the money. How long would it take for the transaction to post?

He slipped the phone back into his pocket, thoughtful.

The burner phone began to ring again. He thought it might be Illari, but he saw a new number with an association to Lund and realized it might be his daughter's burner phone. She was still hiding downtown with Lund.

He answered the call. "Hey, girl. Can't sleep?"

"Dad!" Suki whispered, her voice frantic.

"What's going on?" he demanded, his whole body instantly on alert.

"We finally got away. We're at the high school."

"Away? From whom?"

"Some bad dudes. They passed us on Main Street and chased after us. Um . . . Mr. Lund drives like a maniac. But he got us away. The car's damaged, though, and the engine's smoking. We hid a few times and then had to ditch it in the faculty parking lot."

"Why are you at the high school?" Roth asked.

"To hide."

"So Lund is still with you?"

"He unlocked the door and is checking things out inside. I'm waiting outside. Dad, I'm so scared. This feels like last year."

Roth grimaced and felt a shudder go through his body. This was his fault. He'd knocked over the first domino. He hated that Suki wasn't here with them. "You're going to be okay, sweetie. Just stay with Lund. Do what he tells you. Moretti's coming up from Salt Lake with some firepower. He should get there in a few hours. Just hunker down and stay out of sight. You know that school. Is there a place you can hide?"

"Yeah. We're going to the theater."

"You do that. Just stay quiet."

"How are Brillante and Lucas?"

"They're asleep."

"Lucky. I'm so tired. I haven't slept at all."

"You're going to be okay. Just trust your instincts, like you did down in Mexico. You have power you can use, Suki," he added, putting emphasis on the words. "Use it to keep yourself safe."

"I'm still scared of it, Dad."

"I know. I know. But you've got to use it if they find you there. Promise?"

"I promise," Suki said. "Love you, Dad."

"Love you too. I'll let you know when Moretti gets to Bozeman. And I'll text Lund to let him know he's on his way, okay?"

"Okay. Bye."

Roth ended the call and sent a quick text to Moretti, informing him that Suki was at Gallatin High School, hiding in the theater. He told him to go there *first*. Roth felt like he and the kids would be okay at the cabin. They could stay there for a long time if needed. But the

Agent Sanchez situation was still a problem. He texted Lund to let him know Moretti was coming to Bozeman with backup.

His phone was running low on power. With the generator running, he could plug it in. Once the sun rose, they wouldn't need the generator anymore. The solar panels would provide enough electricity to keep things running, and they were much quieter than the generator.

He looked over at Agent Sanchez. She was holding the mug in her left hand. She'd been listening to everything he said.

"Let me call someone to protect your daughter," she said. "I know you don't trust the FBI, but what about the sheriff's department? I can have someone at the high school in minutes."

Roth stared at her, still not sure whether to trust her. Her reactions to everything he'd shared with her seemed within the realm of normal.

She was right. If she wasn't crooked, she was in a position to help Suki and Lund immediately. But if she was working for or with Jacob Calakmul, then it would be incredibly dangerous to tell her anything about Suki.

Outside the cabin, he heard a sound that brought a chill to his heart. The howling of wolves.

CHAPTER SEVENTEEN

Bozeman Yellowstone International Airport

Bozeman, Montana

December 26

"Do you want me to call his cell phone again?" Angélica asked.

Jacob wanted to leave the Pegasus. The jet was refueling and would transition to the hangar. Perhaps he would transform into a snow leopard and prowl the tarmac at the airport? No, he preferred being a true jaguar. They had survived for millions of years and could handle any terrain, any environment. He couldn't leave the plane in his human form, for his presence in the United States needed to be kept secret. It was not time to conquer the greed-sick country. Not yet.

"He won't answer," Jacob said. "I know he won't. But I have an idea for how we can *make* him answer."

"We can't stay here much longer," Angélica cautioned. "The risk is too great. Thankfully, the blizzard at Jackson Hole provided the alibi we needed to land here, but immigration officials will be coming soon."

"They will search the jet and find nothing," Jacob said. He wasn't worried. His magic could mask what needed to remain unseen.

Jacob looked out the window at the dark sky. The sun would be rising in a couple of hours, and the city of Bozeman would awaken. He wanted to have the Roths in hand by the time it did. He'd assumed that they would have been caught before the Pegasus reached Montana. But once again the famous author was testing Jacob. He'd escaped on snowmobiles to somewhere in the mountains. But Jaguar Priest K'oxol would hunt the Roths down. There were predators in those mountains that would help him find them. Jacob was certain of it. The tracks of a snowmobile would not be difficult to follow.

But what was Mr. Roth's end game? What was his plan?

Jacob sipped from the mug of *xocolatl*, replenishing his strength, invigorating his mind.

"We're vulnerable here," Angélica whispered, gazing out the window. He could smell the scent of fear coming from her skin. It had been a great risk to breach the borders of the United States. He had no passport, no identification of any kind. His presence in this country was illegal. But it was still his birthright.

Jacob wasn't worried for himself. He could transform into a bird and fly back to Mexico if need be. Nothing could be allowed to stand in the way of the prophecy being fulfilled. It would be a problem if Angélica were detained, however. She knew too much. He would kill her before he let that happen.

He reached out and touched her knee. He didn't want to kill her. His feelings for her had grown more complex over the past several years of working together. "We'll be fine. The bureaucracy in this country renders it easy to manipulate. We can bribe the officials if need be. Turn your thoughts elsewhere. What does Mr. Roth hope to gain here? Why did he go to Dresden for the prophecy?"

"Proof that he's not crazy?" she suggested. "We both know his daughter can control the magic. Maybe she revealed the glyphs?"

"But who will he tell? He clearly doesn't trust the FBI, or he would have told them. He refused to divulge what he knew in front of Agent Sanchez when she presented him with the search warrant."

"But he's gone away with her now. What if he *has* told her? We wouldn't know. Agent Garcia is still waiting at the house in Bozeman in case they return."

Garcia was their connection in the Bozeman office. Jacob had arranged for him to be transferred to Agent Sanchez's satellite office following the match last year. He was the one who had signaled K'oxol to attack the Roths' house and kill the agents sent there to protect them. K'oxol would have killed Agent Sanchez too if she hadn't escaped with the family.

The FBI didn't realize that Garcia was still alive. Nor would they. His connection to internal comms was providing the inside information Jacob and the MS-13 gang needed. The agent had let the jaguar priest know which members of the family were present and also sent the gang to look for Suki. He was their eyes and ears.

Angélica's phone rang. She answered it. "Hello, Garcia?" She paused, listening. Jacob could hear the deep tenor of the man's voice, but he was speaking very low. Angélica bent forward, deep in concentration. Then she smiled.

"Excellent. I will tell him. Meet us at the airport at the FBO run by . . ." She paused, looking out the window at the fuel truck. "Jet Aviation. It's not in the main terminal. Your badge should get you through security. You'll fly with us back to Cozumel."

Jacob held up his hand.

"Wait," Angélica said, pausing, looking to Jacob for instructions.

"Tell him to wait at the house in case they return. We will call him back when it's time to leave."

"Did you hear that? Good. Await orders. Well done." She ended the call.

"News?" Jacob asked, smiling. It was about time they got some good news.

"Suki is at the high school. The MS-13 gang just arrived."

"There will be alarms at the school," Jacob said. "How long before the police go there?"

"It's a school holiday. They'll send one car to check it out. Not a problem for the gang."

"What about the FBI reinforcements coming from Salt Lake?"

"Garcia said they're not due to arrive for hours. We have time."

Jacob nodded. "Close, but we'll be gone in time. We must find out what Roth wants with the Dresden Codex." He rubbed his chin, then took another sip from the mug. "He needs someone to translate it."

"We've monitored his phone calls and e-mails. Nothing."

"So he's been using a burner phone," Jacob said. "What else has his security, Mr. Lund, provided him?"

She pulled out her tablet and activated it. "If he's been using a burner phone and a laptop we don't know about, he could have been purchasing things and doing research without us knowing about it."

"His home and phone internet traffic show he hasn't been researching for another book."

"No. Mostly looking at news. YouTube. He researches diabetes and comas."

"He wouldn't have found anything about my family online," Jacob said. "Our people monitor the internet constantly. Has he been working with law enforcement?"

"Wouldn't we have noticed that? He doesn't travel. He goes to coffee shops during the week, but the only big trip he's taken was to Germany."

The pilot called out from the cockpit. "Looks like immigration got here early," he said. "A car is driving up."

"The FBO must have a contact," Angélica said. "That's customer service." She straightened out her winter attire, the outfit she'd worn in Switzerland, and grabbed the coat and put it on.

The pilot came out, looking bleary-eyed.

"Have some more *xocolatl*," Jacob told him.

After Angélica freshened herself by the door, she undid the latch. Cold wind knifed into the jet. The car pulled to a stop at the side of the Pegasus, and some official-looking people came out. Jacob invoked the magic of the *kem äm*, using it to enact a glyph of invisibility around himself. Just like the glyph protecting the most important parts of the Dresden Codex. Their eyes would pass over him as if he weren't there.

One of the FBO employees entered the aircraft. "We apologize it took so long, but this is Frank Dodd from US Immigration. He'll need to see your passports, please, then we can park the jet in our hangar, and you can finally use the lounge. We're sorry the storm put you off course, but we hope you have a pleasant stay in Bozeman, Miss . . . ?"

"Torres. Call me Angélica." She smiled pleasantly and backed away, letting the others enter. The customer service agent was a young man in his midtwenties, and he was looking at Angélica with obvious appreciation. Mr. Dodd, from immigration, was a gray-haired bureaucrat who looked unpleased and kept honking his nose into a handkerchief.

"Passports," Mr. Dodd said sternly.

Angélica and the pilot handed their documents over. The man began to peruse them, looking at the stamps.

"Thank you. Need to scan these back at the airport. Please stay here until you're cleared."

"Of course," Angélica said politely.

"There's no one else on board?" Mr. Dodd asked. He honked and blew his nose again.

"You can check the lavatory," Angélica suggested with a small smile.

"Don't mind if I do," said Mr. Dodd. He walked right past Jacob, oblivious to his presence. There was a single restroom in the back.

The young man reached out and stroked Angélica's arm. "Are you meeting anyone in Jackson Hole? A ski trip at the Four Seasons, maybe?"

Jacob wanted to rip out the young Romeo's heart. He invoked the magic, causing a feeling of danger to throb in the air.

The young man blinked in surprise and yanked back his hand.

Mr. Dodd came back. "Where were you headed again?" he asked.

"A storm prevented them from landing in Jackson Hole," said the young man. His eyes were dancing with a combination of fear and interest. He didn't understand what he was feeling. But the sense of danger made him possibly even more attracted to her.

"Yes, a storm," Angélica said. "A blizzard that was unexpected."

Jacob smiled. It was a storm that *he* had caused.

CHAPTER EIGHTEEN

GALLATIN HIGH SCHOOL

BOZEMAN, MONTANA

December 26

Suki had never been to the high school in the middle of the night before. The normally bright and sunlit common areas were now veiled in darkness with just the illumination of security lights. They'd entered from some rear doors near the faculty parking lot. Nervousness thrummed inside her. Calling her dad hadn't helped quell her anxiety. She slipped her phone back into her pocket.

Gallatin was a new high school, built recently through a bond measure costing over a hundred million dollars. The school had a large central area where the three different wings met. From there, they jutted out at different angles, each wing three stories tall. The exterior was a combination of brown brick and gray metal siding, but the front facade was all windows. During the day, it showed a panoramic view of the mountains.

The sound of their feet walking on the smooth and polished concrete floor echoed softly as they moved.

"Theater arts is that way?" Mr. Lund asked, gesturing to the left.

"That's the basketball arena, actually," Suki said. She pointed to the right spot. "Theater . . . those doors."

The theater was adjacent to the large central quad with its wide and angled stairs, some of which were colored a bright blue. The sitting-area tables were also brilliantly colored—reds, oranges, yellows—all muted in the darkness. The quad had a second level too, with additional seating and places to hang out. She looked over at the table by the big windows where she and Brice usually ate lunch together. It was so different from the old schools she'd attended in Fremont, California. Cold War schools—cramped and cracked and graffiti-sprayed.

Suki walked to the big wall of windows, seeing a little reflection of herself and Mr. Lund as they drew nearer. Bozeman was still asleep, the day after Christmas. Her stomach throbbed with worry. She was desperate to be with her family, but there was no way to get to them without a snowmobile—and no way to get a snowmobile before dawn.

"Let's get to that hiding place you mentioned," Mr. Lund suggested calmly. He was holding a shotgun he'd taken from his trunk. She'd seen him thrust another handgun into his belt as well.

"You're loaded for bear," Suki said, nodding at the shotgun.

Mr. Lund wrinkled his brow in confusion.

"My dad sometimes says it," she explained. "It means you're preparing for a fight."

"Better to have it and not need it than to need it and not have it," he replied.

The streak of headlights moved through the parking lot of the high school. The nervous feeling in her gut suddenly intensified. A white SUV was pulling into the main entrance of the school. The same SUV that had chased them earlier.

Mr. Lund frowned. "Let's find that hiding place, shall we?"

Suki nodded quickly and marched to the corridor leading to the sports and theater arts wing, just to their left. She walked with purpose to the correct metal door.

While the exterior of most of the high school was brown and gray, the theater building was silver. There was a bank of windows, set at an odd triangle in the corner. One facade had a grid-design and another, angled slats. Very artistic. She opened the doors and then pulled out her cell phone and triggered the flashlight.

"Big theater," Mr. Lund said. "How many does it hold?"

"Seven fifty," she said. "It's legit."

Mr. Lund had a handheld flashlight, which he switched on. The curtain on stage was open, revealing the set for the upcoming school play. The opening was a chorus number, a fun song that invited the more squeamish members of the audience to consider leaving before the murders started. The thought made Suki wish she had *another* place she could go.

"That way," she said, pointing when the light from his flashlight hit the recessed door in the back wall. It was kept locked because of the expensive sound-stage equipment up there, but she knew where the hidden key was kept and quickly retrieved it and unlocked the door.

The interior stairwell was pitch-black, but with her phone light, she climbed the steep steps and Lund followed behind her. It was a cramped space.

The eerie quiet made Suki's skin crawl, but she knew the space. She was the stage manager and had been up here a hundred times. Once she reached the lighting booth, she opened the door and went in. A large plate-glass window looked down on the theater.

There was a huge control board for sound and lights, with about a million different buttons and switches. It was a state-of-the-art system.

Mr. Lund entered next and checked out the area. There were some heavier boxes, full of equipment. He tested them and nodded.

"These can be used to barricade the door."

"That's what I was thinking," she said. She also thought about the magic she could summon with the ring and bracelet. The magic usually worked when it needed to, when her need pushed her past her anxiety. "This stairway is the only way up here."

"I'm going to stay down in the theater itself," he said. "If they come in as a group, one blast from the shotgun will do the most damage, and then it's just cleaning the carpets."

"Weird flex, but okay," Suki said.

"If they're smart, they'll come separately, and I'll have to pick them off one by one with a handgun."

"Please don't destroy my school's theater," she begged. "We have a play starting after the holiday break."

"I'm hoping it won't come to that, Suki. I reactivated the alarm system. They'll trigger the perimeter alarms when they get here, and if they try to break in. I hope local police will arrive while we stay out of sight. Your dad's friend from Salt Lake is on his way. He's sending him directly to the school, so we'll have a SWAT team here pretty soon. With any luck, this will all be very boring." He turned to head back down.

"If you're going down there, then let me grab a headset," Suki said. "The stage team has them so they can communicate with the booth." She went to one of the lock boxes, flipped the latch open, and withdrew a couple of headsets.

"Smart thinking," he said with an approving nod.

Suki set them to the same channel. She slid one of them over her ears and adjusted the volume. Then she handed the other to Mr. Lund.

"I saw a glowing exit sign on the wall by the stairs," he said, adjusting the headset and mic. "Testing . . . testing?"

She heard him loud and clear. "The small pup gnawed a hole in the sock," she said back.

He looked at her in confusion.

"The fish twisted and turned on the bent hook," she said.

"I'm confused," he admitted.

"This is a *real* sound check. We don't say 'Testing one, two, three.'"

"Ah. You test the syllables and diction to make sure they come through clearly."

"Press the pants and sew a button on the vest."

He repeated it. "Press the pants and sew a button on the vest."

"See? You're getting good at it already."

"Thank you . . . I think."

Suki grinned, but the expression wavered as a wave of premonition engulfed her. "They're coming."

Mr. Lund nodded. "Those seats provide a lot of cover. Where are the exit doors?"

"There, there, there," she said, pointing to the illuminated signs through the window.

"I'm going to roam around a bit down there. Lock the door after I leave and then stay up here. If you see anyone enter, tell me which direction." He pointed as he said, "North, east, south, west. Just give me a general sense. I'll keep them busy and away from here. I know this school really well. If someone other than me comes up these stairs, barricade the door and call 911. Got it?"

"Roger, roger," she said, using a robotic voice. Her nervousness settled a little. He seemed so confident, so capable.

She followed him back down the stairs and then locked the door behind him, pocketing the key. Then she went back up to the lighting booth and hunkered down.

She heard Lund's voice through her headset. "The rain in Spain is mainly on the plain."

"That's from *My Fair Lady*," she replied. "And you got it wrong."

"It's the only rhyme I know."

"Her purse was full of useless trash," Suki said.

"This garbage bin is full of useless trash."

She looked through the windows and saw him and his Maglite maneuvering through the rows of seats.

"Do you have a bulletproof vest on?" she asked.

"Is that another sound-check question?"

"No."

"I do not. Are you worried about me?"

"A little."

"Your dad texted me that they might have some sort of technology capable of deflecting bullets. Do you know anything about that?"

The sickening, intense feeling was growing stronger. "I think they're almost here. And it wouldn't surprise me if he's right about that."

"Your dad also said you get strong feelings of warning when danger is close, and that it started in Mexico."

"Yup. My hunches always seem to pan out too."

"Interesting, because I just got a text from someone in immigration who said that a Pegasus private jet chartered from Mexico is on the tarmac at the airport. I think it's more common for the rich to visit Cancún during the holidays than Bozeman."

Suki's heart clenched with dread. "Um. Yeah. And a Pegasus can take off like a helicopter."

"I think our drug lord friend is in town. He's come after you guys himself. Very interesting and stupid on his part. I've asked my friend to detain him."

Suki swallowed. That meant Mr. Calakmul wanted them very badly. "Be careful," she warned.

"I'm going to let your dad know. My friend Stoker works as the manager of air traffic control at the airport. Gotta hold that jet." He sounded more than a little excited. "This . . . this is a good thing. He came to *us*. I'm sure we can find a good reason to arrest him."

"You think so?" Suki asked. She remembered Jacob transforming into a jaguar. He would not be easy to catch. But she didn't tell Lund this. He wasn't supposed to know . . . and she didn't think he'd believe her if she told him.

"School alarms are going off," Lund said. The Maglite switched off. One of the angled-wall windows shattered in a hail of glass.

CHAPTER NINETEEN

Beck Cabin

Bozeman, Montana

December 26

The only animals Roth had personally seen near the Beck cabin were a few deer and a single moose. He knew there were gray wolves in the mountains, but they were incredibly rare, and he'd never heard them before. Had the wolves been drawn to the noise of the snowmobiles and lights in the middle of the night? The keening of their howls made his insides clench with dread. It was an irrational fear. They were perfectly safe inside the cabin.

He wasn't the one in danger. His daughter was.

He fully trusted Steve Lund to keep Suki safe. But he couldn't shake the horrible feeling that this was his fault for taking those photos, especially after what Illari had told him about the translation. He went back to the counter, filled another mug with steaming water, and scooped some hot chocolate powder into it for himself. What he really wanted was a cup of *xocolatl*. It wasn't a caffeine hit. The drink was restorative.

Weariness was starting to creep up on him again. Adrenaline was better than a cup of coffee, but even that wore off in time.

He stirred the drink and then went and sat back at the table, across from Agent Sanchez. Her mug was half-empty.

"Let me help your daughter," she said again, more gently this time. "MS-13 is a dangerous gang."

"Didn't think they'd be in Bozeman," he replied. "Thought they were more a Southern California gang."

"You'd be surprised," she said. "Twenty years ago, most of the meth produced in Montana was homegrown. The stuff we're finding now is purer, which makes it far more addictive and dangerous. It's cartel grade. Mexican origin. Truth is MS-13 has been here for a while. Your friend Moretti would tell you the same. When the task force goes after a bust, they have to wear body armor and go in like Navy SEALs."

Worry itched at Roth. She was saying this on purpose. He sipped some of the hot chocolate, letting the flavor swirl across his tongue before he swallowed it.

"Jacob Calakmul said that the jaguar priests were running the cartels," he told her. "All the meth, heroin, stuff like fentanyl. They're drugging our country so we'll be easier victims. The obesity epidemic too."

"You mentioned that before. So, what, he's making Americans eat fast food?" she asked in a skeptical tone.

Roth patted his own gut. "I can't say I know how it all works. But I've been to the arena. We played the game. The Beasleys were supposed to win. They played willingly, because they were told they'd be made rulers of some kind after the bloodbath started."

"Bloodbath?"

"A second civil war. You work for the federal government. I don't. But I see what's going on in the news. The race riots. The paramilitary types. The anger between political parties. There's no trust anymore. Hasn't been for a long time. My wife's family is from Mexico originally. Her great-grandparents picked fruit and worked in orchards in San Jose."

"Mine worked ranches in Texas," she said with sympathy. "Life in Mexico was hard back then. There was more opportunity here. But if you think politics here are bad, they were even worse down there around that time. I don't think my *abuelita* would have dared dream that one of her granddaughters would end up in the FBI."

The howling of the wolves was getting closer. It was truly a creepy sound. He rose from the chair and went back to the cabin door to make sure it was locked and bolted.

"Is that the only door in and out?" she asked. "I don't see another one."

There was a tunnel beneath the cabin, a crawl space that led into the woods. But he wasn't going to tell her that.

"That door can withstand a bear," Roth said. "No wolf is going to break through."

"I've lived in Bozeman for years," Agent Sanchez said, "and I've never seen a wolf in these hills."

"You're right. That's why I'm a little on edge. My friend's dad was a missionary at a Navajo reservation. He used to tell us stories about the Navajo. The skinwalkers."

"Those are just myths," she said bluntly.

"I'm afraid I'll have to disagree with you," he said. "I've seen a man turn into a jaguar. After that, anything is possible."

"Or you *thought* you did," she suggested. "Did they give you anything strange to drink? Something laced with hallucinogens maybe?"

He lifted the mug and gestured it toward her. *"Xocolatl."*

"Like the pure kind? From actual cocoa beans?"

"Yes."

"Or were they from the coca plant? The same used by the cartels to make cocaine?"

"No . . . it was chocolate. I wasn't drugged out. What we experienced was real. And we all almost died."

She frowned. He could tell she was trying to reason with him. To make him doubt what he'd been through. He didn't blame her for not believing him—it really was the kind of thing you needed to see to believe—but he still had to try.

He sighed. "Agent Sanchez, the strongest thing I take is ibuprofen. A drug test would prove it."

"Then let's prove it, Mr. Roth. Let me go, and I'll bring you to a safe house. There's a witness protection program. There are hotels in the area where you can stay while we look into this. If you're worried about this drug lord hurting your family, let us help."

"The problem, Agent Sanchez, is I can't be sure whether you're working with them. It could be someone else in the FBI. I thought I was a pretty good judge of character, but that trip to Mexico convinced me I'm just as gullible as most people are. The book *Talking to Strangers* shows just how easily we're deceived. Fidel Castro fooled the CIA for decades with double agents. I want to trust you. But I can't trust myself. If I let you loose and give you a gun, you'd probably turn it on me."

"No, I wouldn't." She leaned forward. "You may be deluded. But I can tell you're sincere and you're smart. Trust me. I've interrogated bad people, Mr. Roth. I've seen the *evil* behind smiling eyes. I've been sworn at, threatened with gruesome death, and on more than one occasion, I've known the only thing keeping me alive was a sturdy pair of hand-cuffs separating me from a lunatic." She shook her head. "You aren't one of the bad guys. And neither am I. Being an FBI agent requires a lot of trust. I had to prove myself trustworthy to get this position, and I have to prove it again every day. Allow me to get your daughter to a safe place. If you let me make a call, right here in front of you, you'll see that I mean what I say. Trust is built piece by piece. We'll start by helping your daughter."

Roth was so conflicted. He felt, in his gut, that she was being hon-est. That she both wanted to help and had the means to do so. But he'd been deceived by the ill intentions of others before. He remem-bered how polite and helpful Jacob Calakmul and Angélica had been upon their arrival at the Calakmul resort. How friendly and inviting the

Beasleys had been when they'd first met their neighbors. Roth hadn't seen the evil behind smiling eyes.

He heard snuffling sounds at the door. Panting. Claws scratching at the wood.

Agent Sanchez turned her head and looked at the door worriedly. "What's drawing them to a cabin?"

The woodstove was generating ample heat now, but it couldn't be that, could it? Wolves were predators looking for food. A rabbit. Mice. Rarely would they try to tackle larger game in the middle of winter. It made no sense that they would feel compelled toward a cabin in the woods. He rubbed his chest, trying to ignore the sound. The question.

"You know, every culture has their own beliefs regarding the supernatural," he said. "Water turns into wine. Leprosy is healed. Fire from heaven consumes an offering. Zeus is responsible for thunderbolts. The Maya are one of the oldest civilizations who left a record. The Aztecs came after them. Do you know where they came from?"

"I have no idea." Her gaze was still glued to the door. "I studied psychology and minored in criminal science."

Another scratching sound at the wood. Roth shuddered. "There's not a lot of evidence, but I've been reading everything I can through the library at MSU. The Aztecs *came* to Mexico. Scholars think they originated farther north. The legend about the snake and the eagle—the symbols on the Mexican flag—you know that, right?"

"Like I said, I grew up in Texas. So no, I don't."

"A group of people, tribes, came from a cave in the north. One of those tribes was the Mexica, and they followed a prophecy that was supposed to lead them to their new land, a place they could be safe. The prophecy said to look for an eagle with a snake in its beak on a cactus or by a lake. They found an eagle eating a rattlesnake and built the city Tenochtitlán. Modern-day Mexico City. But where did they come from before? Well, the story is that the Aztecs came from a mythical land called Aztlán. Some scholars wrote about it as a paradise. Others said it was ruled by a tyrannical elite called the Azteca Chicomoztoca. A priesthood of sorts. They could supposedly transform into animals. Not just one kind."

"These are the jaguar priests?" she asked.

"Possibly. There aren't many jaguars that far north these days. Most are extinct because of game hunters, but they did exist back then. But there's also speculation that Aztlán was here in the US. Somewhere in Arizona, New Mexico, Utah. Maybe even Idaho."

"Interesting," she said, her tone intrigued. Then more scratching drew her gaze back to the door.

"My friend's dad, the one who told us about the skinwalkers, served in the Four Corners region. You know where that is?"

"I've been there on vacation."

"That's where the stories of the *yee naaldlooshii* come from. Moretti's dad told us about this missionary he knew who heard an animal following him when he came back home at night. He got back to his hogan and—"

"What's a 'hogan'?"

"It's a living structure, made of dried mud. They made them into mounds with a single door going in and out. No windows. Just a hole in the roof for smoke to escape."

"Sounds dirty."

"Yeah. The missionary built a fire, but he heard human voices calling for him to come out. According to Moretti's dad, one of the *yee naaldlooshii* jumped up on the roof, but the smoke and fire kept him out. The next morning, the guy found wolf tracks all around the hogan. Not footprints."

"It could have been a practical joke," she offered.

Another scratch came at the door. Roth pushed away from the table. "I'm waking Jordan up. All this scratching is creeping me out."

"They can't get inside," Agent Sanchez said. "You said the door's too thick."

"I know. But I'll feel better if he's out here. He's a good shot."

"I'm not too bad myself," she said.

"Guess we'll never know." Roth chuckled. He went to the next room where Jordan was snoring softly on the leather couch. He roused him with a quick shake to his shoulder.

Jordan grunted, his eyes opening. He lifted his head. "It's so dark. How many hours has it been?"

"There are some wolves outside. One is scratching at the door."

Jordan slung his legs over the couch, rubbing his face with his hands. "Oh." He checked his pistol and then made sure Agent Sanchez's gun was still in his pocket. "You want me to go outside and scare them away?"

"No. Just open the storm window and look."

"How's Agent Sanchez doing?"

"I freed one wrist so she could have some hot chocolate."

He rose swiftly and marched to the kitchen. Roth followed. For a moment, he feared she would be loose. She lifted the cup to her lips and nodded to Jordan.

"Morning, soldier," she said to him.

Another scratching noise came to the door.

"Dad?" Lucas called from the bottom of the stairs, his voice groggy. "I don't like that sound. What's out there?"

"Gray wolves probably," Jordan said. He looked exhausted, but he managed a smile. "Cool, huh?"

"Wolves?" Lucas asked as he came downstairs. He went to Roth and gave him a hug.

Roth patted his curly hair and hugged him back. "It's okay. They can't get in."

The howling grew louder and louder, as if the wolves were all gathered just outside the cabin. The feeling of danger intensified. Lucas began to tremble.

"Why are they doing that?" He gasped.

Jordan went to one of the storm windows by the front door.

"Be careful," Roth said.

Jordan unlatched the barrier. He stayed behind it and swung it open a few inches so he could peer outside.

"Whoa, big one," Jordan said in surprise, looking in the direction of the front door.

"A wolf?" Roth asked.

"Yeah. It's pretty sweet. It's prowling back and forth."

The howling intensified.

"I see . . . another one over there." He opened the window wider and switched sides. "And another one smelling the snowmobiles."

"How many do you see?" Roth asked.

"Three . . . four . . . Sounds like more than that. Must be a whole pack. Wait, there's something glowing out there." His voice became more tense. "Is it electronic or . . . ?"

"What?" Roth demanded.

"I don't know. It's coming from the woods. Stationary, like—"

"Shut the window," Agent Sanchez said. "You're a target to anyone outs—"

A bullet cracked through the window and struck Jordan in the shoulder. He spun and went down, groaning in pain. The bullet ricocheted off the woodstove. It had gone completely through him.

"Down!" Roth shouted, pulling Lucas to the floor.

CHAPTER TWENTY

BECK CABIN

BOZEMAN, MONTANA

December 26

Jordan grunted with pain as he scooted himself backward across the kitchen floor, smearing blood as we went, his uninjured hand pressing against the wound in his shoulder. Roth helped direct Lucas under the table and then arm-crawled to the window.

"Cut me loose!" Agent Sanchez implored, wrestling against the remaining zip ties.

As Roth reached the window, a cold wind came in from the broken glass. He reached up and pushed the storm shutters closed. Latched the lower half. Another bullet struck the glass and thumped into the wood, but the shutters were reinforced with a metal lining that rendered them bulletproof. Roth stood and secured the other brackets to keep them closed.

His mind was racing now. Someone had tracked them in the deep snow all the way to the cabin. That should not have even been possible. Hiking through deep snow would quickly exhaust anyone.

Of course, the people he was dealing with had access to uncanny powers.

"We need to stop the bleeding," Agent Sanchez said urgently. "The bullet went right through him."

"*He* knows it did!" Jordan barked in pain.

"Mr. Roth—you have to let me help. I've had field training for this."

She was right. Sarina was the nurse. Not Roth. He didn't know what to do.

"Lucas—wake up your brother and get him down here," Roth said.

Another bullet struck a different window. He could hear the cracking of the glass, the thump of the bullet against the barrier. He realized he was starting to hyperventilate and that a panic attack was on the way. It was hard to calm your breathing when someone was shooting out the windows in your cabin. When you were a sitting duck in your own safe house.

Lucas scurried up the stairs, head low.

Jordan had reached the wall and was scooting himself up. A grimace of pain twisted his mouth. He pulled back his hand, saw the blood, and swore under his breath.

"Mr. Roth!" Agent Sanchez urged.

"I'm thinking!" he snapped back at her. If she were with Calakmul, letting her free would be disastrous. She could put a bullet through Jordan's temple and then subdue the family from the inside. But without her help, Jordan might bleed to death. No ambulance could get out there. It would have to be a helicopter.

The howling of the wolves had been a deliberate ruse to get them to open the shutters to investigate. He was mad at himself for falling for the trick.

"Any suggestions?" Roth asked Jordan.

"Since I'd rather not *die*," said the other man, "you take the Glock. Have one of the . . . *nnnghh* . . . boys cut her loose."

"I am *not* going to hurt anyone!" Agent Sanchez protested.

"Now's your chance to prove it, Agent Sanchez," Jordan said. He extended the pistol to Roth, who took it.

The howling had stopped. Maybe the gunshots had frightened the wolves away.

Lucas and a bleary-eyed Brillante came hurrying down the stairs.

"What's going on?" Brillante demanded.

"There's a pack of werewolves outside trying to kill us," Lucas said.

"Dude . . . seriously?"

"I don't know! That's what it sounds like. Someone shot Jordan!"

"Lucas," Roth said curtly. "Go get the first aid kit. The big one. It's in the storage area."

"I know where it is." He bounded away to get it.

"Brillante. Get the knife from that drawer where I put it. You're going to cut the agent's zip ties. Start with the ones at her ankles first."

His son looked at him as if he were making a mistake. "We're letting her go?"

"I'm feeling lightheaded," Jordan said.

"Do it," Roth said. He stood by the stove, pistol lowered but ready. He didn't want to shoot her, but if she attacked anyone, he would. "Stay behind her and out of reach."

"Got it," Brillante said. He retrieved the box cutter and then knelt next to Agent Sanchez's chair. He cut the ties on both her ankles and then stood next to her. Roth could see the anxiety in Brillante's eyes as he glanced at the last zip tie, then at Jordan, then at his dad.

Roth nodded to him.

Brillante bit his lip, slit the last tie, and then quickly backed away, brandishing the box cutter.

Lucas returned with the first aid kit.

"Put it by Jordan," Roth said.

Agent Sanchez rubbed her wrists and then looked at Roth. "I'm going to help him, that's all. But he's going to need a hospital. Let me call for backup."

"Stop the bleeding first," Roth said.

"I'll do my best."

She knelt by Jordan and opened the large first aid kit. The first thing she did was put on some latex gloves from a packet. Then she removed some gauze and stripped off Jordan's parka. His shirt underneath was soaked around the entrance wound. She wadded up the gauze and pressed it against his back.

"Lean into the wall," she told him.

"Don't you need to elevate his legs?" Roth asked.

"Nope. That'd make it bleed faster," Agent Sanchez said. "Press hard." Jordan pressed against the wall, bending his knees slightly.

"This is going to hurt, but I'm not trying to kill you," she said as she quickly took out another wad of gauze. She put the gauze against his chest, up near the shoulder, and then positioned her knee against it, like she was kneeing him in the chest.

Jordan moaned with pain, his head thrashing back and forth.

"Sorry," she said. "It takes a lot of pressure to stop the bleeding. If it was just your arm, I'd use the tourniquet kit, but that won't work where you were hit. It's okay to yell."

"I'm not going to yell," Jordan grumbled angrily.

"Don't be a hero. Yell if you need to." She pressed harder, her face tensing with the effort.

"I think you're enjoying this," Jordan muttered, then started coughing.

"Maybe a little," she said back. "Mr. Roth, are there any roads leading to this cabin? What's the nearest one?"

"We're snowbound," Roth answered. "Only a snowmobile can get in or out. Or a chopper."

"You didn't answer when I asked earlier if that's the only door, so I'm assuming there's another way out?"

She was good. He grimaced.

"Okay, so we have a secondary exit," she confirmed. "Are the windows upstairs secured?"

"Boys?" Roth asked.

"Yes," Brillante said. "They're all closed. It's pretty dark up there."

"How far is the nearest cabin? Are there people living up in these mountains during the winter?"

"I don't know," Roth said. "I've seen some other cabins, but not many, and I wouldn't be able to find them in the dark."

She glanced at her watch. "Won't be dark much longer."

"Do you have to press so hard?" Jordan asked.

"At least you didn't get shot in the head," she answered. "And be thankful it wasn't an AR15, or we wouldn't be speaking right now."

Jordan looked at Roth. There were some AR15s in the bunker below. But would what they were facing even be hurt by one?

The gun was getting heavy in Roth's hand, but he kept it pointed down, still ready.

"You served in the 82nd?" Agent Sanchez asked Jordan.

"I did," Jordan replied through gritted teeth. "Was with the Old Guard before that."

"In DC. Nice. How long have you been out of the army?"

"Four years. I'm almost thirty. How old are you, Agent Sanchez?"

"Thirty-four. Been with the FBI since college."

"Where'd you go to school?" he asked her, but his voice was thready and faint, bereft of his usual confidence.

"Texas A&M. College Station."

Jordan's head lolled to the side, his eyes fluttering closed.

"What's wrong?" Roth asked in concern.

"He passed out. Loss of blood or pain . . . or both." Agent Sanchez was still applying pressure with her knee. "It takes a while to stop the bleeding. You might need to spot me."

"I'm good," Jordan said suddenly, rousing, his eyes blinking fast. "Ugh. Anyone have any Taco Bell?"

"You want Taco Bell?" Brillante asked.

"My insides are already burning," Jordan said. "I wouldn't notice it now. Can't think of a better time to eat it."

Lucas snorted and began to chuckle, and then so did Brillante. It was obvious they were nervous behind it, frightened, but grateful for the opportunity to pretend that everything was all right. Jordan was good at that.

"You've lost a lot of blood," Agent Sanchez said softly.

"I've had worse," he replied bluntly.

Roth pulled out his burner phone. He called Moretti, who picked up after a few rings.

"Hey, Roth," his friend said. Roth could hear the noise of the road coming from the phone.

"How far are you from Bozeman?"

"Couple hours. These roads are nasty. You okay?"

"I've been better. One of our bodyguards was shot up at what's supposed to be our safe house."

"I'm fine!" Jordan said, raising his voice.

"Shoulder wound," Roth said. His eyes were fixed on Agent Sanchez, watching to see if she tried to take advantage of the situation. But she was completely focused on stopping the bleeding.

"Where's the agent?"

"She's trying to stop the bleeding."

Silence. "Be careful, Roth."

"I'm doing my best. Do you have any medics on your team?"

"No, but we can summon an ambulance for you wherever."

The phone vibrated in his hand, and he pulled it back and saw Lund's name. "Hold a second. I need to take another call."

"No problem. I'll wait," Moretti said.

Roth switched the call. "Jordan's been shot."

"Who shot him?" Lund ground out. "A federal agent?"

"No, not a federal agent," Roth answered.

"They would have missed!" Jordan hollered. His words were a little slurred, though, and his head was starting to loll again.

Roth gave him an impatient look. "Someone tracked us to the cabin."

"Get down to the cellar," Lund said. "A Pegasus jet that originated in Cozumel, Mexico, landed in Bozeman. I think Calakmul is here."

Roth couldn't believe the news. "Really?" It was a terrifying thought. But if they could turn the tables and get law enforcement to arrest him, the whole situation would change.

"Really."

"You've got to get him, Lund!"

"Working on it. I gotta go. MS-13 just showed up at the high school."

"Suk—"

"Suki's safe. Just can't talk right now."

"My friend Moretti is a couple of hours outside of Bozeman. I'm having him go straight to Gallatin."

"That's appreciated, but it won't be fast enough," Lund said. "The alarms will bring in local police. Don't worry. I'll keep her safe. I promise."

"Thank you," Roth breathed. He ended the call and switched back. "Moretti—remember, I need you to go to Gallatin High School first thing. Lund is holed up there with Suki. That MS-13 gang just arrived."

"That's not good. I'll take some of my men and go directly there," Moretti promised. "There's a contingent of FBI coming along also."

"There's more. Calakmul may be at the airport. *The* Jacob Calakmul."

Silence. "The guy from Mexico you wouldn't talk about?"

"Yes. Lund is going to try and have him arrested. If we could get him—"

"That's incredible. Okay, we're driving as fast as we can on these roads."

Agent Sanchez extended her hand and pressed two fingers against the side of Jordan's neck, checking his pulse.

"Normally . . . a girl buys me a drink first," Jordan said with his dizzied voice. His body was starting to tremble.

"Pulse is weak," Agent Sanchez said. She looked at Roth frantically. "Give me my phone."

Roth had flashbacks to that night at Huellas de Pan. Of his wife lying on the couch at that orphanage. Of watching her life slip away before his eyes. He started to hyperventilate again.

Lucas came up and gave him a hug. "It's okay, Dad. It's okay. They can't get in."

It wasn't getting in that was the problem.

They needed to get *out*. Or Jordan would die.

Brillante sat down by the wall. He looked so tired. They were all exhausted. Jacob Calakmul was determined. And his erratic actions also suggested he was worried. Roth had made the jaguar priest *worry*. Good. He'd been lured out of his home territory and into Roth's. That gave Roth an important advantage.

"My phone," Agent Sanchez insisted.

The door handle jiggled. The wolves began to howl again.

Roth reached into his pocket and started to pull out the phone, but at the last second, he let it drop back in. This could be a life-altering decision.

CHAPTER TWENTY-ONE

Bozeman Yellowstone International Airport

Bozeman, Montana

December 26

Jacob grew more and more restless. The Pegasus had been relocated to the FBO hangar. The high fluorescent lights produced an annoying buzz and the heaters were struggling to compete with the ambient cold shrouding Bozeman. The jet had been refueled already, and local mechanics were doing a thorough inspection of the craft.

Jacob walked around the hangar, his magic concealing him from prying eyes. Mr. Dodd had requested that Angélica join him in his office, and she had yet to return. Some hiccup with the computer system, he'd said. The pilot had gone to take a quick shower at the executive suite. Jacob, whose presence was unknown to everyone but Angélica and the pilot, had been left alone.

An unsettled feeling gnawed inside him. The hangar, although huge, still felt like a cage.

The concrete floor had been polished to a shine. The comforts of technology surrounded him, but he missed the jungles of the Yucatán—his homeland.

The ancestor whose name he bore had overrun a corrupt political empire that had poisoned the Maya. The ruler had been deposed—assassinated—and the people had scattered into tribes based on familial alliances and prestige.

The collapse of that civilization had begun almost two thousand years ago and had been meticulously documented in various records. Until the Spanish had burned nearly all of them. But Jacob knew about his ancient ancestor—and the prophecy about his people returning to prominence to reclaim what was theirs. He relished the idea that this new empire, built on steel and slivers of silicon, would one day bend the knee to the Calakmuls. The Jaguar Prophecies were about to be fulfilled.

One of the office doors opened and several men in uniforms emerged. Not the pilot. Jacob frowned. They wore tan slacks, black windbreakers, and had sidearms strapped to their hips. Four men in total. They all had crew cuts and were of varying ages, but the oldest one seemed to take the lead. Jacob watched them approach the Pegasus, and when they passed him, he saw the words on the backs of their jackets: "Department of Homeland Security—Police." Beneath the jackets, he saw each was wearing a Kevlar vest.

One of the maintenance employees cleaned his greasy hands on a rag and approached the four. "What's up?"

"Got a warrant to search the jet," said the lead. "There may be a stowaway on board."

"For real?" the tech said. "There's no one in there, man."

"Just open the luggage bay. Johnston and Flaig, you search the interior."

The two obeyed and climbed up the portable stairs to enter the Pegasus. Jacob was grateful his restlessness had prompted him to exit the jet earlier. This explained why Angélica hadn't returned yet. She'd probably been detained by these security people.

An unexpected feeling grew inside Jacob's stomach. It was unfamiliar to him. A stranger in the world of emotions.

Worry.

Far away, in his ancestral homeland, the games were being played. Maybe one of the families had already won. The matches were usually settled on the first day. The game the Roths and Beasleys had played the previous year had been an exceptional one. His gut had told him that Mr. Roth would make trouble, and he should have listened to it. He'd underestimated the author once again. And that infuriated him.

But even the fury was tempered with worry.

The Department of Homeland Security was inspecting a foreign jet for a stowaway. Was this a trap Mr. Roth had set to catch Jacob unawares? Had he intentionally lured him to America so he could be investigated, questioned, and imprisoned?

Jacob clenched his hands into fists. He burned to transform into a jaguar and maul these pitiful security officers. To rip out the throats of the mechanics who would witness the scene.

But he had to get Angélica back first. She knew everything about the Calakmul operation. She was his confidante. She wore the most luxurious clothes during their travels and the most attractive native dress when down at the ruins. The thought of her in an orange jumpsuit in prison was intolerable.

Ah, so *that* was the source of his disquiet. He was worried about losing her. There was no real danger of imprisonment for Jacob. He could transform and fly away. If they shot at him with their bullets, he could summon the *kem äm* and defend himself. She had no such protection.

The idea of losing her caused a squeamish feeling. He'd once feared she would betray him. If she did so now, under threat of imprisonment, then the full attention of the US government would be turned his way too early. The thought was unconscionable. The plague had been let loose, but it would be weeks before it began to spread exponentially. And then the sacrifices would begin. The most powerful leaders in the world would be slain, leaving the people desperate and worried, as they should be. They'd spent years cultivating at least one asset within the upper echelon of each of those governments to help ensure the final result they desired.

Jacob began to head toward the doors he'd seen the DHS agents come from. Their presence at the jet meant something was going wrong. It was probably Mr. Roth's security guy who was causing trouble— the one who had helped rescue him in Germany. Another debt Jacob intended to collect from Mr. Roth.

He opened the door and smelled the sickening stench of coffee. That noxious drink from a little chrome vat tasted like motor oil compared to *xocolatl*. The interior of the offices looked like a maze of cubicles, cheap carpet, and a few conference room doors.

He clenched his fist again, summoning the magic through his ring. Angélica had a tattoo of a glyph on her shoulder blade. Through that glyph, he would always be able to find her. It was part of the troth she'd willingly entered into when joining his family.

His magic-enhanced senses discerned the direction, and he began to walk. A few of the morning staff were at their desks, yawning and tapping on computer keyboards.

"I hate this job," one of the men muttered. "No one should have to work on Christmas."

Jacob had heard similar complaints down in Cozumel, a popular destination for winter travelers. The locals celebrated their version of the holidays in the early weeks of January, after the crowds of tourists had left.

Jacob felt a little like a tourist himself now. Another unfamiliar sensation.

He walked across the thin carpet toward a bank of conference rooms. He felt attracted to one of them. It had large plate-glass windows facing the interior, but the blinds were down. There was just enough of a gap in the window for him to peer inside.

Angélica sat at a conference table, her formfitting winter fleece hugging her body, her jacket slung over an adjacent chair. There were two DHS guards talking to her, one of them a woman. Angélica had the stiff posture and folded arms of someone enduring an interrogation. He felt his heart throb as he saw her shake her head no.

Could he kill her if he had to?

A year ago, he would have answered with an unhesitating yes. But they'd grown closer now that the prophecy was on the verge of being fulfilled. The promise of having her as his queen had begun to paint fantasies in his mind. She was luscious and beautiful, the type of woman a man coveted, and also smart, capable, and incredibly diligent. She anticipated Jacob's needs and was well versed in the technology of the day, which was as foreign to him as his magic was to her. He needed her to represent him when governments began to topple.

Suddenly, both of the agents went to the door and opened it. Jacob tensed. He was still cloaked in the invisibility magic, but had they somehow sensed him at the window?

Both of the agents left and started down the hall away from him.

"She's lying," the more heavyset one said to his female companion.

"You're right. She's good at it, though. She's not a ditz like some of these billionaire girlfriends can be. She went to Stanford."

"How long can we hold her, Mitchell?"

"Until the FBI gets here." She looked at her watch but didn't say how long that might be.

The FBI.

Jacob's man in Bozeman had already been compromised. If more federal agents were coming in from the Salt Lake office, Garcia would be unable to act without suspicion.

After they disappeared down the hall, Jacob opened the door and saw that Angélica was alone inside. He dropped the magic, which instantly made his muscles relax.

"Jacob!" she breathed in relief. She rose from the chair and came to him, hugging him. She was trembling. He breathed in the fragrance of her perfume, felt her softness. The hunger inside him awakened all of his senses.

"It's so cold here," she said, shuddering. "I want to go home."

He wished they were back at the Jaguar Temple as well.

"They're searching the jet," he told her, stroking a lock of her hair.

"What?"

He nodded. "What have they asked you?" He tilted her chin up. He felt like kissing her, but he restrained the urge. He hadn't kissed her yet, although he'd come close several times. He wanted complete control over the moment.

"They're asking questions about *you*. If you were also going to Jackson Hole. When you were expected to land. They've notified air traffic control to look for another private jet." Her fingers dug into his shirt. "We have to get out of here!"

"Not without Roth," Jacob said firmly. "His trespasses cannot go unpunished."

"Please don't abandon me," she whispered worriedly.

"I won't," he said. That was true. His emotions yearned to hold her, to comfort her. To soothe her fears.

"They have my passport. I cannot leave the country with—"

He put his finger on her lips. "Shhh. Don't be afraid." He could break her neck so easily.

Kill her before she betrays you, his inner voice warned. *You can find another queen.*

Yes, that was true. But it would take time. And she had served him faithfully for years. They were *so* close to fulfilling the prophecy.

No, he would break Mr. Roth's neck instead. Just envisioning that moment—the satisfying crack of it—made him feel better.

"I will not leave you," he whispered to her. He bent his forehead down until theirs touched. Her eyes closed. He could feel her breath on his face. Could feel her leaning into him.

He *could* kiss her. The act of tenderness appealed to him.

Maybe . . .

The door opened suddenly, and the young Romeo from earlier entered with a cup of the steaming filth. He paused, blinking in shock at seeing Jacob embracing her.

"Oh . . . I'm sorry . . ." he stammered and started to retreat.

Jacob released her and stepped forward, grabbing the young man's wrist with one hand and the coffee cup with the other so it wouldn't spill. When he gestured to Angélica, she instantly took it from him.

The young man tried pulling his arm away, but Jacob was stronger and wrenched him into the room. He'd obviously hoped to find her alone. To be *friendly* with her. The coffee was a pretense.

"Let me go," the young man said, his voice quavering in fear.

Jacob snapped his neck and dropped him to the floor.

CHAPTER TWENTY-TWO

GALLATIN HIGH SCHOOL

BOZEMAN, MONTANA

December 26

Suki hunkered down at the sound and lighting panel, peeking over the top edge into the auditorium below. The theater was very dark except for a slash of brightness from the security lights in the parking lot shining through the broken windows in the corner.

She saw two of the gang members. One was stalking down an aisle toward the stage. He had a gun in his hand, fist pointed up toward the ceiling. Another gang member was going up the steps toward the upper seats. They were searching, row by row.

Suki whispered into her headset. "One heading your way."

Lund had told her he wouldn't respond due to the risk of being overheard. But he'd asked her to give direction on what she was seeing.

Suddenly, the auditorium lights flicked on. She saw a third man by the door, his hand on a switch. With the illumination, she could see the tattoos on their faces and necks. It was scary to see people so heavily tatted. They looked frightening, but she imagined that was the point.

Mr. Lund rose from his hiding space between the rows. She saw the muzzle flash, heard the distinct crack of the pistol being fired, twice . . . then a third time. The gang member closest to him was struck three times in the chest and went down.

The other two began firing into the empty theater, but Lund quickly ducked down.

"Kill the lights," Lund whispered into the headset. She could hear the muffled thud-thud-thud of bullets through the glass of the control room *and* through the headset.

Suki searched the control panel, found the lighting switches she needed, and killed the house lights again.

Another few shots were fired, then Lund was running, staying low so he could take cover from the seats. She barely saw his shadow. More gunshots sounded. The lights came on again, but Suki slammed them off, overriding the wall switch below. Lund returned fire again, and then he slammed the far door open and was out of the auditorium.

She heard his gun fire twice more. "Got another one," he said curtly. She could hear him panting as he ran.

The man from the upper aisle came running down the corridor. He slammed into one of the lower seats, which he hadn't noticed in the dark, and yelped in pain. But he got up and took off after Lund. The first guy that had been shot wasn't moving at all.

The lights came on again. She turned them off.

A flashlight flicked on. The guy by the wall had one. He had his pistol out, aiming ahead, the flashlight held alongside the muzzle. He began sweeping the room with the beam of light.

"You okay?" Lund asked in the headset. He was still running.

"One guy still here in the theater," she whispered. "He's looking."

"Distract him. I'm being chased."

"Stay safe," she said. She didn't want anything to happen to Mr. Lund. Her stomach was knotted with fear, and she felt vulnerable being in the theater alone with the gang member. But she'd already barricaded the door with equipment boxes.

The panting sound in her ears changed. He was running up some steps to an upper floor.

He'd be okay, she told herself. He knew the school. These bozos didn't.

Peering down, she saw the gang member approaching the wall where the stairs to her room were located. She activated the sound system and then cranked the microphone receivers all the way up, causing an ear-splitting shriek to rip through the room. She grinned as the gunman clamped his hands over his ears, wincing in pain. She twisted the volume knob up and down. Hopefully, it was giving him a headache. It was a powerful sound system. State of the art.

"I hear that noise all the way over here," Lund huffed. "You're mean."

"Thank you."

She could tell he'd reached a carpeted area. Then she heard a door beep, and he went inside and shut it.

"The security systems are going off," he said. "Like for the school-shooter drills." He was still puffing for air. "All the doors are locked, so stay put. It's also notified the 911 dispatcher."

"Can the gangsters get into the room with you?"

"If they shoot through the door, yes. But they don't know which one I'm in."

"Nice. This guy is still looking around trying to find me with the flashlight, but he can't hold both ears while he does."

"Excellent. You might turn the sound down, let him think it's over, then hit him again."

"Now you're being mean. I like your way of thinking."

"Just saw one guy go by," he said in an undertone. "Nope—make that two. There's probably five or six in total. I've shot two. One is with you. So maybe these are the last of them."

Suki twisted the dial and lowered the volume. The man's shoulders had been hunched in pain, but they relaxed slightly. He looked around and began scanning with the flashlight again. She could see enough of his face to tell he was pissed off.

She cranked the volume again, making him scowl in pain. But he endured it, focusing on the flashlight, heading toward the stairs leading to the sound booth.

"He found the stairs," she said softly.

"I'd better come back for you," Lund said. He sounded worried.

"You got three or maybe more out there looking for you. Only one in here with me, plus the door is blocked and barricaded. The police should be getting here soon, right?"

"I don't know how quickly they'll respond. I'm guessing most of them are over at your house, looking into what happened to the FBI agents—crap."

"What?" she asked, fear weaving through her veins.

"One came back," he whispered. "They're trying the doors and shining flashlights in the window."

A single shot was fired, removing the locked door below as an obstacle. Her guy was coming up the stairs now, slowly but steadily.

He was going to reach the booth. Yes, she'd locked and barricaded it, but he looked pretty tough. He would be able to shove those things aside. Maybe she should yell something at him and knock him back down the stairs?

The door handle rattled. Then a fist banged against the door, startling her. He wasn't going to let another locked door stand in his way. She knew that.

Maybe there was another way to stop him.

That idea, which was incredibly foolish and dangerous, sparked another. Images flashed in her mind from the games in Mexico. The huge ball court with carvings of the ancient players in the stone. The hoops fixed to the walls for the ball. The golden nets of magic.

The *kem äm*. If something touched it, it would be violently repelled.

Although she hadn't been able to summon the magic much since returning, she'd done it in Dresden, then again at Brice's house earlier . . . Using the magic, enacting the power of the bracelet from Cozumel and the ring her mother and great-great-grandmother had worn, made her feel closer to them. It made her feel like they were connected across space and time, and even the line between life and death, though she hoped her mother was still alive.

Mom. Grandma Suki, I need your help again, she thought silently in the dark, confined booth.

Staring at the door, she summoned her courage and lifted her hand. The magic was totally weird. It felt like it was alive. Like it could hear her thoughts.

Fear coiled tightly in her stomach. Her mouth was dry. She wanted to run, to hide, but she was so tired of running from these people.

She stared at the black-painted door.

Grandma. Abuelita.

Since returning, she'd tried to find out more about her great-great-grandma from her grandmother. Suki had come to California as a teenager in the 1920s to pick fruit for orchards in Santa Barbara. That's where she'd met and married her first husband, a man she'd later divorced after having two children with him. A *borracho*. A drunk. She'd taken her children from Santa Barbara to the Bay Area and worked hard, saving every penny, until she was able to buy a little home in San Jose. She paid it off as quickly as she could. Then bought another to rent out. And then another.

Grandma Suki had been eccentric too. She'd once knocked a chicken unconscious, plucked it while it was still alive, then dropped it into the pot on the stove so that when it revived, her sisters thought it was possessed of the devil. This was a totally different time, though. It wasn't a prank to be played on sisters. It was a life-and-death situation.

Focusing on the door, Suki flooded her mind with all the memories of that powerful and strong-willed woman. Soaking in her great-grandmother's strength. Her mother's strength. Her own. Little motes of light began to swirl around her outstretched hand. She didn't know how to direct them, but she tried to imagine them filling the doorframe the way they had in the arena down in Mexico.

A gunshot rang out and the lock exploded, along with splintered pieces of wood.

Suki strangely didn't feel any spasms of panic. The flow of the magic inside her caused a thrill, a rush, a feeling of dangerous power. It was that combination that made her fear it. Like handling a gun when her dad had taken them all to the firing range to practice.

A body thumped against the door. It held. Another thump.

The magic of the *kem äm* filled in the space, obeying her direction. The black-painted door shimmered.

Another blow.

The door hinges split, driving inward.

And Suki watched as the entire door immediately exploded backward. The magic had ripped it from its hinges, smashing the jamb and throwing the gang member down the stairs. Drywall dust filled the air. The speakers' shriek filled the room.

Suki turned the dial down and stood up, peering through the haze.

The guy had been knocked down below, only his arm and one leg visible beneath the broken door.

"What was that noise?" Lund asked in her headset.

"I'm good," Suki said with a smile. "Got him."

CHAPTER TWENTY-THREE

Beck Cabin

Bozeman, Montana

December 26

Roth had to admit to himself that he was impressed with Special Agent Sanchez. She'd managed to stop the bleeding from the gunshot wound, and when the question arose of how they'd bring him downstairs since Roth was reluctant to relinquish the gun, she'd slung Jordan over her shoulders in the classic fireman's carry. Gritting her teeth, she'd maneuvered the much heavier man down the steps to the basement. Roth had almost insisted on carrying him, but relinquishing control of the firearm would be risky. And she'd offered to do it.

Brillante, watching her do this, wagged his eyebrows in astonishment. "Bruh," he whispered to Lucas. "She's cracked!"

"Just get down there," Roth said, shoving them toward the stairs. He was watching the door, pistol at the ready. The flames in the woodstove were getting low, which was causing the temperature to drop.

Dim light from the coming dawn slipped in through the barricaded window frames.

Lucas reached the bottom of the steps, clearing the path for Roth.

The cabin door and windows exploded inward as if struck by a missile.

Roth held up his arm to cover his face, feeling the sting of shards of wood. There was no deafening sound, but the whole cabin shook like an earthquake. Roth felt stings on his face and neck. He hurried down a couple of steps, his heart in his throat, and then turned and shoved the door closed behind him. Locked it. There were deadbolts lining the wall, heavy metal bars that were secured in metal rungs and pegs.

He was no longer sure that was enough to keep them safe.

"What the actual heck!" Lucas bellowed, his eyes blazing with fear.

Agent Sanchez settled Jordan on the floor against the wall, and he moaned in pain, his head lolling to the side.

The basement was nearly the same dimensions as the upstairs of the cabin, though a little smaller. There were cots hanging from racks on the wall. Food storage cases. Racks lined with tinned food and dehydrated goods. Guns. Military gear, including collapsible shovels, knives, and canteens. The well on the cabin property provided water into the basement too.

A panic room filled the short end of the farthest wall, its door open. It was the last line of defense.

Agent Sanchez rose to take a look at the display of weapons. Before he could do anything, she'd grabbed an AR15 from the wall.

Roth brought the pistol up and aimed it at her. "Put it down, Agent Sanchez."

"Are you going to shoot a federal agent, Jonathon?" she demanded. She didn't raise the assault rifle, but neither did she put it down.

The sound of boots thumped overhead. Roth kept the barrel trained on her. With that weapon, she could kill all of them within two seconds.

"Boys, listen to me," Roth said.

"Dad," Brillante said nervously. "Don't shoot her!"

"I want to help you," Agent Sanchez said. "Whoever is up there killed my squad. I'm not going to be defenseless. I'm going to help take them out if it comes to that. Now, lower the gun."

He screwed up his face, hating the situation they were in. If the man upstairs was one of the jaguar priests—and the uncanny events of the past ten minutes suggested as much—then he needed all the help he could get. But if Agent Sanchez was one of them, then he and his sons would be in even more trouble if he took the gun off her for an instant.

He had a decision to make . . .

"Jordan, how are you feeling?" Roth asked.

"I'm not at my best right now, boss," Jordan said. "I'm about to faint again, to be honest."

"He needs a transfusion," Agent Sanchez said, "and I'm not a medic. We need to get out of here. Where is the exit? I don't see a door."

Roth hesitated, still anguishing over the situation.

"Jonathon," Agent Sanchez said, shaking her head. "Please. I don't want to die either. And I don't want anything happening to your kids. *Trust* me."

He lowered the handgun.

It was the look in her eye. The sincerity in her voice. Maybe he was a fool, but he believed her.

Agent Sanchez breathed in relief. She approached him, the barrel of the AR15 pointed down, and put her hand on his shoulder. "I know that wasn't easy. But you did the right thing. Is that a Swisher shelter?" she asked, nodding to the metal vault in the corner of the basement. There were buckets of MREs in there, as well as a huge drum of water.

"I don't know the brand, but yeah," Roth answered. "It can withstand an EF5 tornado."

"I've seen those before," she said, smiling. "Maybe the boys can go in there for now. If bullets start to fly, they'll ricochet around here."

"I'll go in with them," Jordan grunted. Clutching his chest, he started to struggle to his feet. Lucas and Brillante helped him stand, but he was already swaying. They headed back to the safe room together.

"We need to call in help," Agent Sanchez said. "Maybe even a sniper to take these people out. But I need my phone to do that. We're on the same side, okay?"

Roth stared her in the eyes for a long moment, then handed her phone over. There was a noise at the basement door, and he turned to face it.

Agent Sanchez looked at the phone he'd already given her. "No signal down here."

"This basement was designed to withstand an EMP," Roth said. He pulled out his burner phone and saw that it also had no signal. "Or a nuclear bomb. We're about thirteen feet underground, and the floor is several feet thick. Concrete and steel."

"So what's the other way out?"

"There's a tunnel that goes into the forest. The boys can grab a shovel and check the tunnel for debris or a cave-in. See if you can lift the vault cover. Then call for help."

Agent Sanchez sighed. "Okay? Where?"

"Over there," he said, pointing to a crawl-space door. "The guy who built this place was expecting a doomsday scenario. He ended up dying of heart failure. Lund heard about it and purchased the property for himself. I've been leasing it from him with crypto to keep Calakmul from tracing it."

"Makes sense. It's surprisingly easy to follow most money trails for the majority of people. Everyone has a credit card or an ATM. But preppers trade in gold, silver, and sometimes cash. Didn't know they were using crypto too."

"So I've discovered," Roth said. He listened for noises coming from above.

"If that panic room can survive an EF5, it'll protect against an AR15. We've got to get Jordan to an emergency room. That's our first priority. I can get a helicopter over here to pick him up so we don't have to take the snowmobiles down."

"So we need to leave through the tunnel," Roth agreed.

"What about us?" Lucas asked, emerging from the safe room. "We've got to stay here with that dude walking around upstairs?"

"Basically, yeah," Brillante said glumly as he followed him out. He gave Roth a hopeful look. "I could make sure the tunnel hatch opens?"

"I'll help!" Lucas volunteered.

"That's actually a really good idea," Agent Sanchez said. "It's probably covered in snow. If we can clear the opening, I can call the team and get some help up here. The GPS on my phone can help them find us."

Roth was relieved he'd decided to trust her. She hadn't turned the tables on him and strapped him and Jordan with zip ties. She could have done it easily.

Roth went to the supply rack and pulled down one of the collapsible shovels and showed his son how it worked. "In case the tunnel is blocked. Hopefully you can get through the snow."

"How far does the tunnel go?" Agent Sanchez asked.

He pointed. "It goes about fifty yards that way and ends past the tree line. There are bushes covering the opening, so it's not easy to find even in the summer. It's in the shadow of a fir tree, so the snow may not be too thick."

"Cool," Lucas said.

The door shuddered. Roth felt the vibrations down in his feet, but it held. "I hope he can't get down here, Agent Sanchez."

She looked around. "I think we're on a first-name basis now. Call me Monica. Why don't you take the AR15, Jonathon, and go into the safe room while the twins clear the path. I'll be in that corner"—she pointed to the one she meant—"so that if he comes down the stairs, I can shoot him from behind. Just keep the door partially closed so you'll be protected when the bullets start flying. Aim for his legs. I want this guy alive, but I don't care if we leave him on stumps." She offered him the AR15.

Roth took it and handed her the pistol. She quickly checked the magazine, ejecting it and then reinserting it.

"You know how to fire that?" she asked him.

"Yup," he said.

The boys went to the crawl-space door and released the latches that held it closed. When it opened, a cool breeze blew inside.

"Take some of these too," he told Brillante, opening a drawer stuffed with hand-warmer and body-warmer packets. "It'll be cold."

"Perfect," Lucas said. He stuffed some into his pockets and then ripped one open to expose it to air so the chemical reaction would start. "It's still chilly down here."

Brillante snagged a headlamp, strapped it around his forehead, and switched it on. He grinned at Roth and began to crawl down the tunnel with the shovel. Lucas followed him. It actually relieved Roth that they were leaving the cabin. They still had all their winter clothes on, despite having slept. If necessary, they could walk back down off the mountain and go to one of the neighbors for help. The noise of them scurrying away began to fade.

Monica went to the safe room to check on Jordan. She felt his pulse and then shook her head worriedly.

"Not good?" Roth asked.

"I'm *fine*," Jordan mumbled.

Monica crouched by him. "Sure you are, tough guy. You need some more fluids. Any Gatorade down here?"

"Actually yes," Roth said. He went to a storage box and pulled out a six-pack and brought it to her.

She unscrewed the lid of one and handed it to Jordan. "Drink."

"Won't it leak out of my chest?" he asked jokingly before sipping some and wincing. "Hurts to swallow."

Another vibration rattled through the basement. Both of them looked back toward the stairs.

"Persistent," Monica said.

"You have no idea," Roth agreed. He tilted his head to the side, studying her. "Thank you."

"Thanks for trusting me," she said. "I can see you've been through a lot, Jonathon. I'm going to research what you've told me. Verify what I can. As I said, you don't act like some of the bad people I've dealt with in my career. I don't know how much of what you've said is true, but if I can confirm any of it, it'll mitigate some of what you've done."

"So it's not a hundred percent I'm going to jail?" Roth asked.

"We're probably at fifty-fifty," she said, her nose wrinkling as he smiled. "Let's see if we can lower the odds?"

"Deal," Roth breathed.

"I'm going to make a hidey hole in the corner now," she said. "Keep an eye on those stairs. You stay here and let me know if his condition changes. Where are the blankets? I'm about to start shivering."

"By the cots. The green wool ones they use in the army." He pointed them out. She retrieved several for him and Jordan and then wrapped one around her own shoulders before going to the corner of the shelter to clear some space.

"She's kinda hot," Jordan whispered thickly.

"Settle down, Romeo," Roth murmured back, watching Monica as she quickly arranged boxes of food stores into a little wall to protect herself. She'd chosen the denser items, like the sugar, to create a barricade. Smart thinking.

Sitting down next to Jordan, Roth settled the rifle on his legs, the barrel pointed toward the door. Jordan was deeper into the safe room, out of sight. Still, Roth pulled the door a bit more so the gap narrowed. Another rumble came. Stronger this time. A ripple of fear quickened his pulse.

The jaguar priest was getting frustrated.

CHAPTER TWENTY-FOUR

BECK CABIN

BOZEMAN, MONTANA

December 26

Roth jerked awake from a light sleep and looked at his watch again. He was so tired that he'd nodded off. How close was Moretti to Bozeman now? He wiped his eyes and shifted to get more comfortable. The boys had been gone for about a half an hour.

He glanced through the crack in the door but couldn't see Monica in her place of concealment.

"How are you feeling?" he asked Jordan in a low voice.

"Like I've been shot. Hurts to breathe. At least the guy didn't blow my brains out."

"Don't say that."

Jordan snorted. "Just being realistic. Could have been worse."

Roth hadn't felt any more vibrations, and there were no sounds of footsteps from above. The bunker was holding. Was their attacker waiting to see if they'd pop out?

Noise from the tunnel announced the arrival of one of the twins. Roth struggled to sit up and then stood with the rifle, planting his hand on the edge of the metal wall of the safe room. He slid the door open and saw Lucas entering the basement.

"It's open," he announced, grinning.

Monica rose from her barricade with the handgun held at her side. "Let me go ahead so I can call and get some support up here."

She was asking him to trust her again.

Roth nodded. "I'll drag Jordan through the tunnel. He's so heavy it'll take me a while."

"You're calling *me* fat?" Jordan said in an injured tone.

"Lucas, you carry the gun, okay? Just don't use it."

"Okay, Dad," Lucas said and took the weapon from him.

Monica went down on her hands and knees and started through the crawl space. Roth knew this was going to hurt the ex-soldier.

"Won't be fun," Roth apologized. "But if we can get you to where you can be medevaced, they'll bring you to a hospital. I'm sure they'll give you a few of those little Jell-O cups."

"Oooh," Jordan said with mock delight. "Tasty."

Roth grabbed Jordan under his arms and heard a hiss of pain, but there was no way to make this comfortable. He hoisted Jordan up a little and then started to drag him away. The noise of moving feet tapped on the floor above again. Roth gazed up, wondering what the guy was doing.

Lucas trailed behind them. Roth hunkered down on his knees and then started to pull Jordan, yard by yard, through the escape tunnel. A strong smell of dirt filled the air. The tunnel was circular, made from concrete vault pieces put down together. Dirt and moisture had seeped into the seams and cracks.

"Shut the door behind us," Roth told Lucas, straining with the effort. It was cold in the tunnel, but soon he was sweating and breathing hard. Jordan groaned when the pain became unbearable. Roth pressed on, pausing to catch his breath at times. It was dark, but light came from the other end of the tunnel, where a ninety-degree angle brought the vault up to ground level.

"Almost there," Roth said. He yanked and pulled Jordan until they reached the crook of the tunnel. It had taken a while to get there, pausing for frequent rests. Sweat dripped down his face and chest. He wanted to rip off his coat.

When they reached their destination, Roth peered up. There were rungs set inside the vault, drilled into the concrete with bolts. It was very narrow. Cold seeped down the throat of the vault.

"Dad?" Brillante called down from the opening above.

"Can you see us?" Roth asked.

"Yeah. Agent Sanchez told me to wait here."

"Where'd she go?" Roth asked, worried.

"She's closer to the cabin, watching. I can see her."

"Tell her I need help getting Jordan out."

"Sure!" Brillante left, and Roth could hear the crunch of his boots in the snow.

Jordan craned his neck, gazing up the shaft. He looked pale and weary. It was about ten feet to the top. Maybe more.

More crunching noises followed, and Monica returned with Brillante.

"A helicopter is on the way," she announced. "One sniper from the Bozeman PD Special Response Team and three SAs from the office. They thought I was dead too."

Roth gazed up at her, feeling a tingle of hope. "What'd you tell them?"

"I said we were in a bunker beneath a cabin and the signal couldn't get through. They know about the danger here. Moretti and his team are coming up the highway now, less than an hour away."

"Thank goodness," Roth breathed.

"I didn't tell them you guys zip-tied me," she said. "But I will in my report. Right now, we needed help fast. Can you lift Jordan onto your shoulders?"

"I'll try," Roth said. He maneuvered Jordan to the ladder and helped him stand. "I'm going to try and get you up."

The younger man nodded, grunted in pain again, and then grabbed onto a rung with his right hand. Roth tried to lift him, but Jordan was too heavy. How had Monica managed it?

"Let me try climbing," Jordan offered. "Just push. Ready?"

"Ready."

Jordan pulled with his one arm and managed to get his feet up on the lower rungs. Roth pushed Jordan's rear end with his shoulder. One step. Two. Monica reached down into the tunnel.

"Almost," she urged. Her hand slipped on Jordan's, and he nearly tumbled back down, but Roth was standing at his full height now and used his hands to push up on Jordan's bottom.

"Got you!" Monica said in triumph. She pulled, Jordan moaned, and then he was high enough for her to grab him beneath his arms and pull him out.

Roth sagged, gasping for breath. He motioned for Lucas to hand him the rifle and slung it over his shoulder with the strap. His son clambered up the shaft and into the morning air.

Roth thought he heard a sound coming from the tunnel.

A surge of panic filled him.

He wasn't sure what he'd heard, but the effort of dragging Jordan and his own heavy breathing would have made it difficult to pick up on anyone entering the basement. He started to climb the thin ladder. He felt bulky against the rungs, and his heart hammered as adrenaline surged.

Monica returned to the opening and held out her hand.

"I think someone else is behind me!" he said.

Monica grabbed Roth's wrist and helped him out of the tunnel. Immediately, she whipped out her sidearm and aimed it down the shaft.

Roth felt the sting of the cold on his nose. The sky was starting to lighten, but he was too anxious to do more than notice it. Then he heard the noise of a helicopter approaching. Could it have arrived so quickly? Maybe the helicopter had already been in the area searching for them?

A flashback from Mexico struck him. A helicopter had found them when they were at the top of the pyramid on Cozumel. On that day, they'd run by going *down* a shaft, not up one.

Roth backed away from the hole.

Monica knelt at the edge, pistol aimed down.

She fired three quick shots into the shaft.

Roth flinched, and Lucas quickly backed away.

"Did you see him?" Roth asked.

"It was . . . an animal," she answered in confusion. "Its eyes were glowing."

"Did you hit it?"

"I don't know." She looked frightened.

A growling noise came from the tunnel.

"Close it," Roth urged. She was by the metal manhole cover, which was hinged and hanging open, the snow and debris pushed away from it. While she aimed the handgun down the shaft, he circled around behind her and pushed the lid down. It clanged loudly as it sealed, metal on metal, the echo thrumming down the concrete tube.

Roth could see a glimpse of the cabin through the trees. The snowmobiles still sat in front of it. Jordan was leaning against the tree, hand clenched against his bloodied shirt. He pulled a Sig Sauer out of his holster.

"I'll watch the hole," he said, pointing the pistol at it. "Get the twins out of here with the snowmobiles."

Roth considered it, but the plan felt too risky. The snowmobiles started up fast, but he didn't want to take the chance of getting caught if their attacker made it back fast enough.

"Was that animal . . . *him*?" Monica asked Roth worriedly. "Its eyes were . . . glowing."

"You didn't believe me earlier," he answered.

Monica's phone buzzed, and she quickly answered the call. "I hear the chopper," she said. "How close are you?"

Roth brought the AR15 into his arms and backed away from the manhole cover. "Boys, go hide by the trees over there."

They both nodded, their expressions scared, and hurried through the snow. Jordan's arm was shaking as he held the pistol.

"Roger that," Monica said, looking up through the trees. "There's a single door leading in and out of the cabin. Have the sniper ready as you land. Is the ER ready to receive us? Good! Thank you! Get down here fast."

Roth listened to the approach of the helicopter. The breeze was tranquil and calm. It was truly a beautiful morning. But his heart thumped with panic.

That's why it took him several seconds to notice his pocket was buzzing.

He fished out the burner phone and saw a text from Illari Chaska. It had been sent a while back, but it hadn't been delivered to his phone while they were underground.

First translation.

Excitement shot through Roth as he clicked the screenshot of hand-written words. Some of the words were crossed over, with replacements above, showing Illari had struggled to settle on various aspects of the translation.

As the cold bit into his ears and frosty breath came out of his mouth, he stared at the image taken from a notepad on her desk.

The god Huracán hath commanded that I, the god Kukulkán, should give unto you this land for your inheritance. I say unto you, that if the alien foreigners do not repent after the intercession which they shall receive, after they have scattered my people—then shall ye, who are a remnant of the house of Jacob, go forth among them and shall be in the midst of them who shall be numerous; and shall be among them as jaguars among the beasts of the forest, and as a young jaguar among flocks of sheep, who, if he goes through both treads down and tears in pieces. And none can deliver them.

It was antiquated language, but Roth was accustomed to it. He'd read translations of the Popol Vuh, which had similar biblical-sounding terms in it. The reference to the house of Jacob stood out to him. According to Jacob Calakmul, his family had lived back during the time of the Aztecs and Maya. They had witnessed the destruction caused by Hernán Cortés and other conquistadors. One could say that the Spanish had scattered and decimated the Mesoamericans.

Jacob was a Hebrew name. Had it been adopted by the family after the Spanish had come and many Indigenous people had been forced to convert to Christianity? But then how did a biblical name end up in a pre-Cortés prophecy?

This was a *prophecy*. *The* prophecy. Men like jaguars reclaiming their conquered lands . . . gods . . .

The thrum of the rotors grew louder. The trees obscured the chopper's appearance, but the sound thrummed in his ears. Roth's chest clenched with dread. He read the translation again.

As jaguars among the beasts of the forest.

Roth had first heard the term "jaguar priests" in Mexico, at Huellas de Pan.

The helicopter appeared over the tree line. One of the doors was open, and a man in tactical armor leaned out with a sniper rifle. The rotors whipped up snow from the trees, causing a blizzard of ice shards to scatter.

A sense of dread sickened Roth.

The helicopter was coming to save them, and yet . . .

From the cabin, a man stepped outside onto the threshold. Gold dust enveloped him in a swirl of leopard-like patches.

He was a younger man, maybe thirty, wearing boots, jeans, and a long coat that appeared to be made from a wolf pelt. He looked Mexican.

Then he lifted his hand, and what must have been a gold ring on his finger began to throb with light.

The sniper took a shot at him.

CHAPTER TWENTY-FIVE

Beck Cabin

Bozeman, Montana

December 26

The sound of the sniper rifle cut through the throb of the helicopter rotors. Roth couldn't see well through the blur of snow that had been kicked up.

One shot was all that had been fired. The jaguar priest just stood there with the glowing ring. Unmoving.

The helicopter swiveled around sharply, the tail swinging around nearly 360 degrees. Wind began to kick against the trees. The snow-laden branches bucked, sending down cascades of white. Roth's stomach clenched with dread as the helicopter spun another full circle and began to careen to the side.

It seemed like an invisible hand was pushing down on the aircraft, bringing it lower and lower as it spun it around like a top. Roth heard yelling coming from the craft.

Monica stared in astonishment, her mouth hanging open.

Roth's brain was already spinning for a way out. The tunnel was compromised now. Even if they could use it to get back to the basement, it would be no good. They could hide in the steel panic room, true, but it no longer felt secure.

The helicopter spun around again, this time striking the edge of the cabin as it swooped in too close. The tail rotor snapped off. His eyes on the cockpit window, Roth could barely see the pilot as he wrestled with the controls. A howling wind blew into the meadow, sending snow everywhere. The helicopter bucked and attempted to rise, but the wind or some other force was holding it down.

"No," Monica said with growing horror.

Roth thought about his boys and was grateful he'd already told them to hide. Jordan was struggling to stand up, his cheeks puffing out with the effort.

They had guns, which made them feel better, even though they might be useless against their foe. The snowmobiles parked by the cabin were their only way out now.

"We've got to get to the snowmobiles," Roth said. "Have to outrun him."

"It'll take too long to drag Jordan to the sleds."

"Then leave me up here. I can shoot," Jordan said. "Get the boys to safety!"

Roth was undecided and then gasped when the helicopter flipped over. The rotors broke off and one flew toward them. They ducked out of the way, and it whacked a pine tree and stuck there. Roth shivered with cold and fear.

"Snowmobiles are the best option," Roth said decidedly.

"I'll cover you," Monica said. "Go."

"What about you?"

She shook her head. "I'm here to protect you guys. And we have agents in that chopper. Maybe we can take him out together. Hand me the AR."

"Just don't shoot directly at him," Roth said, pulling it off his back. "The bullets could bounce right back at you."

"Got it," she agreed. "Come on."

She holstered her handgun and started moving toward the cabin ahead of him, AR15 at the ready.

The engine from the helicopter was dying. The aircraft was on its side. The door facing the sky was open—it was the one where the sniper had been hanging from, but that man was no longer visible. Roth saw someone climbing out of the wreckage.

The wind was still blowing snow everywhere, but it had started to calm again. The jaguar priest strode toward the helicopter with purpose.

Monica motioned toward the cabin with one arm, the barrel of the AR pointed at their opponent. They were approaching the scene from the far corner. If the jaguar priest turned, he might see them, but his focus was on the wreckage. Roth could hear the crunch of their boots in the snow and winced. But there was still the noise of the fading helicopter engine, the shudder of the trees, the loud thump of snow falling. It helped mask the noises they were making.

Monica gave him a sharp hand signal to hurry. She aimed her AR15 at the jaguar priest's feet. She fired several rounds into the snow. Roth started to jog through the deep snow toward the snowmobiles. The jaguar priest didn't slow at all, as if the bullets weren't a concern to him.

Another FBI agent jumped down from the helicopter. Roth could see he was bleeding from his forehead. He had his sidearm out and aimed it at the jaguar priest.

"Hands up!" the agent ordered, his face contorted in pain.

The jaguar priest kept coming toward him.

Monica fired the AR15 again in a sweeping pattern. Several more rounds went toward the jaguar priest. Roth saw a sizzle of light, and the bullets ricocheted back. Because of the angle at which she'd fired, the bullets didn't strike Monica but instead hit the cabin, cracking windows and blasting chunks of wood away.

"Don't shoot him head-on!" Monica shouted to her colleague, lowering the rifle. "The bullets will rebound at you!"

The jaguar priest turned his head and looked at her, then noticed Roth charging toward the snowmobiles. Frowning, he resumed stalking toward the agent by the helicopter.

Monica fired three quick shots again. No effect.

The other agent shot once, straight at the oncoming man's chest. The bullet immediately ricocheted right back at him. Monica had warned him, but the panic of the moment had prevailed. He grunted in pain, struck by his own bullet. He was wearing a bulletproof vest—Roth could see it—but the bullet had pierced it. Blood bloomed on the front of the vest, and the man's face went slack.

The jaguar priest reached him and snapped his neck.

Monica threw down her rifle and pulled out her phone.

The jaguar priest started toward her.

"This is Sanchez, the chopper is down—repeat—chopper is down!"

Roth reached the first of the snowmobiles and jumped astride it. He pressed the starter switch, and the engine roared to life. Panic-stricken, praying he'd have enough time, he jammed it in reverse and hit the throttle. The reverse beeping sounded, and Roth launched backward from the cabin. Monica was approaching the jaguar priest, hands held up, ready to fight.

Roth felt the exhilaration from the acceleration as he rushed away from the scene. He didn't want to leave her stranded, but if he could get the twins away, she could try to escape too. He twisted the handlebars so he could sweep in a circle and then go forward. But his stomach lurched when the sled banked too hard, too fast, and tipped over. One second he was moving, the next he was falling. His back crunched into the snow, his left leg pinned underneath the snowmobile. The weight of it slammed on him, and he grunted in pain. His leg wasn't broken—the snow was cushioning it, but as he tried to push it away, he only fell deeper in the snow.

Idiot! he screamed at himself. He'd never been pinned before, although he'd heard it was a risk.

He pushed up on the handlebars, the engine still coughing exhaust, and managed to get his other knee up. He tried to leg-press the snow-mobile off himself, but it was too heavy. His stomach ached with fear. When he tried rocking it back, he just pushed himself deeper into the snow. He was burying himself.

Another gunshot sounded. Judging from the sound of metal against metal, the ricochet hit the helicopter.

"Guns don't work, Anderson!" Monica yelled. "Help me subdue him!"

"Who is this guy?" the other agent asked, bewildered.

"I'll explain later. Help me subdue him."

Monica stopped and watched the jaguar priest approach, both arms raised in front of her face as if she were a boxer shielding herself from a punch. Roth again pushed against the snowmobile, but he still couldn't leverage it off his leg. Grunting, he tried rocking it back, frustrated and fearful. Monica was risking her life to save him and his boys. If she died because of his accident, he'd hate himself.

"Come on, big guy," Monica said to the jaguar priest. "Let's see what you've got!"

The other agent was running through the snow toward them, but he wouldn't get there in time.

Monica turned and ran. Roth knew instinctively that she was trying to draw the jaguar priest after her. The man turned, putting his back to Roth, and started after her.

The other agent, Anderson, rushed to intercept as Monica turned abruptly and charged back toward their attacker.

Roth swore with frustration, heaving against the snowmobile. He felt it start to lift. His muscles quivered. The sound of hand-to-hand combat intensified his efforts. He heard Monica gasp in pain.

No, no, no.

The snowmobile slumped down on him again. He gasped for breath, sweating from the effort. He looked back toward Monica and saw the two agents were fighting the jaguar priest. The swirl of golden leopard spots that had hung in the air were gone. Then Agent Anderson went down, his arm torqued. The cracking of his neck filled the air. Monica shouted in rage and flung herself on the jaguar priest's back, wrapping her legs around his waist and putting a choke hold on his neck.

He broke it effortlessly and flung her from himself. She landed in the snow, unmoving. Roth tried heaving the snowmobile off himself again, and suddenly it tipped and went down, freeing his trapped leg. Disbelief surged through him.

"Hurry, Dad!" Brillante urged.

The boys had come! They'd snuck up and had pulled the snowmobile off him.

Roth scrambled to his feet, his leg sore. The snowmobile engine was still activated. It was a two-seater, but all three of them would need to fit. He straddled the front seat, and the boys stood on the runners on each side of the snow mobile, grabbing onto him and the armrests of the back seat. That would help keep things balanced.

Roth gunned the engine, and the sled immediately began to churn through the snow.

He looked at Monica and saw the jaguar priest grab her head and lift it. Swiveling, she punched him in the face. She'd only been playing dead.

The blow surprised the man. Maybe even stunned him for a second. Roth felt the snowmobile accelerating. He needed to save his boys. But it grieved him to abandon Monica and Jordan. Both of them would die.

"Go! Go!" Lucas wailed in fear.

The jaguar priest rubbed his mouth where she'd punched him, then his eyes lit with ferocity and started to glow. He was going to transform again. Roth knew it. Fangs sprouted from behind his lips. An awful, terrible gloom sprang to life in Roth's heart. The haunting image of Eric

Beasley being savaged by Jacob Calakmul flashed before his eyes. In his wolf form, the jaguar priest would easily be able to pursue the fleeing snowmobile. It's how he'd gotten to the cabin so easily.

Monica screamed in terror.

A pistol crack sounded from the grove.

Jordan's bullet struck the other man in the temple.

Killing him.

CHAPTER TWENTY-SIX

BOZEMAN YELLOWSTONE INTERNATIONAL AIRPORT

BOZEMAN, MONTANA

December 26

"Ma'am, where do you think you're—?"

Jacob halted and released his grip on Angélica's arm. The agents had returned faster than anticipated. Jacob had shoved the body of the man he'd killed beneath the conference room table, but it would be found quickly enough.

The agents were behind them, having just come around the corner. The sound of rustling could be heard—a weapon being drawn.

"Hands in the air, sir," warned one of the agents.

Jacob had not summoned the invisibility magic again. He'd made the choice purposefully. He slowly turned, seeing three agents in black shirts and tan pants. The female one had a Taser pointed at him, readied in a combative stance.

"Who are you?" asked one of the other agents.

"I'm the one you've been looking for," Jacob answered. He stepped in front of Angélica, a slow, deliberate action.

"Hands in the air!" ordered the agent again.

Jacob clenched his fist and summoned the magic with his ring. A whorl of *kem äm* came to him, creating a shield between him and the others.

"I don't think so," Jacob answered smoothly. "We're leaving."

"Sir, this is your *last* warning. Or you'll know what fifty thousand volts feels like."

An inspired thought. Jacob used the magic to tap into the electricity feeding the bank of fluorescent lights along the ceiling and sent it into the woman with the Taser. It would feel like getting hit by a lightning bolt.

The agent stood there, energy sizzling down her arms, her hair steaming, her body trembling violently. The power winked out as the circuit breakers shut it off. The agent collapsed onto the carpeting.

The other two agents stared, stunned, as the power flickered on again.

And Jacob was already there. He slammed the heel of his hand against the next agent's nose, breaking it and snapping his head back. The third agent reached for his firearm, but Jacob stepped forward and grasped the man's wrist. The other man was bigger, more muscular. It didn't matter. The magic surged through Jacob's body, and he hurled the fellow into the conference room window, shattering it. The man fell in a pool of glass beads on the other side.

The man whose nose he'd smashed was trying to get his radio off his shoulder, pinching off the blood streaming from his nose. Jacob kicked him in the knee, breaking it, then swiveled his hand around and struck the man's throat, crushing his windpipe.

All three agents were down, but more would be coming.

Angélica stared at him in awe. She'd seen him transform before. But she'd never witnessed how deadly he could be in human form. All the jaguar priests had been trained in hand-to-hand combat and survival skills. Jacob had been through the most rigorous regimen of all, both in the moves perfected by the ancient class of warrior-priests and modern special-ops tactics.

The primary goal wasn't to subdue someone into tapping out.

It was to kill them efficiently and quickly.

"The Pegasus?" she asked in a whisper.

"Yes."

"What about the satellites? Radar? They'll be tracking us."

He understood her worry. For years, the Calakmul family had operated in the shadows. The Mexican government had been thoroughly infiltrated, officials bribed to turn a blind eye. Here, they did not have that protection.

"It takes time to get anything done in this country," Jacob said. "We'll exploit that. You'll see. I'm not leaving you behind."

She gazed at him, her features softening. "Thank you," she said huskily.

A TSA employee with the traditional blue shirt came around the corner just ahead of them, radio in hand. "Power surge, I think," he said into the device. He didn't have a soldier's physique and was carrying a lot of extra weight. He saw them, saw the man on the ground past them. He looked confused at first, squinting.

Jacob rushed him, yanking the radio out of his hand before performing a judo arm grab and flipping him onto his back. A choked noise came from the man's mouth, then Jacob smashed the radio against the man's head to disable the radio and kill the agent.

Jacob reached for Angélica's hand, and she gave it to him. They started running down the corridor, fleeing past the cubicles of office workers. Only some of them took notice of the two figures running past them. Jacob pushed open the metal door, and the two of them slipped past it and started down another corridor heading to the exterior doors and the hangars.

Blue emergency lights began to flash. Strobes too. Someone had triggered an alarm.

Jacob frowned with impatience, and when they reached the doors at the end of the corridor, he paused to look outside.

A new vehicle had arrived. A black Suburban. Several FBI agents, clad in their telltale jackets, loitered in the snow by the SUV. And the hangar door was still open.

Time was precious, but Jacob refused to leave Bozeman without Roth and his family. He looked up and saw the security camera by the door, its baleful little gray box and lens innocuous against the gray paint of the corridor. Invoking the magic, he short-circuited the device. No recordings. No evidence.

He needed to take out the agents quickly. He didn't doubt his ability to do so.

"After I transform, open the door for me," he said to Angélica. "There is a moment before I can control my mind again, when I cannot think as a man. I'm vulnerable then to the bloodlust. Once I'm outside, I'll remember. Are you ready?"

"Would you attack me?" she asked worriedly.

"No. But I cannot use the magic for anything else for a moment or two. It makes me vulnerable to attacks. To bullets. Ready?"

"Ready," she agreed, nodding vigorously.

Jacob yielded himself to the darkness of the magic. The itching to transform had been growing steadily. It was a powerful feeling to become part of nature itself. The ancient sorcerers of the Aztec and Maya had mastered these secrets. They could become birds to fly long distances. Aquatic animals to swim. Predators to hunt and kill. And the creatures of nature also responded to the magic. Vicious allies could be summoned.

But Jacob did not need those. He was strong enough in the magic to deal with this situation. Strong enough, even, to control the weather. It was a powerful, heady sensation. It made him feel like a god. But he was only a vehicle for their power. The ring bound him to a covenant, giving him access to otherworldly power.

But there were consequences. There were always consequences.

Jacob succumbed to the intoxication of the magic and transformed into a jaguar. The rush of the magic was thrilling as he became the beast. For a moment, he could only experience the raw nature of the animal as he adjusted to its additional faculties—its sense of smell and sight, and the unfamiliar sensation of having a tail. But then that moment passed, and he remembered his purpose.

A low growl came from his jaws.

Angélica pushed open the doors.

Jacob bounded out, charging the FBI agents with ferocity. His animal form radiated a power that instilled fear and terror in his victims. It wasn't just the danger of a wild animal. It was a manifestation of the gods' power.

One of the FBI agents saw the blur of silver and black charging toward him, dropped his cup of coffee, and reached for a weapon. Jacob savaged him with claws and fangs, then caught the next man after he started running around the vehicle to escape, screaming for help. The noise on the tarmac was loud, full of the shrill noise of engines, fuel trucks, and baggage carriers. The jaguar let out a shriek that couldn't pierce the noise.

Another agent was inside the SUV in the driver's seat. Cowering.

The side door was still open. The jaguar leaped inside, and the man cried out in fear, honking the horn before he was silenced forever by deadly claws.

The jaguar left the SUV and started padding toward the open hangar. Angélica emerged from the doorway and started to walk swiftly across the snowy tarmac, her phone to her ear. When they reached each other, he strode next to her, huffing in the cold air. He imagined he looked like the ferocious pet of a very wealthy woman.

"Suki is still at the high school," Angélica said. She knew he could understand her in his animal form. "The MS-13 gang is having trouble getting her."

A low growl emitted from the jaguar. Jacob transformed back into his human form. The magic gave him energy. It filled him with blood-lust. In that moment, he could have killed Angélica and the pilot and not cared until the feelings ebbed. The thrill of the magic was more powerful than mere human sentiments.

The pilot was standing in the open doorway of the Pegasus. His eyes widened with surprise as he watched the transformation complete.

"Take us to the high school," Jacob said, panting slightly. "Gallatin High School."

Mr. Roth would not win, and Jacob would exact another price for such willful disobedience. He would turn the man's own daughter against him.

CHAPTER TWENTY-SEVEN

GALLATIN HIGH SCHOOL

BOZEMAN, MONTANA

December 26

Suki peeked through the broken doorframe and down the steps. There was no movement or noise coming from the gang member who'd been trying to reach her. Was he dead? Had the magic killed him?

The phone in her pocket began to buzz. Pulling it out, she saw it was a call from Brice. She shook her head and rejected the call.

"You still there?" she whispered to Lund through the headset. Her gut told her it was time to flee. This was one of those feelings she got, the ones she'd learned to trust.

"They're having problems breaking open the doors," he said. "You okay?"

"The door's gone. And he's waking up."

"Wait. He got through?"

"Not exactly. It's difficult to explain. The door blew up in his face and knocked him down the steps. I thought he was dead, but he was only unconscious." The warning to run grew stronger.

She saw the gang member push the door aside and sit up, rubbing his face.

She knew she risked him hearing her if she kept whispering. "He woke up."

"I'm coming, Suki. Stay there."

"He could come back up the steps. I'd better run."

The choice was made. She knew she could summon the magic again to block the door, but if these men also had the power of the *kem äm*, then he could easily disperse it. She'd caught him off guard before. She might not be so lucky again. That meant she needed to get out of there and hide. Now. There was a whole lair beneath the stage. She knew how to use the mechanism that operated the trapdoors. This guy didn't.

"Stay where you are so I can find you!" Lund hissed.

Nope, she thought to herself. Glancing around the booth, she grabbed a heavy storage box with latches. It had equipment in it that weighed about fifteen pounds. She ran down the stairs quickly, hefting the box.

The gang member looked up at her and started to rise.

She threw the box at him as hard as she could.

He caught it with both hands the instant before it struck him in the head. As he lowered it, he shot a menacing stare at her. Blood trickled from his eyebrow.

"Come here, *chiquita*," he said to her. *"Vámonos."*

She was halfway down the stairs. He blocked the bottom with his body. He was twice her size.

"Oof," she muttered to herself, then swung over the railing and jumped. The man rushed to intercept her.

Suki landed, rolled, and started running to the nearest aisle. The fixed seating would provide a barrier. She heard him coming after her, choosing another row to run down. Suki reached the end first and went up two more rows before going down one in the center block of seats. He was right behind her, but she was smaller and faster. At the end of the row, she sprinted toward the stage.

He said something nasty to her in Spanish. She wasn't sure what, but it sounded like a curse word. Her heart was pounding as she raced as fast as she could.

Through the headset, she heard gunfire. Lund was having his own problems.

Ahead of her, at the bottom of the aisle, was a wooden stair box constructed for the play. It was painted black, but she could see it in the dim light. She ran up the steps and quickly cut right toward the thick stage curtains. One of her jobs for the play was to control the curtains. She knew the ropes and the layout backstage intimately. When she hit a gap in the wall by the curtains, she heard the man's hard breathing and his steps pounding behind her.

The thick velvet offered interference. She felt his hand grabbing for her, but the folds of the curtain blocked him from seizing her. Suki almost started crying in fear, but she got through the barrier and then released the trapdoor lever. She heard the click-clack of the trapdoor dropping. Turning, she sprinted onto the stage, dodging a set piece, and then jumped into the hole.

She landed with a grunt. The trapdoor was spring-loaded, so it was easy to push it back into place. It clicked and locked. The noise of the man's footfalls came right overhead, and then he stopped where he'd probably seen her fall.

"*Chiquita,*" he said menacingly. "Oh, *chiquita.* You are clever. *Muy inteligente.*"

Suki stared up at the flooring above her, trying to calm her breathing. Another barrier lay between them. That meant something.

"Can you hear me, *chiquita?*"

She didn't answer, but she was gasping for air. He didn't know how to get down. She'd thrown the lever when he was still obscured by the curtain. But would it matter? Could he blow up the stage?

"*El jefe* is very interested in you, *chiquita*. You can control the *kem äm*. That's how you knocked me down. I realize that now. The jaguar priest wants to see you. It's a great honor to be invited to meet with him, *chiquita*. Come with me."

As he spoke, she felt a sense of gloom churn in the air. Magical fear radiated from the man above her as he walked in slow circles around the trapdoor.

Suki knew of a prop crate nearby to throw something at him. Could she find it in the dark? She began to carefully back away, but then her shoe chirped against the concrete.

"I *hear* you, *chiquita*. Don't run away. Come with me."

The fear felt as if leeches were clinging onto her body, sucking her courage away. Blackness whirled around her. She thought she heard chittering laughter. This was an evil man. A horrible man. He'd murdered people, she sensed. He'd murdered children. He could do terrible things to her when he caught her.

Grandma, Suki thought desperately. She backed away, sniffling, trying to control her body, which was beginning to tremble. She bumped into something and fell.

"Oh, *chiquita*," crooned the gang member. "I'm coming for you. I'm coming."

The urge to run and escape flooded her body. Like she was a jackrabbit and he was a wolf. She clamped her hands on the headset. A high-pitched squeal started deep within her, growing louder and more frenetic.

Run.

Run.

Run!

Grandma, Suki pleaded in her mind. Magic began to envelop her in motes of golden dust.

She heard the sound of another gunshot through the headset.

Lund grunted in pain.

Her protector had just been shot.

CHAPTER TWENTY-EIGHT

Beck Cabin

Bozeman, Montana

December 26

The metallic blue of the Life Flight helicopter contrasted with the pristine snow, and the whirling rotor was kicking up a blizzard. Two EMTs carried a stretcher with Jordan strapped to it. Roth walked alongside it, limping on his injured left leg. A third medic was in the chopper, getting a blood transfusion ready.

All of the workers wore blue jumpsuits and sunglasses.

"That was a great shot, Jordan," Roth complimented, squeezing Jordan's wrist. If the bodyguard hadn't acted so quickly, so resolutely, Agent Sanchez would be dead. And Roth and the boys would have been captured.

"I still got the goods," Jordan said over the noise of the helicopter.

Monica had been talking to the pilot in the Life Flight helicopter, but she emerged from the cockpit, the wind blasting her dark hair into her face. The two EMTs hoisted Jordan's stretcher into the helicopter, where the medic was waiting with the IV. Neither of them climbed in. Their duffel bags of gear sat on the porch of the Beck cabin, by the injured pilot of the FBI helicopter, who sat holding a piece of bloodied gauze to his forehead. Roth was surprised to see that he was even alive.

"Back away!" she warned, holding her hands up to direct Roth and the boys away from the helicopter.

The blue Life Flight rose from the snow and headed over the trees back to Bozeman. The two EMTs went to grab their gear and help the injured pilot.

Monica looked exhausted. She had smudges under her eyes and was shrouded in weariness and sadness. More FBI agents had been killed in the helicopter crash and the fight with the jaguar priest.

The corpse of the priest was still in the snow, placed in a body bag. After the kill shot, his body had reverted to human form. Roth stared at the bag, fearful the man might come alive again like in a vampire story. Just to be sure, he'd asked Monica to handcuff the body before they'd removed the gold ring from his finger and zipped him up.

Putting her hands on her hips, Monica looked at Brillante and Lucas. "How are you two holding up?"

"Feels a little like the death game all over again," Brillante said.

She looked at him thoughtfully. Did she believe them now? "Except no ball and hoops, huh?"

"Where's Suki?" Lucas asked worriedly. "Is she still at Brice's house?"

Roth shook his head. "No, she's with Lund. At the high school. I'm worried about her."

"You all need some sleep," Monica said. "I'll send a tactical team to the high school if one isn't already on the way."

"Thanks," Roth replied. "You look exhausted too."

"I've done stakeouts that lasted weeks. A little coffee, and I'll be fine. After the Life Flight brings Jordan to the hospital, it'll come back for the other injured agents and the EMTs." She looked at her watch.

"Our Salt Lake support should be arriving anytime. We need the manpower more than we knew."

"Do you believe me now?" Roth asked her seriously.

She looked at him with firmed lips. "I can't explain what happened, but I know what I saw. A helicopter was made to crash. Bullets bounced off him like he was Superman. And he was turning into an animal when Jordan shot him. Director Wright is going to be asking a lot of questions, Jonathon."

"Is he the FBI director?" Roth vaguely recognized the name, although the only details he could recall about the man were that he had red hair and had been leading the FBI since the previous administration.

"Yeah. And he's more of a skeptic than I am."

That wasn't good. "I hope you don't arrest me today," Roth said.

She gave a weary smile. "Not today. But no promises about tomorrow. I am going to put a travel ban on you, though. And your kids. No leaving the country."

"Fair enough. I can assure you we're in no hurry to leave."

She looked over at the EMTs working on the injured pilot, then turned around in a full circle. "Beautiful view. But one heck of a crime scene. It'll take them a long time to process it. We need to get you and your boys to a safe place."

"Can we go back home?" Lucas asked.

"Sadly, no. It's a crime scene too. I'm sorry."

Lucas's mouth drooped. "That's okay. But where are we going to stay?"

"A hotel?" Brillante asked.

Monica nodded. "There are several downtown that the bureau uses to protect witnesses." Her phone rang, and she quickly answered it. "What's going on, Bobby?"

Roth could hear the voice crackling on the phone, but he couldn't make out the words. She turned around so he couldn't see her face. But he'd seen the shocked look in her eyes a split second before she managed to conceal it.

"Have you called in the National Guard?" Monica asked firmly. "No? Then do it! Call the Gallatin Readiness Center in Belgrade. We need boots on the ground!" She paused, listening. "Then call the governor! Close down the airport. You can't let him get away! Uh-huh. Roger that, Bobby. Thank you."

Roth's anxiety continued to spike.

She ended the call and stuffed her phone into her pocket.

"What's going on?" Roth asked.

"The TSA has men down at the airport," Monica said angrily. "The enforcement agents sent to investigate Calakmul's jet have been killed. Necks broken. They're acting like it's an active shooter event. We have a jurisdictional nightmare on our hands."

"You can't let Calakmul escape," Roth said desperately. His mind was whipped into high agitation.

"They say he wasn't on the jet. Just the woman. But the trail of deaths proves otherwise."

"Angélica is his personal assistant," Roth said. "If she's there, he's definitely there. Trust me."

"Bobby's going to lock down the airport," she said. "No flights authorized to take off or land."

Roth laughed at that. "He's not going to ask for permission to leave. Disable his jet."

"I can't do that without a judge's order," Monica said.

"If you don't do it immediately, it'll be too late to get a judge's order," Roth said. His weariness had drained away.

"You don't know about bureau protocol," she snapped. But her expression told him that she shared his frustration. "Right now, we need to get you and your family to a safe place. The snowmobiles are the fastest transportation back right now."

"You're coming with us?" Roth asked.

"Of course. My duty is to protect and serve your family until the threat is over. I want this Calakmul guy in custody, Mr. Roth. Believe me. I've lost several friends because of him. And I've seen what you've all been through. This is crazy stuff. I've warned the other agents to spread the word that he can't be apprehended the way we typically do things."

"Too bad you shut down the X-Files division in 2002," Roth quipped, referencing the TV show from the early '90s.

"Funny. But no. That's not real."

"*This* is real," Roth insisted.

"I know. Let me check on Andy first. Get the snowmobiles fired up." She walked over to the injured pilot.

Brillante shook his head. "This Christmas break is almost as bad as last year's."

Another text arrived on Roth's phone. He pulled it out and saw Illari Chaska's name with another screenshot translation.

He remembered a stretch of words from the last batch. *A remnant of the house of Jacob will go forth among them . . . as jaguars among the beasts of the forest.*

One jaguar priest had taken out a sniper and multiple FBI agents who were trained to take down murderers. Only Jordan's lucky shot during the transformation had killed him. These monsters were immune to bullets for the most part.

Another part of the message flashed through his mind: *And none can deliver them.*

He was terrified for Suki. He pulled out the cell phone, his heart pounding, but he didn't know if he should call. What if someone overheard her talking and caught her?

She's with Lund, he told himself. *He knows what the* kem äm *can do. He'll protect her.*

Moretti would too, once he arrived. He had to believe that. He couldn't bear if something happened to her, especially after the way he'd lost Sarina.

He texted her. *Are you safe? Help is coming.*

No immediate answer.

"Fire up the snowmobiles!" Monica said.

Roth slid the phone back into his pocket.

"Were you messaging Suki?" Brillante asked. "Is she okay?"

"She's with Lund, and Moretti will be with her soon," Roth told him. "She'll be safe. You boys follow me on your sleds."

He took the boys to the snowmobiles. The front of the Beck cabin had been riddled with bullet holes. All the windows on that side were broken. He'd imagined the prepper cabin as being a true safe house, off the grid, a place where Jacob Calakmul couldn't find him.

He'd been wrong. A jaguar priest had broken into the cabin in his hunt for them. He'd even broken into the basement. One man. How many more jaguar priests were there? How many more of them were coming for them?

And none can deliver them.

Roth watched the boys straddle their sleds and fire them up. His was still back where he'd ditched it. Jordan's had been left behind. After going to his snowmobile and firing up the engine again, he waited for Monica to slide onto the back seat.

"Where to?" he asked her over his shoulder.

"Back to your house," she said.

"I thought it was a crime scene?"

"It is. But there are plenty of agents there. Safety in numbers. We'll take one of the bureau's SUVs to the hotel."

Roth's phone buzzed in his pocket. He almost didn't feel it with the rumble of the snowmobile, but he fished it out.

Suki had texted him.

Lund is shot. I'm hiding.

Roth began to hyperventilate. His anxiety was through the roof now.

"What's it say?" Monica asked over his shoulder.

"Lund is shot. Suki's hiding at the high school." He squeezed the phone in his hand, full of fury and terror. He called Moretti next. It rang twice before the call was answered.

"Hi, Roth, we're almost there."

"Where are you?" Roth asked worriedly.

"On 191 heading north. Just passed Atkins. We're about thirty minutes out."

Roth knew that highway. It was the most direct road to Bozeman, directly to the west of the Beck Cabin.

"We're leaving the cabin now on snowmobiles," Roth said. "We'll try to meet you off the highway before you get to town. Look for us, but don't wait for us if we're not there. Suki's alone at the high school."

"What happened to the bodyguard?"

"He's been shot. We need to get her out!"

"Driving as fast as I dare, bud. One of the cars already went off the road and flipped because of the ice. But we'll get to her, Roth. We'll get all of you. Call me when you get to 191 so I know you're there."

"Will do. We'll hurry."

He ended the call and revved the engine again. He and the boys took off across the snow.

CHAPTER TWENTY-NINE

Aspen Ridge

Bozeman, Montana

December 26

It was a beautiful scene—snow packed among the fir trees, the profile of the mountains jutting toward the enormous "big-sky" horizon. A slate-gray river cut through the canyon, half of the water frozen, half turbulent, completely blocking their way forward.

Roth's face was numb from the wind. The motor on the snowmobile was idling, the exhaust coming out in gray puffs. Brillante and Lucas pulled up next to where he'd stopped at the edge of the ridge.

"Are we lost?" Monica asked, sitting on the back seat, gripping the handrails.

"Dad always gets lost," Lucas said. "We practiced going from our house to the cabin and back again dozens of times. Never been out here before."

Roth pulled out his burner phone and opened Google Maps. It pinpointed their location. He could see *US Highway 191/Gallatin Road* on the map to the west. It came from the southwest at a forty-five degree angle before turning due north to Four Corners, Montana, where it turned ninety degrees to the right, due east into Bozeman.

"I'm not lost," Roth said, shaking his head and staring at the phone. "I just wasn't expecting a river or this ridge. I thought we'd be in the valley by now."

"Valley's that way," Brillante said, pointing to the lower ground where a few farm pivots could be seen amid the snow-covered fields. There were a couple of neighborhoods down there, but it was primarily farmland.

Roth scratched his beard, thinking. Crossing a river on a snow-mobile was dangerous unless it was frozen enough. It would be sturdy enough to bear the weight of the snowmobiles at eight inches thick. More than twelve inches, and he could have driven his Denali across it. But without an auger to measure the thickness, there was no way to tell whether the river was safe to cross.

"Do I need to call in another helicopter?" Monica asked dryly.

"Let's be safe," Roth said. "Follow this river north and see if there's a bridge we can cross. Once we're in the farm fields, it'll go fast."

Brillante revved his engine.

In seconds, all three snowmobiles were spraying chunks of ice and zooming downward along the ridge toward the valley. Hiking through such deep snow would have taken hours, but the sleds cut a path quickly. His nose hairs froze again, and he grimaced at the sting of wind against his cheeks. It was cold, but with the sun finally up, he could feel the warmth seeping into his jacket.

They reached the valley floor and followed the river north. Roth hoped they'd reach 191 before Moretti. He didn't want to sit on the sidelines while Suki was in danger, especially not when he knew Jacob Calakmul was in Montana.

They needed to catch him. They needed to. This was their chance to stop his plan.

To find out what had happened to Sarina.

Once they'd reached the farm fields of the valley, they made faster progress. The river entered a series of canals, directing its flow away from the fields. Roth increased his speed and broke west. They flew down the gently rolling hills, under the huge farm pivots, dormant during the winter. Evidence of other snowmobile tracks could be seen the deeper in they went. Snowmobiling was a popular winter activity in Bozeman.

Roth noticed a small dip ahead with a taller hill on the other side. When they reached the top of it, he hoped they'd finally get a view of the highway.

"Hold tight!" he called over his shoulder.

The drop was steeper than he was expecting, and they picked up speed. As they reached the bottom, he realized the snow had concealed the steepness on the other side as well. What had seemed to be a gentle rise came up at him like a cliff wall.

Roth's heart sputtered with terror as they hit the rise hard. Snow exploded into his face, blinding him. It felt like they were going vertical and would topple over backward. Roth hunkered down closer to the handlebars and gunned the engine in his panic. He'd heard some terrifying snowmobile stories before, but he'd never been in a situation like this one.

The sled settled, though, signaling that they'd made it past the steepest part. He had snow all across his face, his jacket, everything. He slowed down and then stopped so he could wipe his eyes and turned in time to see Brillante shooting up the same edge. There hadn't been time to warn the boys.

Brillante cleared the top too, whooping in joy as he came up, splattered with snow. Roth heard the engine of Lucas's snowmobile. He waited. He watched. But no Lucas.

"That was sweet!" Brillante crowed as he stopped next to them.

"Where's Lucas?" Roth asked.

"He was right behind me," Brillante said, confused. He turned his neck. "I'll go find him."

"Wait. That's pretty steep."

"You don't have room for him on yours. I'll go get him if he fell off!"

"Just be careful!"

As Brillante sped back down the little ravine, Roth looked back at Monica, who was trying to get the snow out of her hair.

"That was terrifying," she announced.

"Yeah, sorry. I didn't see how steep it was."

"I couldn't see it at all until we hit it," she said. She looked around him. "That's 191, isn't it!" she said, pointing.

Roth followed her direction and saw the highway. "That's it."

A caravan of law enforcement cars, lights flashing, could be seen north of their position.

Roth punched the handlebar. "We were so close!" Frustration seethed inside him. He'd counted on getting a ride with Moretti. Although he knew Lund and Moretti were both better qualified than him to help Suki in the present situation, he wanted to be there. It would feel better if he were close. If he could see her with his own eyes.

"I know where we are," Monica said. She pointed again. "That's Cottonwood Road." Her finger moved. "That's the road to your home. There's a restaurant at the corner of 191—the Jump. We sometimes go there for drinks after duty."

"Yeah, you're right. Never been there, but I've seen it."

"Let me call and get one of the bureau SUVs to meet us there. They can pick us up."

That made sense. They could ditch the snowmobiles in the parking lot and call the restaurant owner later, after they opened.

"Good call," Roth said. More of his anxiety dissipated when he heard another snowmobile approaching. That was a good sign.

Monica pulled out her phone and placed the call. "Hi. Yeah. We need a lift. Can you send someone in a bureau SUV to the Jump? Yeah. Corner of 191 and Cottonwood. I've got Mr. Roth and the boys. We just saw the cavalry pass us. They're at Four Corners by now. Thanks, Bobby."

She ended the call.

Brillante came riding up with Lucas sitting behind him.

"What happened?" Roth asked.

Lucas shook his head. "I chickened out."

"Where's the snowmobile?"

Brillante eased up next to them. "Left it down there. We can get it later. Let's go."

"We're going to a restaurant," Roth said, pointing across the fields.

"Good, I'm hungry," Lucas said.

"Not to eat. One of the FBI vans will pick us up. We need to get Suki. But Moretti just arrived, along with the backup from the Salt Lake field office."

"Let's get moving," Monica said, nodding forward.

Roth gunned the engine again, and soon the two snowmobiles were flying over the fields. There was a small pivot right at the corner of Highway 191 and Cottonwood. The parking lot of the restaurant hadn't been plowed recently, and there were no cars in it at all. They slowed down and crossed Cottonwood, then eased into the back of the parking lot and killed the engines. Roth took the snowmobile key out so that no one could steal it, then took the other sled's key after they'd settled in.

It felt good to stretch his legs. He pulled out his phone and called Moretti, gazing up Cottonwood Road. A black SUV could be seen in the distance, heading their way.

Moretti answered on the first ring. "Didn't see you on the highway," he said. "You okay?"

"Yeah. We just missed you. We're at a little restaurant nearby. Where are you?"

"We're about to hit Bozeman. Some of my men are going to Gallatin High with me. Some are going to the FBI office, but a large group is heading straight to the airport."

"You've got to catch him," Roth insisted. Brillante was making a snowball. Roth shot him a warning look and shook his head.

Monica walked away from the snowmobiles toward the restaurant, watching as a black SUV approached.

"Some TSA agents are down at the airport," Moretti said, "but we've got a tactical team with some big guns on the way. He won't get away with this, Roth. Trust me."

"Yeah, well, he can deflect bullets, so don't shoot directly at him if it comes to that. We just learned there's a weakness, though." He paused. Moretti didn't know Calakmul and his men had the ability to transform. Telling him over the phone wasn't ideal, but his friend needed to be prepared if he was going to fight them. "Remember those stories your dad told us, Moretti? About the skinwalkers? Calakmul and his followers . . . they're like that. I know what it sounds like, but they can transform into animals. I've seen it happen with my own eyes. If one of them starts to transform in front of you, that's when you attack. That's the only moment they're weak."

"So the *yee naaldlooshii* aren't a myth," Moretti said slowly. He sounded surprised but not disbelieving. "And using silver bullets won't work?"

"Ha ha. Just be careful."

"This is why you wouldn't talk about Mexico?" his friend asked in a contemplative voice. "You saw them transforming?"

"Among other things," Roth said. "Sometimes seeing is believing."

"If you say it's true, I believe you," Moretti said. "There's never been anything wrong with your eyes."

Warmth surged in Roth's chest. It made him feel better that his friend knew. It made all of this feel more doable. "Whatever you do, don't let Calakmul's jet take off. It's a Pegasus. It can take off vertically."

"We've got some gear that can handle it," Moretti said. "I'll call you when I've got Suki. It's all going to be okay, Roth."

"Thanks, bud. Our ride just showed up. Talk to you later."

The SUV entered the parking lot.

"Boys," Roth said, gesturing for them to come to him.

Monica was walking toward the Suburban, craning her neck to see the driver. She started in recognition and then immediately reached for her pistol.

Metal glinted from the open window. A gun fired.

Monica fell to the snow.

The Suburban stopped. Roth recognized the driver. He'd seen him as part of the FBI squad the night before during the search. Agent Garcia?

The man aimed his pistol at Roth's chest. "Get in, Mr. Roth," he said with a menacing scowl. "Mr. Calakmul would like to see you."

CHAPTER THIRTY

Bozeman Yellowstone International Airport

Bozeman, Montana

December 26

"We need to get going!" Jacob shouted as he entered the cockpit. The hangar doors were still open. The engines of the Pegasus were hot. As soon as Angélica returned from moving the FBI vehicle into the hangar, they'd be ready to remove the stair ramp and leave. They'd already moved the agents' bloodied bodies onto the hangar floor.

"I'm trying to find the high school and figuring out where to land," said the pilot, staring down at an aerial map he'd pulled up on his phone.

"It has a parking lot, surely," Jacob said.

"This isn't a helicopter! If I hit anything and damage the plane, we'll be stuck. I need more time, Mr. Calakmul!"

Jacob seethed with frustration. He watched as the SUV pulled into the hangar and Angélica left the driver's seat.

"How fast can we get back to Mexico?" Jacob asked.

"A few hours. I've disabled the transponder so the jet will not identify itself on radar, but if the military sends jets to hunt us down, I don't know what—"

"Fly beneath radar, just as you did running drugs across the border. If any military jets engage us, leave them to me," Jacob said. "Just get us across the southern border as quickly as possible after we've picked up the family."

"I think we can be across the border in two hours. Now please let me study the map. I need to concentrate!"

Jacob felt a flash of impatience, but he tempered himself. He could kill the pilot after they were back in Cozumel.

The pilot was still studying his phone. "All right. I think I can find it. The high school is really close to the airport, though. Shouldn't we wait until MS-13 catches her and brings her in?"

"No!" Jacob insisted. "We cannot stay here. We go . . . now!"

"Tell her to hurry and get inside," the pilot shot back.

Jacob nodded and left the cockpit entry. The feeling of anxiety was powerful, but he was good at mastering his emotions. His training as a jaguar priest had ensured it.

When he glanced out the door, Angélica was striding past one of the bodies of the dead agents. She didn't look down at it, but her mouth wrinkled in distaste.

"Hurry," Jacob entreated, then saw the "dead" FBI agent lift his head and raise his arm. His bloodied hand gripped a handgun.

"Look out!" Jacob yelled, summoning the magic from his ring to protect himself.

The agent's arm was quivering. It wasn't clear who he was aiming at—him, her, the jet. The crack of the pistol shot reverberated through the expansive hangar.

Angélica was struck, the bullet going straight through her, and she crumpled to the ground, her face twisting with surprise.

Jacob stared in shock for a moment as more bullets sprayed from the gun, then sprang from the open door of the jet with a pulse of magic. Leaping like a panther, he made his way to the agent. He stomped on the man's arm, breaking it, then bent down and smashed the man's windpipe.

The agent's neck was still ravaged from the previous attack, but he'd survived—he'd only been playing dead. But he was truly dead now. His eyes stared vacantly, blood dribbling from his mouth.

Jacob rushed immediately to where Angélica had fallen. She lay on her side, legs pulled up, gasping for breath. The bullet had pierced her winter coat from behind, gone through her ribs and out through her chest, below her breast. A wild, stricken look was in her eyes. She was struggling to breathe. Her lung had probably collapsed.

He gripped her hand, peering into her face. In that moment, he had a taste of what Jonathon Roth had been suffering. The fear of permanently losing her pierced his heart more surely than any bullet could. He was accustomed to her ways. Her sly smiles, the scent of her perfume, her brilliant mind and adaptability to both technology and the ancient ways of the Maya. The original Malintzin had been faithful to the jaguar priests, even though her role had cost her. He didn't want Angélica to pay the ultimate price for serving him. They weren't lovers. Not yet. But he wanted so much more from her, with her.

Her breath was coming in little pants. She stared at him fearfully, realizing she was bleeding to death.

He would not let the gods of Xibalba have her. She was a flower meant for sunlight, not the deep cenotes and their underground grottos. He could save her life. He *had* to. Living without her, he realized, would be too painful.

The image of Sarina Roth, lying on a stone table in the shrine of Ix Chel, came to his mind. She'd lain there for weeks before the magic had finally healed her.

He put his hand on Angélica's breast and invoked the healing magic in his mind. *"Utzirisaj,"* he whispered, summoning his own strength to lend to hers. He could mend a broken arm. Fix serious injuries. But he'd never tried to heal a bullet wound before.

Angélica slumped to the concrete floor, lifeless.

"Utzirisaj!" Jacob commanded, his voice beginning to quiver with dread. She wasn't dead. She couldn't be. He felt a little throb of her heart beneath his palm.

The magic closed the bullet hole, fusing the flesh together. The blood that had been spreading across her fleece jacket had stilled. He still felt her internal injuries, though, the magic telling him the healing was not done. There was more damage.

"K'ijij," he whispered pleadingly. The magic of repair. Bone cleave to bone. Sinew to sinew. *Heal. Fix. Mend.*

He heard the pilot's voice through the intercom in the cabin.

"They're coming, sir! Leave her!"

Jacob twisted his neck and saw emergency vehicles heading toward the hangar. Lights flashing blue and red. SUVs mostly, but there were military vehicles too—one with a machine-gun nest attached to the top and camo paint on the sides.

He felt the throbbing of her heartbeat stop. Her breath guttering out.

The pain that wrenched him was unimaginable. He had killed his own father to become the Ajwäch, the head of the jaguar priests. His father had also been named Jacob, and at one time, he'd hoped to fulfill the prophecy himself. In order to claim his birthright, Jacob had needed to slay him.

It hadn't been like this. Losing his Malintzin was unbearable.

The vehicles charged toward the hangar to stop them. Jacob stared, held out his hand, and invoked a web of *kem äm* to cover the entire opening. The goldens strands of magic suffused the area just as the first vehicles reached it. The drivers either didn't notice or were too bent on reaching the jet inside the hangar to let it stop them.

When they struck the *kem äm* at that speed, the lead vehicles flipped backward with an ear-piercing sound of shattering glass and mangled metal. Jacob watched with little enjoyment as the debris ricocheted backward into the oncoming vehicles.

It was as if a missile had struck. Gas tanks exploded. Shredded tires ripped from spinning wheels. Airbags ballooned and popped.

The sound of the carnage happening outside the hangar meant nothing to Jacob. He scooped Angélica's body into his arms and lifted her up. He felt the power of the jaguar magic filling him with strength and determination as he carried her up the steps. In his mind flashed the remembrance of the Aztec legend of Popocatépetl and Iztaccíhuatl, a warrior and a princess who had fallen in love. The imagery of the warrior carrying his dead lover to her grave was popular throughout Mexico.

This must be how Popocatépetl had felt upon losing his beloved.

Jacob understood better than he ever had the powers of the heart. The rage of loss. The hopelessness of despair. He hoisted her body higher and finished climbing up the steps. The pilot was waiting for him, eyes wide with fear and awe at what he'd just seen.

"Get us out of here," Jacob said intently. "Hover near the hangar door, and I'll release the barrier."

Climbing in past him, Jacob brought Angélica to the back seat, the same one where Mrs. Roth had been strapped in just over a year ago. The irony tasted like copper in his mouth. He heard the sound of the cabin door closing and locking.

He laid Angélica down on the seat and brushed the hair from her forehead. The gods could revive the dead, but that power was beyond Jacob. He could only petition for it.

A thought came to his mind in a whisper.

Witz'itz'il.

She was not dead. Her heart had only stopped. A little touch of magic could start it again. A true sorcerer could manage such a thing.

He put his hand on her breast again, staring down at his ring. His father's ring. Passed down from master to master for millennia.

"*Jutz'it koyopa,*" he said, thinking the Mayan words first. A little lightning. Just a little.

He felt the magic of the ring extend from his hand into Angélica's chest. And then he felt it again, the throbbing of her heartbeat. He started to choke up with relief, amazed it had worked.

Angélica's eyes fluttered open. She took a breath, and he felt her chest expand a little. But still she struggled to breathe. Her insides had been ravaged by the bullet. She needed time to heal. To mend.

She needed a hospital, but there was no way he would take her to one.

There was another place, though. A place of healing. A place that had the most powerful magic of all. Aztlán.

He stared at her, relieved she was conscious again. The protective feelings thrumming through him were overpowering.

"I . . . I'm dying," she whispered, gazing up at him with growing terror.

He shook his head. "I won't let you."

The rotors embedded in the wings of the jet screamed with power. He felt the wobble of the craft as it rose from the hangar floor.

"Take us away," Jacob called to the pilot. He released the webbing blocking the hangar.

The jet roared through the gap, flying through smoke as the Pegasus took to the skies once more.

CHAPTER THIRTY-ONE

GALLATIN HIGH SCHOOL

BOZEMAN, MONTANA

December 26

"*Chiquita . . . chiquita . . .* where are you hiding?"

The sound of the man's gravelly voice made Suki's spine tingle with fear. She had thought she'd tricked him because he went back and searched the theater aisles for a while, but now he'd returned to where he lost her. Through the headset, she could hear Lund breathing heavily. He was still alive, at least.

"Suki . . . you still there?" Lund asked through the headset.

She wanted to answer him, but she was afraid of revealing her position to the gang member on the stage above her. The gentle tread of his footsteps echoed through the space around her. She backed away slowly, and her heel banged on a metal pole, sending it rolling noisily across the floor. She bit her lip, angry at the mistake.

The sound of the footsteps followed the clacking of the rolling pole. Then it stopped.

She nearly yelped in terror when another round of gunshots sounded over the headset. Two . . . three . . . four shots. They sounded like they'd been fired in her ears. She closed her eyes, fearing the worst.

"Sorry. Had to shoot both of them. I think there's one more up here with me. Maybe two. And the one by you." She heard the heavy breathing again. "I'm coming for you. I'm assuming you aren't talking because the battery died or you're afraid of being overheard. I just left the computer room, and I'm walking down the main corridor toward those colorful stairs. Just stay put."

She knew he was injured, but he wasn't giving up on her. She felt grateful that the man who'd been a total stranger to her until the last few days was risking his life to protect hers. She owed him a milkshake at the very least.

"*Chiquita* . . . let's stop playing hide-and-seek. No more games. If you come out right now, I won't hurt you before bringing you to Mr. Calakmul. But if you make me find you, I'll give you pain. You have no idea."

Horror and revulsion shot through her. A feeling of blackness and darkness radiated from above her.

"There are things I could do to you, *chiquita*. I will. I've tortured so many I've lost count. You'll scream for mercy."

She closed her eyes, shuddering. She could imagine his eyes—a shark's eyes, cold and flat. She could hear his footsteps heading away from her.

There was a stage door, a way to access the trap room without triggering the trapdoor she had used. It was the only other way down or out. He was walking right toward it.

"Suki, I'm coming down the steps," Steve Lund said through the headset. "No one has followed me. Heading toward the auditorium."

Suki's mouth was so dry she could hardly swallow. The stage door opened and tendrils of golden light began to snake down into the trap room. He was coming down.

She was trembling with fear. "He figured out how to get to me," she whispered into the headset mic.

"Get out of there!" Lund said in her ear.

Suki ran to the trapdoor and triggered it from beneath. The door flopped down. She heard the sound of the gang member running toward her, but he crashed into a plastic crate.

Suki dragged another crate to the opening, stepped up on it, and jumped. Grabbing the rim of the opening, she pulled herself up onto her stomach and then swung one knee up.

His hands grabbed her foot before the other leg could make it out.

She cried out involuntarily as he wrenched on her leg and pulled her back down into the trap room. She could smell his acrid sweat, the stale cigarette stink of his clothes. He grabbed her by the front of her shirt and hauled her off her feet. Suki squirmed, trying to break his grip, but it was like uprooting tree roots.

"I'm at . . . the auditorium," Lund wheezed. He was out of breath.

The headset was wrenched off her head, stinging her ears. He tossed it away and then brought a knife to her throat. The blade was made of obsidian, a double-edged piece about six inches in length with a wooden handle carved with glyphs.

The golden power swirled around them both. He pulled her against him, his muscled arm across her chest, the dagger a breath from her throat. The tendrils lit the way back to the stairs, and he marched back to the steps and went up, bringing her with him.

Her mind was blank with fear. She'd been caught. Just like down in Mexico. They would take her back there, but this time she'd be missing a finger or two. Obsidian blades were sharp enough to cut through bone. She remembered the night Lucas had been caught by one of

Calakmul's warriors, who'd threatened to cut off his head. The memory almost made her throw up.

When they reached the top of the stairs, she saw Lund running down the center aisle, holding his pistol.

"Freeze!" he shouted, dropping into a stance. She saw blood on his arm. Light surged through the broken windows.

But Suki's captor held her in front of himself, and the swirling motes of gold would deflect a bullet.

"Shoot me, go ahead," teased the gangster. "Might hit the *chiquita*, though."

"The police have just arrived," Lund announced. "The school is surrounded."

Was it a lie? Suki didn't know.

"You think I care?" scoffed the gangster.

"You care about going to prison?" Lund quipped back.

"No. The shoe will be on the other foot soon. The jaguars are coming. Do you know how many of my brothers are locked up? How many spider monkeys are about to be set loose? When the jaguars come, it's all changing, man. You'll be shanked now."

"You think someone will bust you out?" Lund said, coming closer, the pistol aimed right at them.

Please don't shoot, Suki thought. She wanted to shake her head no, but she was afraid she'd cut her own neck on the dagger blade.

"We're all getting ready for freedom," cackled the gangster. He kept inching forward, step by step, toward the edge of the stage curtains. "Revenge day is coming, man. Better go hide while you can. All the cops will be rounded up. Shoe's on the other foot! See how you like it."

"Let's make a deal," Lund said. "Let her go, and you'll walk away. No arrest. You're the last one standing."

"You're the last one *bleeding*," sneered the other. "Ain't nothing. I'm going to bash your head in with a crowbar. Not enough to kill you. Just enough to make you wish you died."

Suki could see the determined look in Lund's eyes. He wasn't going to back down. And neither was this guy.

"Shoot me," her captor taunted. "You're thinking about it. Can you make the shot? Are you good enough? Just shoot me. Shoot me!"

Suki felt the compelling urge from the magic. Lund had no defense from it. He was going to do it—and the bullet would bounce right back at him.

Suki closed her eyes and summoned the glowing tendrils of the magic around them to her bracelet and ring.

The pistol fired. She saw the flash on her closed eyelids. She felt the bullet whip past her and then heard the sound of something wet hitting the floor behind her. The gang leader had collapsed, shot in the head.

Lund lowered the pistol.

Men charged into the auditorium wearing tactical gear. Red lights crisscrossed from the opening.

"Police! Hands up!"

Lund raised both hands. She saw blood trickle from the cuff of his sleeve.

"I'm Steve Lund!" he shouted. "Suki Roth is right in front of me. 'Bout time you guys got in here! Where's Moretti?"

"Right here," said a voice that was familiar to Suki. Her dad's friend had visited them before, both here in Bozeman and in California. Her shoulders slumped with relief.

She was so grateful he'd made it.

"My men are sweeping the building," Moretti said as he marched up the main aisle. He had a buzzcut, a widow's peak, and enough gear on him to stop a tank by himself. He was large and fit for a man her dad's age. He looked like the kind of guy who could do the Ironman competition. He probably had. "Any threats left?"

Lund began to relate whom he'd shot and where. They were all, to his knowledge, dead.

"You didn't leave any for us?" Moretti said. "The van driver is cuffed and in a car. That one was easy."

"Good," Lund said. "Can I lower my hands now?"

"Of course. Stand down, gentlemen."

Lund holstered his pistol and turned, gripping his injured arm. He leaned back against the edge of the stage. "I need an ambulance. Got grazed by a 9 mm."

"Ouch." Moretti looked up and down at Lund and then glanced at Suki. "Last time I saw you was in January . . . at the funeral. You okay?"

Suki nodded. It had been Bryant Westfall's funeral in Boise. Roth, Westfall, and Moretti had been close friends in high school back in Fremont. Westfall had been her father's financial advisor, killed as part of the jaguar priests' scheme.

Suki had an uneasy feeling. "Where's my dad?" she asked.

"We were supposed to meet him on the highway coming in," Moretti said. "He asked me to come get you and bring you to him."

The bad feeling intensified. She knew intuitively that this wasn't just anxiety—something was wrong with her brothers and dad.

"I'd really like to see them," Suki said. "Can you take me?"

"Sure thing, Suki. The FBI went straight to the airport to bag a suspect. Let's get to my car, and we can call your dad from there, okay?"

Suki nodded with relief. She started to leave, then turned to Lund. "Thanks."

He gave her a shallow nod, clearly in a lot of pain.

She held out her palm as if to give him a high five. He reached out and gave her one, but she shook her head and pressed her palm against his and then wrapped her thumb around his hand.

"Introvert's hug," she said to him.

Lund chuckled and tapped his thumb against her hand. "You okay, kiddo?"

"I will be when I see my family again," she said nervously.

She followed Moretti up the aisle and out through the broken window. A bunch of law enforcement vehicles were parked in front of the high school, lights flashing. Another officer, also in tactical gear, came up to Moretti.

"You see that?" he said, pointing to the horizon.

Moretti looked toward the mountains, snow-capped and beautiful—except for the plume of black smoke rising up from a location several miles away.

"What's that?" Moretti asked.

The officer shook his head. "It's coming from the airport."

Moretti frowned. "The Feds went in with guns blazing? Or did something go wrong?"

The other officer shrugged. "Don't know. No reports have come in yet. What's the situation inside?"

"Lund took out the MS-13 gang all by himself. Take the van driver to the field office for questioning. I'm going to bring Suki back. Tell Travis to wait for orders."

"Roger that."

"This way," Moretti said to Suki, gesturing to a silver Crown Victoria sedan. "That's mine." She felt like she should leave. *Immediately.* The feelings of dread were intensifying.

He pulled the radio from his shoulder holster and spouted off a bunch of police talk. Codes of some sort or other.

Moretti started the car. He pulled out his personal cell phone and made a call. She couldn't make out the voice from the other end, but it didn't sound like her dad.

"I got her. Where should I meet you?"

She pulled the door handle to open the door, because suddenly she knew the warning wasn't about her dad and brothers. Or some sort of danger that was coming. It was about danger she was already in. She had to get out of the car.

But the security switch had already been positioned. The door wouldn't open.

CHAPTER THIRTY-TWO

Cottonwood Road

Bozeman, Montana

December 26

As Roth stared at the barrel of the pistol, he felt his phone begin to buzz in his pocket. His hand twitched, involuntarily starting to reach for it.

"I will shoot you, Mr. Roth. Don't. Move. Tell your boys to get in."

Roth felt how close he was to death. One shot, one bullet, and he was a dead man. He lifted his gaze from the handgun to the FBI agent's cold gaze.

"I'm not going back to Mexico," Roth said forcefully.

"You don't want to see your wife?"

It felt as if the man had punched him in the gut. "What are you saying?"

"She's alive, Mr. Roth. She's at the Jaguar Temple."

"But she's in a coma still?"

The other man shook his head no.

"What?" Roth exploded with the emotional upheaval that head shake triggered. Why hadn't he been allowed to speak with her? Why wasn't she returned home? Was he lying?

"She's alive. Well. And getting pretty fluent in Mayan, as I understand."

Roth began to tremble with rage and helplessness. "They promised me they'd send her back to Bozeman if she woke up." Was this a terrible lie to confuse him into making a bad decision?

"Boys. You want to see your mom? Get in. Now."

"Dad?" Brillante asked, his voice quavering.

The boys were closest to the passenger side of the vehicle. If they ducked out of sight, they might be able to get to the snowmobiles.

No, that wouldn't work. Roth had the keys in his pocket. He closed his eyes in silent frustration, then opened them and stared at the agent.

"I think you're lying," he said. "I think she died, and Calakmul didn't want to tell me because he'd lose his hold over me. Boys. Get out of here."

"Dad!" Lucas said. "He'll shoot you."

"I think he's planning to do that anyway," Roth said. He took a step toward the agent.

"You think I won't?"

"Maybe I don't know Jacob as well as you do, but something tells me he wants us all alive. Boys—get out of here."

The agent's mouth contorted with anger. He opened the SUV door and came out, holstering the handgun. He withdrew cuffs instead.

"You're coming whether you want to or not," seethed the agent as he marched toward Roth.

Monica rolled onto her back, bringing up her pistol. She aimed it at Garcia's privates. "I don't think so, Garcia."

Roth stared at her in surprise.

"On your knees, Garcia. Hands behind your head. You know the drill. You only grazed me. I won't miss."

"Yaaas!" Brillante cheered. He and Lucas started to approach, but Roth signaled for them to stop.

Agent Garcia slowly sank to his knees, his hands lifted, the cuffs dangling.

"Now lie down," Monica said. "Slowly."

Garcia complied, scowling with fury. Then Monica got up, still pointing the gun at him, and slowly approached.

"Put your hands behind your back."

He did as requested, and she straddled him and handcuffed him with the cuffs he'd produced. Roth was so relieved he almost hugged her. The boys rushed over and wrapped their arms around him.

"I thought you were dead," he said to Monica as he squeezed his boys.

"Even at close range, it's easy to miss a target. I had a bad feeling, so I threw myself to the ground. The bullet nicked me."

She reached into the open driver's door and grabbed the walkie-talkie. "This is Agent Sanchez. This channel has been compromised. Repeat. This channel has been compromised."

Sanchez's cell phone immediately rang. She put the walkie-talkie down and pulled out her phone, keeping her pistol still. "Sanchez," she said. "What the . . . ? Yes, sir. Understood. I've got Agent Garcia in custody. He shot at me and tried to abduct the Roths. The father and sons are with me, yes. Mmmm. Got it. Thank you, sir."

She hung up the call. "The ASAC is on his way."

"What's an ASAC?" Lucas asked.

"Assistant special agent in charge," she said. "I haven't met him before, but his name is Carter. He was ordered to go directly to your home after they arrived from Salt Lake, so he left the caravan and passed by this location not that long ago."

"You have no idea what you're up against," Garcia said with fury, still lying on his chest.

"I know more now than I did last night," Monica replied with equal heat. "You're a traitor to your badge."

Roth heard a vehicle coming in fast and glanced past the SUV. Another Suburban was speeding down Cottonwood Road.

"How do we know which side they're on?" Roth asked nervously.

"We're on *your* side, Jonathon. We're going to find out how this snake slipped through. This must be the van responding to my call."

The SUV came up and several agents got out. A man in his late forties emerged from the passenger seat. He had a serious face, rendered more so by his salt-and-pepper hair and sideburns and his cleft chin.

"I'm Carter," he said, approaching Monica. He looked agitated. Upset.

"Nice to meet you, sir."

"Who's this agent?" Carter demanded, nodding to Garcia on the ground.

"Agent Sam Garcia. He's from my unit and was partially responsible for the fiasco last night."

"We had him listed as missing, possibly kidnapped." Carter shot an angry look at Garcia, then beckoned to one of his agents. "Put him in the back. We'll sort this through later."

The agent hauled Garcia to his feet and marched him to the SUV.

"You look angry," Monica said. "Now give me a moment to explain what's going on."

"Agent Sanchez, my boss just got blown up at Bozeman International along with some National Guardsmen that *we* asked to assist us." He pointed to the horizon. Roth glanced in that direction and saw a plume of smoke in the distance. "I'm now the acting SAC, and I'd very much like to know what on *earth* is going on, so I can tell the director before he sees this on CNN!"

"Sir, I'll explain as best I can," Monica said, "but we've been running for our lives all night. There is a criminal behind this situation named Jacob Calakmul from Mexico."

"Drug lord?"

"I wish it were that simple." Roth chuffed.

"And you're the famous author?" Carter asked, glancing at Roth. He didn't seem impressed. "The one who was nearly kidnapped in Germany?"

"Yes," Roth answered. "You know about Germany?"

"Of course," Carter snapped. "I spent Christmas talking to BND agents from Munich instead of skiing with my kids."

"I was about to take them to a hotel," Monica said. "Only the twins have slept . . . a little. But we just learned that Mr. Roth's wife may be alive and a hostage down in Mexico."

Carter scratched his forehead. "This makes no sense. The drug cartels wouldn't be this foolish."

"What we're dealing with is bigger than any of the cartels," Monica said. "Let me get this family somewhere safe. Then we can start figuring out the pieces so you can brief the director."

Carter's cell phone rang, and he pulled it out. "It's the director," he said worriedly. He turned his back to them and answered the call. "Agent Carter. Yes, sir. Yes, we just reached Bozeman. I don't know what happened at the airport. I've only heard a few things that make no sense. Yes, the airport has been shut down. No flights in or out."

Seeing Agent Carter on his cell reminded Roth that his own phone had rung. He reached into his pocket and saw a missed call from Suki. He tried calling her back, but the line rang a few times before going to voice mail. The recording was a snippet from the cartoon *Phineas and Ferb* with no other distinction.

Roth ended the call and tried again. Then a third time. Suki still didn't pick up. Because it didn't go straight to voice mail, he knew she still had battery life on her phone.

He sent a text. *Are u OK?*

Frustrated, he tried calling Moretti. The call rang, but no one answered. Then again, if there'd been an explosion at the airport, there was probably an emergency response underway. Maybe Moretti was a part of that.

Roth stared at the phone. What if Suki had been involved in the explosion? Was there a chance Moretti had gone there from the school with Suki in the car?

"Yes, sir. Thank you, sir. I'll let you know as soon as I find out." Agent Carter ended the call and turned around. "They're sending the bomb squad and investigators to look at the crash scene. Their plane should be here within the hour. Only one they'll allow in."

"What are you going to tell the director?" Monica asked. "I have info you need to know before you do."

Carter looked at the Roths, then back at her. "Get them to a hotel. Mr. Roth, your family will go down to Salt Lake City tonight. We can protect you better down there."

"My daughter isn't answering her phone," Roth said, looking worriedly at Monica. "I asked my friend Moretti—"

"Will Moretti?" Carter asked, startled. "From Salt Lake? You know him?"

"Yes. He's my high school buddy. She might be with my bodyguard, Steve Lund." He held up a finger. "Let me try calling him."

The man nodded, and Roth lifted his phone to make the call.

Lund answered on the first ring. "I'm in an ambulance heading to the hospital," he said curtly.

"Where's Suki?" Roth asked.

"She's with your friend, Moretti," Lund said. He sounded like he was in pain. "I saw her leave with him about twenty minutes ago."

Roth was relieved at that news, but his stomach was still doing flip-flops. What if Moretti had gone to the airport?

Why hadn't he called?

He felt his phone vibrate in his hand and pulled it away from his ear. Suki was calling back.

"She's calling!" he blurted. "Sorry you're hurt, Steve, but I have to go."

"Take the call. Make sure she's okay."

Roth ended the call and answered the incoming one. "Suki! Are you okay? Where are you?"

Roth heard the unmistakable sound of an engine in the background . . . the roar of a Pegasus jet. Horror flooded him.

"Mr. Roth," Jacob Calakmul said, his voice edged with anger and threat. "I thought you'd answer my call if I used this phone."

CHAPTER THIRTY-THREE

COTTONWOOD ROAD

BOZEMAN, MONTANA

December 26

Jacob Calakmul had Suki's phone.

Roth's stomach shriveled with dread. Panic began to clang emergency bells inside his mind.

"Where's my daughter?" Roth asked with a shaking voice, fearing the response.

"I warned you, Mr. Roth," Jacob said. "Did I not warn you?"

"Where is my daughter?" Roth yelled at him.

"I know you went to Dresden. I know you took pictures of the codex. What have you found, Mr. Roth? Send the pictures to this phone, and I will let you speak to Suki. She's alive. Do as I say, Mr. Roth. For the sake of your wife and your daughter, do as I say *right now*. Send me the pictures."

Roth's ears were ringing. He saw Monica looking at him worriedly. Then the Pegasus passed them with a roar. It wasn't but a few miles away, heading south toward the mountains. They could all see it since it was flying so low.

"How do I know she's with you?" Roth said. "You could just have her phone."

"Ask me a question, Mr. Roth. Something only she would know."

Roth squeezed his eyes shut. His heart was hammering fitfully. "Ask her," he said thickly, "what her favorite anime show is."

There was a pause. Then he heard Suki's voice coming from the phone. *"The Promised Neverland."*

Roth felt the dagger plunge into his chest. He'd lost Sarina in Mexico, and now Suki was being taken from him.

"Did you hear that, Mr. Roth? I think we've established now that she is with me. Send me the pictures you took. Then I will let you speak with her. It may be your last opportunity to talk to her. Do it now."

The call ended.

Monica approached him, a look of concern and fatigue in her eyes.

Carter was on his phone again. "Why was a private jet allowed to take off from the airport?" he snarled.

"Was that Calakmul?" Monica asked.

Roth gritted his teeth and nodded. His sons both looked stricken. They'd clearly picked up on the meaning of the call.

"They have Suki?" Lucas asked in anguish.

"Are you sure?" Monica asked. "Sometimes criminals pretend to abduct girls, and it can be difficult to discern the truth. Did he want money?"

"No, she's with him," Roth said, shaking his head. "I heard her voice. She told me something only she'd know." He rubbed his fingertips against his forehead. The feeling of loss and despair was avalanching inside him. He'd thought he could get away with crossing Calakmul. He'd thought . . .

The truth slammed him so hard his knees buckled, and he found himself sitting in the snow of the parking lot, so dizzy he nearly blacked out.

"Dad!" Brillante called out, and both boys rushed to him.

Monica crouched in front of him and put her fingers to his wrist. "Your heart is racing." She drew her hand back. "Give him some space," she told the boys. "He needs to catch his breath."

"Moretti," Roth said, his mind zipping from one thought to another like fireflies.

"As you know, he's been working on a task force against MS-13," she said. "But he's been solid. Nothing to flag the radar that he was bought and paid for. No fancy cars or anything like that."

Roth's mind ached with the sting of betrayal. When they'd fled Calakmul's compound last winter, Moretti was the one he'd called from the ruins near San Gervasio. He'd left him messages again when they'd fled to Huellas de Pan for shelter. Roth had *told* his friend where they were, and Calakmul's people had appeared shortly after.

The cut was so deep. He'd known Moretti from childhood. The two of them had grown up with Bryant, who'd been murdered on Calakmul's orders. Had Moretti known? Had he condoned it?

Or . . . was it possible he'd been set up as well?

"Dad, you look like you're going to puke," Brillante said with concern. Still, he and Lucas walked a little distance away to give the adults some space.

"I feel like it," Roth muttered.

"We don't have time to argue about this, Sanchez!" Carter burst out. "Mr. Roth, who was the person who called you? Not your daughter, clearly?"

Roth was trembling. "It was Jacob Calakmul. He's . . . he's the ringleader of this stuff. I've already told Agent Sanchez what happened to my family and me last Christmas, and she has the recording on her phone. I *have* to send Calakmul the pictures I took in Dresden, or he's going to hurt my daughter. He has her phone. She was with him. I could hear her voice."

"And you are certain?"

"Yes! I know my own daughter's voice!"

"Show me the pictures," Carter demanded, holding out his hand.

Roth felt tears sting his eyes. He'd let Suki down. His determination to unmask Calakmul had worked, but at what cost?

He didn't know what to do. What to think. Moretti's betrayal was impossible to wrap his head around. He'd trusted him with his life, his children's lives, and he'd handed Suki over to Jacob Calakmul.

"Mr. Roth, I can arrest you right now and confiscate your phone," Carter blustered, "but let's try to work through this as amiably as possible. Show me the pictures. Now!"

Roth didn't object. He unlocked the phone and went to the photo section. There was a selfie of him and the kids and Brice at the airport after landing. The sight of Suki's tired smile as she cozied up next to Brice made the pain in his chest increase. The pain was almost unbearable.

He swiped a few times until he reached the Dresden Codex pages, illuminated by the golden magic of the Maya. He offered the phone to Agent Carter.

"What's this?" Carter asked, wrinkling his nose. He looked confused and annoyed.

"An ancient Maya document on display in Dresden, Germany," Roth said. "That's one of the images Calakmul wants. There were four blank pages on the codex. That's one of them."

"Doesn't look blank to me," Carter said. "It's hieroglyphs?"

"Ancient Mayan," Roth corrected. "I need to send those images to him right now, or he's going to hurt her." He held out his hand. *"Please."*

"What do we do?" Monica asked Carter.

"Send the pictures," he said. "Our priority is safeguarding lives. Protect and serve." He gave the phone back to Roth, whose palms were already slick with panic at the wait.

He swiped through the pictures quickly, then texted them to Suki's phone.

By the time he finished, Carter was on his phone again, his back turned. "I need eyes on Moretti from the Salt Lake task force who came up here. Have dispatch track his vehicle. We need to apprehend him, but be cautious. He's heavily armed. Yes. Yes. Get it done."

———

The hotel shower was so hot it nearly scalded his skin. Roth stood in the cramped shower stall, trying to avoid touching the plastic shower curtain. The steam swirled in the air, and little droplets created by the mist were streaking down the curtain and the wall. He could hear the television on in the room outside the bathroom door, but his thoughts were far away. He'd gotten a single text back from Jacob Calakmul confirming that the photos had arrived and issuing an ultimatum. If anyone pursued him, Suki's life was forfeit. He would be allowed to speak to her once the jet was out of US airspace. More instructions would follow.

What would happen to her? He was pretty sure Calakmul wouldn't kill her at least. He'd been too interested in her ability with the *kem äm*. Calakmul and Garcia, the agent who'd been under his pay, had both implied that Sarina was alive. That she was awake. He hoped with everything in his heart that it was possible, that they would be able to watch out for each other before—

A knock sounded on the door. Roth turned off the water.

"What?" he called.

"Your phone just beeped!" Lucas said, his voice muffled.

Roth yanked the shower curtain aside and quickly dried off. The mirror was hazy with mist as he wrapped a towel around his waist and opened the door to the suite bedroom. The TV was blaring an episode of *Gravity Falls*, a cartoon that the twins enjoyed.

"Turn it down," Roth said. He grabbed his phone and saw the text from Suki's phone.

She will call you at 7pm. Be ready.

The remnants from the hotel breakfast were scattered over the kitchenette table. The boys had been famished when they'd arrived at the hotel an hour ago, but Roth's appetite, usually prodigious, was nowhere to be found. He set the phone down and went to the suitcase on his bed. The boys had shared a queen-sized bed in the adjoining room of the suite, which had its own TV and small bathroom. Their two rooms were linked by a kitchenette. The FBI agents had gone to their house and packed a bag of clothes and toiletries for them after dropping them off. Roth grabbed some shorts and a fresh T-shirt and underwear and went back to the bathroom to change. When he returned, a knock sounded on the door. Roth peered out the spyhole and saw Agent Sanchez.

He opened the door for her. She had a bag full of Subway sandwiches and a two-liter bottle of Mountain Dew. Her presence—and the involvement of the FBI—was partially a relief. The burden of trying to stop Calakmul was no longer on his shoulders alone, even if he suspected no one other than Monica would believe him.

Sometimes you really did need to see to believe.

"Come in," Roth said, stepping aside so she could enter. He closed the door behind her, then turned to face her. "How long do we have this hotel room?"

"As long as we need it. The bureau keeps rooms like this in various hotels to be used by agents or people in need of protection." Her gaze flitted to the dirty breakfast plates. "Did you get any breakfast, Jonathon?"

He shook his head. "Can't eat."

"You need something," she said. "Any news?"

"Just this." He grabbed his phone and showed her the latest text.

She looked at her watch. "That's nine hours from now. Curious."

"What about the jet?" Roth asked. "Any word?"

"They disabled the transponder and are flying below radar. The Department of Defense is fully aware of Suki's kidnapping, and so is the State Department. The ambassador to Mexico has also been briefed." She paused. "That recording you made last night was pretty helpful, actually. We're already starting to reassess the Beasley case."

Roth slumped down on a kitchenette chair, pulled up to the little round table. "How did Agent Carter take the story?"

She sighed and slumped down in the chair across from him. "Let's just say that the fact you're a world-famous fantasy author doesn't add to your credibility."

"You think *I* don't know that?" Roth chuffed.

"What's important is *I* believe you," she said. "I saw what I saw. The airport is still under lockdown. Apparently one of the SUV explosions caused a fuel tanker to explode. It's a mess over there. Our forensics team still made it to the crime scene, though, and they're saying a wild predator killed several agents. There's also the helicopter crash at the cabin. The evidence matches what you've told us, Jonathon. Too bad Mulder and Scully don't work for the bureau anymore."

Roth chuckled. "Any word on Jordan or Lund?"

She nodded. "I visited them both at the hospital. Jordan is going into surgery in an hour. There's some damage to be repaired, but the doctors are optimistic. Lund was only grazed by a bullet, and he'll be discharged soon. He wants to hunt down Moretti, but Carter told him to back off. They know each other. Not a good history."

"Did they find Moretti's car?"

She nodded. "It was ditched in the parking lot of the Family Dollar not far from here. There are footprints for him and Suki leading to the lot behind the store where a Pegasus jet seems to have landed and taken them away. His phone has been shut down. Goes straight to voice mail."

"Unbelievable," Roth grumbled. "He has a wife and kids. He left them behind?"

She shook her head. "Nope. DHS confirmed thirty minutes ago that they were on a flight yesterday."

"A flight?"

She nodded. "To Cancún."

CHAPTER THIRTY-FOUR

Pegasus Jet

Glen Canyon Area, Utah

December 26

I'm so screwed. That was the predominant thought looping endlessly in Suki's mind. She was used to living with anxiety, but this was different. This was a fulfillment of her deepest fears. She'd been torn away from her family—kidnapped by Jacob Calakmul, the psychopath.

The last time she had been in the Pegasus jet, her mom, Sarina, had been lying on the back bench in a diabetic coma. This time another woman lay there, Calakmul's assistant, Angélica. She'd been shot and was obviously in pain. She was probably *dying*, and Jacob Calakmul, who'd always seemed so detached, so cold, was freaking out about it. She saw it in the stress lines on his brow. In his nervous intensity as he hovered over Angélica, invoking the ancient Maya magic over and over to keep her alive.

Suki was strapped in her seat, facing them. Were they still in the United States? She wasn't sure how long they'd been flying—an hour maybe? Two? Her phone was with Calakmul, so she didn't have any way to tell the time. Maybe they'd already crossed the border into Mexico. They were flying low over a brown landscape riddled with canyons. She didn't see any cities or oceans or coastlines. Just ragged, dusty brown with jagged clefts and deep canyons.

Jacob said something in Mayan, stroking Angélica's face with tenderness. Agitation radiated from him. Suki had always been able to pick up on other people's moods. Well, except for Lund, who didn't seem to have any moods. She hoped he was okay. He was being shuttled off to the hospital when she went with Moretti.

Moretti.

What a jerk. A total two-faced jerk. Suki's feelings of danger had gone bananas as she got into his car. Odd, since an authority's car *should* be a safe place. Suki let out a breath, her worry and fear bubbling up again. Tears leaked out of her eyes, but she brushed them away. She wasn't someone who lost it easily. And it would be horrifying and mortifying to start bawling in front of these people.

It was strange to think about, but the school play, and every other aspect of life at home, would go on without her. She wouldn't be involved, wouldn't see it. Under normal circumstances, that would be totally devastating. But something about being kidnapped by a vengeful billionaire assassin who could shape-shift into a jaguar put things into perspective. Especially since she had no doubt Calakmul would use *her* to get her dad and her brothers. And maybe normal life wasn't going to be realistic for anyone anymore.

She twisted the ring on her finger, the one her mom had given her. *Please help me,* she thought inwardly. *Grandma Suki. Mom. Anyone. Help me. Help me get out of here.*

The intercom crackled, and the pilot said, "Sir, we're almost there. I need you to guide me."

Jacob brushed his lips against Angélica's brow and murmured something to her. He rose and started down the aisle toward the cockpit. His expression was strained. Although he glared at Suki as he passed her, he said nothing as he made his way forward and disappeared into the cockpit. With the door open, she could hear them talking.

"Yes, that's the canyon," Jacob said. "Get closer."

"Is there a place we can land? There's nothing out here. It's dangerous."

"We can land down there. Trust me."

"I'm not used to this kind of flying," the pilot said. He sounded worried, like he wasn't entirely sure they'd make it.

"You're too tense! Let me calm you down. *Nake'ik.*"

Suki recognized the word as Mayan, and though she'd never heard it before, it felt familiar. It was like a phantom memory, one that didn't belong to her.

Nake'ik. To be calm. Still. To be peaceful.

She began to repeat it in her mind. *Nake'ik. Nake'ik. Nake'ik.* And she felt a ripple from the magic pass through her. The feelings of dread and loneliness began to fade as peace seeped into her. *Nake'ik. Nake'ik. Nake'ik.*

"Over there," Jacob said. She still couldn't see him but could imagine him pointing. "That's the one. Go into that canyon. The one with the rock bridge."

"But there's a river down there," said the pilot, more calmly now.

"True, but there are also shores. The jet can't go to the cave, but you can land near it. Slow down."

Suki could feel the tremor of the jet as the speed decreased. The wing rotors engaged, signaling a shift from jet mode to helicopter-jet mode. Or whatever they called it. She stared out the window again, seeing the same canyon, webbed with natural bridges. As they came closer, she saw trees—aspen maybe?—growing on the shadowy floor.

The canyon was freaking huge. It wasn't constructed of the red rocks of the Grand Canyon—she would have recognized them by sight—but it was amazing and looked otherworldly, as if they were landing on Mars.

Suki heard Angélica groan again. She didn't know what to do—whether she should call for Jacob's attention or let him do what was needed in the cockpit. Normally that would have made her anxiety spiral, but she still felt calm, at peace. That was very unusual for her.

Her stomach lurched from the motion of the jet tottering as it lowered. But soon they'd landed at the bottom, on a sandy shore next to the river running through the canyon. Those beautiful trees were arrayed around them, interspersed with rock and sand.

The whine of the engine began to decrease, then Jacob emerged from the cockpit and hurried over to Angélica. He started to whisper the Mayan words again, and Suki listened intently.

"Utzirisaj."

That was harder to understand, but Suki repeated it in her mind. *Utzirisaj. Utzirisaj. Utzirisaj. Nake'ik. Nake'ik. Nake'ik.*

The pilot opened the exterior door. There was no landing ladder this time. No airport terminal.

"Are we in Mexico?" Suki asked.

Jacob tilted his head slightly but didn't look at her. "Southern Utah. Come here, Socorro."

He was calling her by her real name, not her nickname.

Anger burned in her gut—he didn't deserve to use her given name—but she unclicked the seat belt and stood up. She walked down the aisle to the rear of the plane, her knees stiff. The outside air smelled fresh and wet.

When she reached the back, Suki saw that the bloodstained jacket Angélica wore had been opened. The bullet wound was closed, but the damage was on the *inside*. The information just popped into her head.

"She's dying, isn't she?" Suki asked in a low voice.

Jacob's jaw clenched. "Yes. I've used all the magic I have to keep her alive, but she's slipping away. That's why we came here. There's a stronger magic here."

Suki's brow furrowed.

"When I was in the cockpit, I felt you invoke the *kem äm*. Your family is blessed by Ix Chel." His expression was intense, probing. "She's the goddess of healing. You need to keep Angélica alive while I figure out where to take her." He turned his head and looked her in the eye. "If she dies, *you* die. Understand?"

Weird flex, but okay, Suki thought to herself. She was grateful for the calming effects of the magic or the threat would have made her tremble. Instead, she felt firm. Confident. She nodded. "The word is . . . *Utzirisaj,* right?"

Jacob's eyebrows lifted. "You overheard me?"

"Yes."

"Excellent. Put your hand here and keep repeating that word. Add your will to it. Your passion. Words help convey your intent, but it's your *will* that matters most. I'll be gone for maybe half an hour. We're close to the cave. If you try to escape, I swear by all the gods, I will hunt you down and rip you to pieces."

"Oof," Suki said, and then clucked her tongue inside her mouth. "Gotcha."

Jacob kissed Angélica's brow again, whispering more soothing words, then rose. He went to the pilot and spoke rapidly in Spanish, pointing back to where Suki had knelt to get more comfortable.

She watched as Jacob transformed into a jaguar right before her eyes and leaped out of the plane. From the window, she could see him padding off in a hurry, following the river upstream into the shade of the canyon and trees before disappearing.

Suki pressed her hand against Angélica's injured skin and began to repeat the word of healing and calm. She figured the woman needed both.

Utzirisaj. Utzirisaj. Utzirisaj. Nake'ik. Nake'ik. Nake'ik.

The pilot closed the door and secured it. "I'm going to the bathroom. Don't try to leave."

"Sir, I have no intention of getting eaten by a jaguar," Suki said.

"Just . . . stay over there."

Suki sighed and turned back to her job. She could feel the glow of the sunlight on her shoulder. When she glanced out the window again, she caught a sliver of moon in the sky, despite the sunlight, and the sight made her more . . . confident? Relieved?

Thanks to Wikipedia, Suki had learned a lot about Maya history and legend since the death game. Ix Chel, whom Jacob Calakmul had said was helping them, was the moon goddess. She was married to the sun god.

Angélica began to moan again and shifted. Suki returned her focus to her patient. Even though she'd been threatened with death, she still felt relaxed. That was very unusual for her, yet another sign of the magic's power.

Utzirisaj. Utzirisaj. Utzirisaj. Nake'ik. Nake'ik. Nake'ik.

Another word came to her mind.

Kunaj.

It was like a whisper in her thoughts. A simple word.

"Kunaj," Suki said, adding her intention to the thought. Her mind and energy.

She felt a pulse of power go down her arm, and Angélica gasped and opened her eyes.

"Whoa," Suki said, removing her hand.

"Suki?"

"Yeah. It's me. How are you feeling?"

Angélica sat up, but she instantly groaned in pain and lay back. "I was . . . shot. It hurts."

"Imagine so."

"Where's Jacob?" Angélica looked around. When she saw they were in the jet, she appeared confused.

"He'll be right back."

"Is the rest of your family here? Where are the twins?"

"Still safely in Montana, I hope," Suki said. She was pleased that her dad and brothers hadn't been captured. But she knew that dipwad Moretti would try to bring them in. She was still furious about his betrayal.

"Where are we?" Angélica asked, panting and shifting on her seat to get more comfortable.

"Utah. In a canyon. Looks like the middle of nowhere."

Angélica stiffened with surprise and then flinched. "We're in the mountains? Southern Utah?"

"Yeah. Middle of nowhere, like I said. Actually, I think 'the middle of nowhere' is on a map. This place isn't."

"We're in Aztlán," Angélica breathed out, gazing through the window.

It sounded like a reference to the lion in the Chronicles of Narnia. "Aslan?"

"No, Aztlán. That's where he brought us."

"Like I said, I'm pretty sure we're in Utah. That's what he said."

"Aztlán is the place where the Mexica came from. The people who founded modern-day Mexico."

"I have no idea what you're talking about," Suki said. "My dad is the history buff."

"I know. I'm just . . . so surprised. The location of Aztlán is one of the secrets he's always refused to tell me. His father showed him where it was. He's never been to the United States . . . well . . . not through an airport or a border crossing. But he came here once with his father." She lifted her hand to her mouth. "He must be . . . he must be very worried."

Suki gave her a knowing smile and nodded. Then she sobered. "Is my mom still alive? Please tell me the truth."

Angélica gave her a serious look. "She *is* alive, Suki, but you should know the Jaguar Prophecies are about to be fulfilled. A great plague has been unleashed. It's already happened, Suki, and it will infect the entire globe within weeks. Your family will be reunited soon. You were *all* going to be protected against the plague." She blinked and looked crestfallen. "But your father has ruined that now. He . . . Jacob is *very* angry with him."

Suki felt her heart sink. She licked her lower lip. "I'm glad about Mom."

Her mother was *alive*. And Suki would be seeing her very soon. That, at least, was something to look forward to. She wanted to hug her mom so much.

At least she'd get to do it before the end of the world.

CHAPTER THIRTY-FIVE

THE PLACE OF THE HERON

COYOTE GULCH, UTAH

December 26

Jacob was haunted by this place, and when he saw a flock of snow-white birds enjoying the cool river water, memories filled his mouth with the taste of blood. His father's blood.

Still in his jaguar form, he padded through the shallows of the murky river, thick with sandy sediment. The birds—a breed of white heron—hadn't noticed the predator yet. His magic shielded him from their senses. The birds made a gurgling sound distinctive for their breed. It was a sound his father had taught him to listen for, a hint that he was nearing the ancient site. The wide, shallow river had its own peaceful sound, but there was no peace in Jacob's heart. The past troubled him almost as much as his fear of losing her, his Malintzin.

The brown walls of the canyon had striations of red, as if weeping blood. It felt appropriate because the history of this place was shrouded in secrecy and myth and *blood*. The legends were so faded now that they seemed impossible. But Jacob knew them to be true. He'd witnessed the magic in action. It was the most powerful magic a human could master, guarded by the most terrible secret.

Some of the snowy egrets, perhaps sensing him despite the magic, suddenly took flight, gurgling as if in terror. The pristine white of their feathers had given Aztlán its name. In the ancient tongue, it meant *the place of whiteness* or *the place of the heron*. The isolated canyons hidden in the vast wilderness of southern Utah would present a formidable hike under normal circumstances. There were no roads leading through or to them. The canyon was susceptible to flash floods due to unpredictable weather conditions that were, in fact, caused by ancient runes to prevent people from coming and finding the place. A sudden storm could fill the riverbed to overflowing within minutes, drowning unwary hikers.

Around the next bend, he saw it—a primordial rock rising above the river, like the fist of a giant pushing up from the depths of the earth, flanked by green- and yellow-leaved trees. There was a cleft in the rock that hadn't been there when Jacob had come with his father.

Time and water ravaged everything.

Jacob transformed back into a man, the magic and invisibility sloughing off him. The water was barely deeper than his shins. He'd already slipped past the protective barrier of the *kem äm* that warded the sacred place, so he immediately went to work.

This particular outcropping of stone was wreathed in olive trees, wild and untamed ones that had been producing their fruit for thousands of years. Even though it was December, he knew there would be fruit. This place, Aztlán, existed within a special nexus of space and time. He was convinced there were other places in the world like it— places where time stood still among the olive trees. Where time could even be *reversed*.

The olive trees were special . . . and so was the stone.

Jacob reverently approached the place where his father had brought him and rehearsed the ritual that would enable him to tap into the special power of the place. Even in modern history, the legend of the undying mountain persisted. The Spanish had gone to Florida looking for the fabled fountain of youth after they'd heard the Aztec legend, but it was not in Florida. It was *here*. And it wasn't a fountain.

Jacob reached the lower trees and began to gather fruit from them, using his shirt to contain them. Olives had been a mainstay in civilization for millennia for their many properties. They could be eaten. Pressed for oil. They also had healing properties through their natural antioxidants and vitamin E. But these olives were even more special and sacred.

After gathering the fruit, Jacob went to the base of the huge fist-shaped boulder. He climbed toward the malformed boulder, careful not to spill the olives, to a level spot on the right side that was higher than the treetops, about a third of the way down. He took his time, carefully preparing himself for the ritual his father had taught him.

Time meant nothing in this place. He would leave Aztlán at the moment of entering it, no time having passed whatsoever.

He emptied the olives into a depression on the stone and then took a nearby chunk of rock and began grinding them into an oily paste, each stab with the pestle reminding him of watching his father do this same thing. The smell of the olives made him shudder.

Jacob had been eighteen years old when he was first brought to this place. By then, he'd already been trained in the ways of the jaguar priests and knew a hundred ways to kill a man. His father had done this very thing, the grinding of the olives, and he'd explained the great secret to him—a person could be made young again, his body age reversing even back to infancy if he climbed all the way to the top of the peak. The ancient Maya and Aztec sorcerers would fly to the Place of the Heron when they were old. They would grind the olives into salve and cover their bodies with it. Then they'd draw the sacred glyphs of youth and vitality onto their flesh with the *kem äm*. And they'd begin to climb the boulder. Going too far was risky because babies were inherently helpless. Some had done it, though, trusting the magical herons to feed them before they toddled out of the mountains as little beings with tremendous wisdom. Theoretically, the keeper of the secret could live indefinitely. Could witness the passage of time on an unimaginable scale. Being a sorcerer was more powerful than being a king, who had a limited lifespan, the opportunity of creating a single dynasty.

But the gods did not want mortals sharing in their gift or their powers. Kukulkán demanded obedience and sacrifice. He demanded *submission*.

Jacob slathered some of the oily paste on his fingertips and smelled it. It was the right consistency. This mountain would reverse the damage Angélica had suffered. Make them both younger again. Jacob had already visited it once and brought himself back to his prime. He could do the same for her.

But there was always a risk. Knowledge like this was heady. It was *powerful*. If he showed her what could be done, there was the chance she would betray him. All of the jaguar priests could transform into animals and wield great power. There were legends of Aztlán and the mountain that could reverse someone's age. But the knowledge of where the mountain was located had remained a secret. Only one was the master of this secret. No one dared murder Jacob because the knowledge of Aztlán's location would then be lost.

Jacob's father had promised to share that secret with him, out of all his brothers. Then at last, at long last, his father had transformed them both into great birds, and they'd flown to Aztlán together. He'd shared the secret knowledge of the ceremony. In that moment, his father had fallen into a trance. It was as if the gods touched him and shared something with him. When his eyes had cleared, he'd grabbed his obsidian dagger and tried to plunge it into Jacob's heart. They'd fought. It was a death struggle between two equals.

In the end, Jacob's father's blood had stained the rock. And slaked his thirst. He'd never told anyone about that moment. People had assumed that the cost of the secret was his father's life.

He shuddered. He'd thought the world of his father. He'd wanted to be like him, and indeed, the two looked so much alike that they'd sometimes been mistaken for each other.

Everything had changed after Jacob returned to Cozumel following his father's death. He was given deference by all. All that his father had owned was given to him, without question. He'd inherited staggering wealth. Resources deep within the most powerful governments. But no amount of wealth could make him forget that moment on the mountain. Despite all he owned and had become, he still didn't know what his father had seen.

Jacob had essentially *become* his father. And he wondered if that secret knowledge would someday come to him too.

———

"Is this Aztlán?" Angélica murmured as he carried her through the river to the bend. When he'd returned to the Pegasus for her, he'd been shocked to see Suki's power had revived her. She'd been unconscious since passing out, bleeding internally.

Suki was strong in the magic. She knew too much. So did the pilot. They would both have to die. It would be a pity to lose Suki.

"Yes," Jacob said. The strain of carrying her in his arms would have exhausted him, but the magic and his devotion sustained him. Time had warped again since he'd passed the barrier. He'd been gone for hours, but only thirty minutes would have passed for those on the line.

"You've been here before," she said. "With your father."

"Long ago."

Carrying her reminded him again of the love story of Popocatépetl and Iztaccíhuatl. The warrior had promised her marriage, but she'd died of grief after being told he was killed during the war. He'd carried her far away, and her dead body had become a mountain.

That was the legend. In reality, Popocatépetl had tried finding Aztlán. He'd failed.

When they reached the bend in the river, he saw the place where he'd ground the olives, but he struggled to carry her up to it. His face muscles tightened, and he moved cautiously, wincing each time she gasped in pain at her internal injuries.

By the time he reached the top, he was dripping with sweat. He needed to rest, so he set her down on the brown, red-flecked stone. Angélica looked around, searching the unfamiliar terrain. She was so pale but still so beautiful.

"This place . . . this place is a great secret," he told her, gazing into her eyes. "By showing it to you, by telling you what will happen, I violate an oath I made to keep it secret. My father brought me here to kill me."

Her eyes widened with shock.

Jacob pressed his lips tightly, struggling with emotion. "Instead, I killed him. Right over there," he said, gesturing to the crook in the stone. "I cannot live without you, Angélica. My feelings . . . my feelings are powerful. I'd intended for you to be my queen." He shook his head. "But no longer."

Her eyebrows flared. "I'm dying, Jacob. The magic couldn't save me."

He sighed. "You will not die. But in sharing this place with you, I'm making you my *equal*. The plague has begun. The prophecy will be fulfilled. Kukulkán's prophecy was about *me* . . . and now it is about *you*."

He dipped his finger in the salve he'd made with the crushed olives. "The founders of Aztlán knew of this place. They were taught of it by the gods. There is a ritual. I must touch your body with this salve and draw the sacred symbols with the *kem äm*. I will show you how. Then we will climb that boulder, and youth and vigor will be restored to us."

A smile brightened her face. "This is Aztlán," she murmured. Who wouldn't crave the gift of endless youth?

He clasped her hand. "It is. And I am not the age you believe me to be. Soon, neither will you be." He smeared some of the salve across her forehead and then down her nose.

Her shirt was already open, still bloodstained. He stroked her neck, his blood surging hot within his veins. He wanted her. He desired her. He would do *anything* to have her.

As he chanted the spell, she closed her eyes, her body swaying beneath his touch, her breath coming faster and faster. She knew the ancient tongue. She would learn the words of restoration, just as he had learned them from his father. It would allow the magic of the olives to do their work.

Magic that would make them young again when they climbed the rock hand in hand.

CHAPTER THIRTY-SIX

Tidwell Hotel

Bozeman, Montana

December 26

The twins were sitting on the queen-sized bed, watching a YouTube video of their favorite online gamers and sharing a bag of microwave popcorn. Roth glanced at his watch. It was 2 p.m. Five more hours before he'd been promised another call from Jacob Calakmul.

This was not going to end well, and it was Roth's fault. He was consumed by the same sense of helplessness he'd experienced after the death game last Christmas, when he'd been unable to prevent Jane Louise's death. He sat on the small, stiff couch that was part of the suite's decor, then rose and began pacing.

The cell phone began to vibrate in his pocket. He quickly fished it out, surprised to see Illari's name on the screen.

"Hey," he said, answering the call.

"Did you get the translation images I texted you?" she asked. "You didn't respond."

"I've been a little busy," he replied, thinking about everything they'd gone through over the last twenty-four hours. "But yeah. I got them. And you saw the donation come through, right?"

"Yes, it did. Thank you. But here's the thing . . ." She fell silent for a moment and then blurted, "Something's not adding up."

Roth scratched the back of his neck, then motioned for the boys to turn the volume of the TV down so he could hear better. "What's not adding up?"

"The Dresden Codex is mostly a calendar. An almanac for planting crops and predicting eclipses and the rising and setting of planets. Venus, for example, was a harbinger of war. Some believed the planet *was* Kukulkán. But the prophecy you sent me was written by Kukulkán. You know, the god they built Chichén Itzá for."

"Yeah, I know," Roth said. "Chichén Itzá was seen as a power center for the ancient Maya."

"Yeah, well the jaguar priests overthrew Chichén Itzá. Why would Kukulkán have left a prophecy about his enemies rising to power? That doesn't add up. The most famous prophecy about him was that *he* would return." Roth knew what she meant. He'd been intrigued by his research into the bearded god who'd given the Maya science, astronomy, art, and fire. In the prophecy of Chilam Balam of Chumayel, Kukulkán had written that he would come to them the second time. He was the word of god. That's why the Maya thought the Spaniards were the actual gods returning. "But Kukulkán didn't come back," Roth said. "So is this translation about the jaguar priests returning or Kukulkán?"

A knock sounded on the door, and then the lock clicked. Roth flinched with dread until he saw Monica enter, holding her cell phone to her ear. Her hair was wet from a shower, and she had on a change of clothes.

"That's good to hear," she said into the phone. "I agree, get a warrant first, and then pick her up. I think it would be better to have that pinned down. Thanks, Arnold. Bye."

"I've got to go," Roth said to Illari. "What you said doesn't make sense to me either, but a lot of this stuff doesn't make sense. There are many different interpretations of Kukulkán, right? The whole obsidian mirror thing where he's tricked into betraying his vows." In the legends, two brothers were fierce rivals. Kukulkán was the creator, and his brother Huracán was the destroyer. The destroyer had tricked his brother with a magical obsidian mirror. These ancient legends, of Kukulkán being tempted and thwarted by Huracán, had reminded Roth of the Bible stories of the temptations of Christ. The rivalry between the two gods was portrayed as an eternal one. "Which story is right? I don't know. Give it some more thought and then let's talk again. Okay?"

"I will. This is really an amazing find. I'll text you later."

"Great. Bye."

Monica shut the door behind her, but Roth had a quick glimpse out into the hall. No one was out there. No one had been out there earlier, either. He'd asked about it, and she'd assured him that agents were at the hotel, and the corridor was being monitored through surveillance cameras. Leaving a guard outside would only tip the hat to which room the Roths were in.

"Did you get any rest?" Roth asked her.

Monica shook her head. "No time for that. We need to get your daughter back. The first twenty-four hours of an abduction is critical. Who was that on the phone?"

"The researcher in LA. She had some thoughts about the prophecy. This case isn't going to be like any you've had before," Roth said.

Monica shook her head with sympathy. "You're right, it's not, and I'm not going to pretend otherwise. But the basic pattern holds true. What we learn now will be crucial for finding your daughter."

Roth studied her. "Who were you talking to just now?"

Monica walked over to the couch he'd been sitting on and sat down. She had a cup of Starbucks in her left hand and sipped from it. Roth looked at it with envy.

Lucas poked his head out the bedroom door. "Any word about Suki?" he asked.

Monica shook her head. "Not yet, but we'll get her back."

"You guys watching MrBeast?" Roth asked the boys. He could recognize the gamer's voice.

"Yeah," Brillante chimed in.

Lucas frowned, visibly worried, sauntered back to the bed, and flopped onto it. Normally the boys were animated as they watched the show, but they were killing time. They were as worried about the next call from Calakmul as he was.

Monica set her coffee cup down. "Interesting coincidence. I just got off the phone with the LA field office. The woman who did your translation . . . what do you know about her?"

"Just that she's a college student in LA. I found her on the dark web, so I imagine she might have a record."

"Not a criminal one," Monica said with a smirk. "She's part of an organization that's on our watch list. They mostly do nonviolent protesting. They show up in Sacramento now and then demanding that California be returned to the Mexican government."

Roth chuckled. "Maybe the Manifest Destiny doctrine was a mistake, and we should redo the whole thing?"

Monica gave him a smile. "A little late for that. California is a $3.4 trillion economy. So no, I don't think they'll be giving the land back. The organization she's part of is called the Mexica. Does that sound familiar?"

He nodded slowly. "The Mexica were the original founders of Mexico. But they were originally from farther north, somewhere in the United States territory. The whole legend of the eagle and the snake and the cactus. The founding of the Aztec empire in Tenochtitlán, which is now Mexico City."

"You know your history, Professor," she said, impressed.

"Let's just say I've been studying it a lot over the last year."

"Have you read *Buried Mirror* by Carlos Fuentes?" she asked.

"I have," Roth answered. The book was a history of Spanish culture and how it had spread throughout the world.

"I read it in college as an undergrad," she continued. "What you've told me about Calakmul, his intention to conquer Western civilization . . . well, it kind of reminded me of that book. There's a lot of history going on here, Jonathon."

"You could say it's *all* about history," he agreed.

"It's important to understand how a criminal thinks in order to predict their next move. Calakmul obviously has resources inside our government. We haven't gotten much from Agent Garcia so far, but his interrogation is underway. He had a burner phone with him programmed with some phone numbers in Mexico. Cozumel, specifically. It's helped convince Carter that we should cooperate with you instead of prosecute you."

Roth sighed in relief. "I need help getting my daughter back. Have you found Moretti yet?"

"No. His tracks end when the jet took off. We're still trying to uncover details on his family and where they went in Mexico."

"I'll bet you a hundred bucks they're in Cozumel," Roth muttered.

Monica nodded. "We've also asked the LA field office to interview Illari Chaska and confirm your story. We'll search her e-mails and make sure that your version squares out. Fair enough?"

"I promised her she wouldn't get dragged into trouble," Roth said. He'd promised her that he would protect her name, her involvement. But he'd been unable to protect his own family.

"She's not in any trouble. We're confirming your alibi. We could also keep an eye on her and provide protection. Our main target is

Calakmul. The director has been in communication with the CIA. We're working on getting satellites over Calakmul's resort in Cozumel. If he lands there with her, we can send in a team—"

"He won't go there," Roth said, shaking his head.

Monica frowned. "You think he'll take her to the jungle in the Yucatán?"

Roth nodded firmly and stopped pacing. He put his hands on his hips. "He's smart. His resort is trackable. It's on Google Maps. The Jaguar Temple is in the middle of the jungle, though, and satellites would be totally useless there."

"That peninsula is *huge*," Monica said. "Hundreds of square miles of dense jungle. You were flown in there on a Pegasus jet, as you said, and saw no lights marking cities. And with the transponder out, we can't follow the jet by radar."

"The only light beneath us was when he lit up the temple with his magic," Roth explained. "But I don't know if the satellites would be able to pick that up. It's not the same kind of light you'd get from a candle or a bulb."

"Satellites are all we have right now. We're working with the State Department to get authorization from Mexico to fly reconnaissance planes over their airspace, but that will take days to arrange. You said your phones were confiscated, so there's no data. I'm assuming there was no record of your trip when you downloaded your info from the cloud."

"Nothing," Roth said. "Everything had been wiped. Contacts. Photos. Everything."

Monica looked defeated. "That means he has friends in Cupertino as well."

Roth understood the reference to the biggest and richest tech company in the world. "His assistant went to Stanford. Did you find anything about her?"

"Just her immigration records. She came to the US on a visa sponsored by the Calakmul family and returned after graduating. She was offered a job at Google but turned it down. No criminal record."

"So you don't know about her family?"

"We've got the State Department working on it, but everyone is still on holiday right now."

A memory flickered in Roth's mind. He snapped his fingers.

"What?" Monica asked.

"Archaeologists have been mapping the jungles of Mexico," he said, his stomach abuzz with excitement. "They've been using the evolving technology of LiDAR to map what's *under* the jungle."

"How's that even possible?" she asked, wrinkling her nose.

"They mount lasers in old airplanes and fly over the jungle. The lasers are attached to servers that track where the light pulses hit. Even though there are a lot of leaves, some of the pulses will still hit the ground and reflect back. They use big server farms to scrub the noise out of the data—the trees, for example—and reveal the changes in topography."

"Topography?"

Roth nodded, more animated. "A topographical map shows changes in elevation. So if the jungle is mostly flat and then there's a pyramid-shaped hill in the middle of an area, that reveals the possibility of a ruin. These researchers have mostly focused on scanning the jungles of Guatemala."

She gave him a confused look. "But what does this have to do with Calakmul?"

"This LiDAR usage in Mesoamerica is very new, but it's already been used to uncover tens of thousands of ruins no one knew about, just in Guatemala. I'm sure that *same* technology could be used to find the Jaguar Temple in Mexico. I watched an episode on the Discovery Channel about this archaeologist who'd used it to find the snake temple, or something like that. I think he was affiliated with UC San Diego."

Monica reached for her coffee cup and took a sip. "Do you want a job working for the FBI, Jonathon? That's an excellent idea. If we get ahold of that tech, we can narrow down our search. I'll have our research team get to work on finding that archaeologist."

Roth nodded, feeling grateful that he'd contributed something. He hated feeling so helpless. Maybe he should have gone to the FBI sooner, but Jacob's threat had frightened him, and he'd been fully aware no one would believe him.

His mind shot to Suki. To the events of last night. If only she'd stayed home instead of going to Brice's house . . .

"Do you think there's a chance, Jonathon, that Calakmul isn't fleeing the country at all? He's clearly a very dangerous man. They finally got the fires out at the airport. He did a lot of damage."

"The explosion?"

"It wasn't just that. He killed several agents. One was electrocuted to death."

"What about the security cameras?" Roth asked.

"He's not on them," she said, shrugging. "But they only showed certain corridors and exits. How do you catch a ghost?" She set down the coffee cup and then rose and started pacing like he'd been doing off and on. "The more we can get into his head, the better chance we'll have of finding Suki and getting her back. We saw his jet fly overhead. But was he even on it?"

"I could hear the engines through the speaker," Roth said. "He was on board. He's a cunning man . . . usually twelve steps ahead. I think I sort of fascinated him because we escaped the resort."

"Because of Beasley's daughter. The little girl who warned you."

He saw that look in Jane Louise's eyes as if it had been only yesterday. Betrayal. He'd wanted so badly to save her, to whisk her to safety, but—

"Jonathon."

Wrestling with his emotions, he glanced at Monica and saw only sympathy.

"In the FBI, we have training on creating profiles for criminals. Even drug lords are predictable in certain ways. But Calakmul doesn't fit into any of the patterns we have. He has powers we don't understand, and frankly, most in the bureau would suggest we're delusional for believing he can do what we know he can." She stepped forward. "You know him the best, Jonathon. If we're going to save your daughter, we need your help understanding this guy's next move. You think he's going back to the ruins. But what if he isn't? You've played chess against the man. Think."

Roth licked his lower lip. He hadn't been able to *stop* thinking. Or worrying. As an author, he had the ability to hold in his mind the traits and personalities of all his characters. He could put himself into another point of view to decide what this or that character would do next in the story. He'd always liked writing his villains, so it wasn't much of a stretch to put himself in the head of one. And yet . . . this was *real*. Suki's life was on the line.

Jacob Calakmul would not risk getting captured. In fact, he'd used devastating force to escape the airport at Bozeman Yellowstone International, leaving wreckage and bodies in his wake. That wasn't his usual method, though—lurking in the shadows, not leaving a trace. Was it a sign of his overconfidence or of his fear of losing all that he'd done to fulfill the Jaguar Prophecies?

Jacob would not have left without forming a plan to recapture Roth and the boys. He wanted revenge. He wanted to *prove* that he was smarter.

Roth pulled the burner phone from his pocket and looked at the last text from Suki's phone.

She will call you at 7pm. Be ready.

Why would Calakmul make them wait so long to hear from her? Why not put her on the phone sooner?

The insight came as a flash in his mind. It was a delaying tactic. Calakmul was stalling. He wanted Roth and the boys to feel they were safe for a while.

Because he was coming after them one more time.

CHAPTER THIRTY-SEVEN

TIDWELL HOTEL

BOZEMAN, MONTANA

December 26

It happened at 4:27 p.m.

The lock of the hotel room door beeped, and Will Moretti came inside, pistol raised. He quickly scanned the room, looking for another target, and then settled the barrel right at Roth's chest.

"Are you really going to shoot me?" Roth asked his friend thickly.

The noise from the YouTube gamer channel could be heard from the other room, the door ajar but not fully open. Roth sat at the desk, leaning back in the squeaky office chair. He looked his friend in the eye.

Moretti lowered the pistol slightly, then used his foot to push the door to the hallway closed until it clicked. "Where's Agent Sanchez?"

"Getting Chick-fil-A," Roth answered. He grunted and shook his head. "But you already knew that."

"The boys in there?" Moretti asked, glancing at the bedroom door.

Roth nodded. "How long have you been working for Calakmul?"

Moretti was a fit man. He'd always been healthy, beefy, and strong. He'd washed out of SEAL school in Coronado and joined the military police in the navy to finish his years of service. He'd joined the police department in Utah after leaving the navy, and he'd been with them for his career, working his way up to a violent crime, antidrug task force. When had Calakmul entered the scene? Had he been involved all along?

"As much as I'd enjoy catching up, Roth, we really need to get going."

"And where are we going?" Roth asked.

"I've got a van parked out the side door. Let's talk on the way. Tell the boys to come out here."

"Did you know Westfall was going to be killed?" Roth watched his old friend for a reaction and was gratified by his immediate flinch. It shouldn't have mattered, but it did.

"No." He shook his head and grimaced. "I didn't, Roth. Men like Jacob don't care about collateral damage."

"Oh, you're on first-name terms with the murderer?"

"I don't have to justify myself to you."

"You don't? We've been friends for thirty years! It wasn't Beasley who set us up for the death game. It was *you*."

"And you *won*," Moretti said, jutting out his chin. "I thought you might."

Roth rubbed his forehead in disbelief. "We almost died down there."

"But you didn't. You made it. There's a whole new world coming, Roth. When the cartels get here, when they get control . . . I tell you . . . some pretty crazy crap is going to go down. Like nothing you can imagine. Anarchy, chaos. *Millions* are going to die. Tens of millions. The death games are only part of it. And you were going to survive, you were going to make it, until you *screwed* yourself and your family." He shook his head, his lips quivering with anger. "You pissed him off, Roth. And now I have to bring you to him."

Roth nodded in understanding. He wiped his eyes and sighed. "Your family is already in Mexico. He's got you by the cojones."

Moretti glared. "Bring the boys. We're leaving. Now."

It hurt to be right. It hurt so bad. As Roth rose from the chair, Moretti lifted the pistol again, aiming at Roth's chest.

"Dude, if you're going to shoot me, just get it over with," Roth said. "I'd rather die in Bozeman than on an altar in a temple in Mexico."

Moretti looked conflicted. Good. Roth was glad for that. Moretti lowered the gun again.

Roth walked slowly to the bedroom door. He paused. "I should bring my burner phone, right? Is Calakmul still going to call me at seven?"

Moretti shook his head. "That was just a diversion. Let's go."

"Fine," Roth said. He poked his head into the empty room. The bed was rumpled. The TV blaring. His boys were safely up on the third floor with Monica, watching and listening to everything from a security camera grabbed from Walmart.

Roth sighed. "Boys, grab your shoes. We need to go."

As soon as he said the words, he ducked into the room, shut the door behind him, and flicked the lock, but it stuck. He backed away quickly and ran toward the bathroom. An FBI agent waited there, gun drawn, beckoning for Roth to come to safety.

"Roth!" Moretti yelled.

Roth clenched his eyes shut as he heard, over the noise of the TV, the electrical discharge of a Taser. Moretti groaned in pain.

Roth's job had been to keep the other man talking as much as he could, to reveal as much as possible. But Moretti was a law enforcement specialist, and it wasn't surprising he hadn't been distracted from his goal of abducting the family for very long.

Behind the door, he heard more commotion as other FBI agents came inside. The agent in the bathroom with Roth nodded. His radio crackled from the signal.

"Got him. He won't be able to stand."

Two taps on the door. "Subject secured!" shouted a man's voice on the other side.

Roth breathed in relief. The agent went ahead, handgun drawn, and unlocked the door.

Agent Carter stood in the opening, a smug little smile on his mouth. "Good call, Mr. Roth. Good call."

Behind him, Roth could see Moretti on the ground, convulsing in pain, his arms twisted behind his back and secured with handcuffs. Two agents were kneeling on him. The pistol was gone.

Roth followed the Taser cable to the far corner of the hotel room, where Lund stood with the Taser in his grip.

"Nice shot, Steve," Carter said, giving him a nod.

"My pleasure," Lund said. He'd been concealed behind the couch, ready to fire the Taser. Roth had pleaded with him not to miss.

Moretti was still groaning in pain from the tase. He had blood on his lips.

"He okay?" Roth asked.

"Bit his tongue," Lund said.

Carter pulled out his phone and called. "Sanchez, how are the twins?" He listened and then nodded. "Good. We're heading to DC tonight."

"Wait a minute, I thought we were going to Salt Lake?" Roth objected.

"After everything that's happened, the director wants the whole family at headquarters. Not only will it be safer, but we'll have more resources to help with the situation. There's a military plane waiting at the airport to take us."

Roth felt a wave of sadness as he looked down at his friend. No, not his friend anymore, but the man who'd been his friend for so many years. "Are we bringing him?"

"Of course, and the two accomplices who were helping him," Carter said. "One to drive the van. Another to watch the corridor.

They're both junior officers, but they were loyal to the man, not the badge. Have you been to DC before, Mr. Roth?"

Roth shook his head. "Been to New York a couple of times."

Carter dropped to a knee near Moretti's head. "Your ears might still be ringing, Officer Moretti, but you have the right to remain silent. If you can even talk. Anything you say can be used against you. You know the drill. You're coming with us, along with your two buddies." Carter rose and glanced at Lund. "I want you to come too, Steve."

"Been a while," Lund answered and nodded. "Can we stop by the hospital on the way to the airport? I'd like to check on my guy."

"The army kid?" Carter asked.

Lund nodded.

"Make it quick. The director is breathing down my neck. We need to be in the air soon. No excuses."

"Part of the job," Lund said, unimpressed. "That's why I retired."

The hospital equipment beeped and chirped all around them, peppered with intercom announcements from the hospital staff. Roth, the boys, Monica, and Lund were huddled in a post-op recovery room where Jordan lay on a hospital bed, wearing a thin hospital gown, with tubes jammed into his arms and an oxygen line at his nose.

The boys were regaling him with the adventures they'd been on since the helicopter had airlifted him away. Jordan looked groggy from the anesthesia, but he listened intently, staring at the twins with the affection of an older brother.

"No way!" he said. "That's nuts!"

"Yeah, and then Mr. Lund tased him in the butt!"

Jordan lifted his eyebrows and shot Lund a humorous glance.

Lund showed no emotion at all. Just gave a little shrug.

"He had a tactical vest on," Monica said. "Didn't want to risk the probe not getting through it."

"You're right, a Taser can't get through Kevlar," Jordan said. "I know. But you can still take someone down with good placement, preferably just above or below the belt. Hitting him in the butt? That was personal."

Monica glanced at Lund, but the man was a sphinx. Still, Roth agreed with Jordan. It *was* personal. Lund had turned Suki over to Moretti, believing she was safe. It had been a lie. That made it personal.

"Thanks for coming to see me," Jordan said. His eyes darted to Monica, and the corners of his lips crept up. "Were you worried about me?"

"He likes her," Lucas whispered, jabbing Brillante in the ribs.

"That's the anesthesia talking, I think," Monica said. Still, a slight blush rose in her cheeks. "But we were *all* worried about you. Glad you're okay, soldier."

"I'm always okay," Jordan said in a dreamy voice. "I feel great. I could do a hundred push-ups right now."

"You were shot in the shoulder," Monica reminded him.

"I could do one-arm push-ups," he said with a grin.

"Bet you he could," Lucas said.

"Bruh," Brillante said. "He's dope."

Lund shook his head. "We need to get to the airport, Jordan."

"Can I come too?" Jordan asked.

Monica smoothed his hair with her fingertips, something that instantly brightened his expression. "Not this time, soldier. Get better." She glanced at her phone and then at Roth. *We gotta go,* she mouthed.

Roth reached down and gripped Jordan's arm. "Thanks for keeping us safe, bud."

"I got the wolf guy," Jordan said. "I hope no one forgets that part."

Roth squeezed. "You got him."

But they hadn't gotten Jacob Calakmul. Where was he now? Where was Suki?

An international manhunt was underway, but it didn't seem like enough. Nothing would until she was safe and with them.

"Let's get back to the SUV," Monica said. She glanced at her watch. "We gotta be there before seven in case he calls your phone."

"Get well," Lund said curtly and then parted the privacy curtain and held it for them.

"Fist bumps, little dudes," Jordan said, closing his hand into a fist. He fist-bumped with the brothers and then with Roth.

Monica started to leave, but Jordan called out to her, and she lingered at the curtain, looking at him.

"Keep them safe," Jordan said seriously, "until I get back."

"I will, soldier," she said, nodding to him.

They were flying to FBI headquarters, the J. Edgar Hoover Building, in Washington, DC. The whole federal government was involved in the abduction case. Satellites were hunting for the Pegasus jet, and Navy SEALs could be deployed at a moment's notice to try to helicopter in and rescue his daughter.

But Roth was worried when he left the post-op room. Despite the assurances he'd had from the FBI, he worried that all the vast resources and professional skills they had at their disposal wouldn't be enough. He would never see his daughter again unless Calakmul was stopped.

But how do you stop a man who'd been fated to win before he was even born?

Another thought slammed into him, this one hitting so hard it jolted him. Illari had said something was off about the prophecy. According to her, it was unclear whether it spoke of the return of the jaguar priests or of Kukulkán.

What if they'd all misinterpreted it?

What if Calakmul was wrong?

CHAPTER THIRTY-EIGHT

LUXURY RESORT, SIAN KA'AN

MAYA RIVIERA

December 26

The Calakmul family owned many resorts in the Maya Riviera, the Caribbean, and other oceanfront locales. They were owned and managed under multiple shell companies, some with ties to Russian oligarchs, others to cartel bosses, and one to a famous American TV personality who had no idea that his golf course was being used to traffic wealthy families into the death games.

The Pegasus jet's engines began to ease after it landed on the helipad at Sian Ka'an. Jacob stared out the window, seeing the golf course near the beach, the luxury hotel, and the swimming pool area with dozens of men and women enjoying drinks, many still wearing their skimpy swimwear at the end of the day. The sun had gone down, but the party was just getting going.

The pilot looked haggard as he emerged from the cockpit. He'd been flying longer than was safe, but thanks to the large supply of *xocolatl* they'd brought, he'd been able to focus for long enough to get them to their destination, the Maya Riviera in the Yucatán Peninsula.

"I need some sleep, *jefe*," the pilot said wearily.

"You've done well," Jacob said, rising from his seat. He glanced at Suki sitting in the back of the jet, gazing out the window. "Get some rest." He was tired of being in the jet. But he was no longer fatigued. He felt ten years younger. He *looked* ten years younger.

Angélica sat in the seat across from his, legs crossed, gazing out the window. She was perfectly healed and also at the prime of life, her appearance reminiscent of the photo he'd seen of her when she'd just started college at Stanford. Their bodies had both changed, altered by the strange magic thriving in Aztlán. But their minds, their experiences, remained the same. He felt his hunger for her stir again. Their tryst in the canyon was a memory he would never forget.

"I may get a drink first, if that's okay," said the pilot. "I need a margarita. I won't drink too much. I'll be ready to fly again in the morning."

Jacob gave the man a convivial smile and gripped his shoulder. "You've earned a vacation, Berto. Stay here for a few days. The resort will provide everything you need." He squeezed the pilot's shoulder. "You've served my family for a long time, and I appreciate it. You deserve some rest."

The pilot grinned with pleasure. "Thank you, *jefe*. After the end times, I'd like a place in Florida. It's very nice in Miami. I don't like the cold."

Jacob pursed his lips and gave him an encouraging nod. "You'll get first pick, Berto. In the Jaguar order, there are many resorts. Many mansions. All of my friends will get one."

The pilot pulled on the cabin door handle and released the lock. With his finger, Jacob quickly traced a glyph on the pilot's back.

The pilot looked back at him in confusion. "I already received protection against the plague, *jefe*."

"I know. This was a blessing. It will give you vigor and strength. Enjoy the resort."

The pilot rubbed his breastbone. Some of the resort crew had gathered outside, and two had dragged a ladder over to the exit. When they saw Jacob standing in the hatch, the concierge started in recognition, clearly stunned to see the master without having received warning. Jacob hadn't risked sending any direct messages for fear of interception by US authorities.

"*El jefe!*" he said, then bowed in reverence.

"See that my friend Berto is given everything he needs or desires," Jacob told the concierge, as the pilot made his way down the steps.

"How long will you be staying with us?" the man asked.

"We'll see," Jacob answered enigmatically. It would not be wise to stay in one place for very long, but he didn't need much time. The disease released on the cruise ships would spread quickly throughout the world. There hadn't been a global pandemic since 1918, when Jacob's grandfather had unleashed a curse on a trip to Spain to try to overthrow the governments of Europe during World War I. That disease had killed millions before the countries had adopted practices to curb the spread. It had been a test to see how society would react to such a devastating illness. A trial run for the end of the Maya calendar and the fulfillment of the Jaguar Prophecies.

This time, with modern travel, it would spread much faster.

"Call Victor," Jacob told Angélica. "Tell him to shut down Villa Sara and move the treasures to the ruins in the jungle. We cannot go back to Cozumel for a while."

"Are we going to stay here for a few days?" she asked. "I was thinking we'd go back to the Jaguar Temple. The game ended. The Barruses won."

"Tell Victor to send the helicopter to get us. This jet is too conspicuous now. We'll fly to Chetumal and then take the Land Rover to the temple. I imagine several spy satellites have been repositioned, but the jungle will hide us."

Jacob's gaze shifted to Suki, who sat in the last row, watching him with her usual enigmatic expression.

"We're leaving soon," he told her.

Suki pushed her glasses up. "You just killed your pilot."

"You saw the glyph?" Jacob asked, impressed. "And you recognized it?" She hadn't studied Mayan. How had she recognized the rune that would give the pilot a premature heart attack?

Suki stared at him. "Are you going to kill me too?"

She asked the question calmly, but her hands trembled in her lap.

"That depends on how useful you are to me, Socorro. Have you been practicing with the *kem äm* as I told you?"

Suki fidgeted. "A little."

"It is powerful magic," Jacob told her. "In the past, more people knew the secrets of the canyon. Of Aztlán and the sorcerers who lived among the ancient Maya. But now that knowledge is carefully guarded. I am the keeper of the great secret. What you have seen makes you a threat to me." He gave her a pointed look. "And if you want your little beating heart to remain inside those fragile chest bones, then you'd best remember to keep what you know a secret too."

He let the threat linger in the air for a few moments. Suki swallowed and nodded.

He didn't trust her. Still . . . he might spare Suki's life if she came to serve him. Her abilities would be useful. Her loyalty could be subverted.

Angélica rose gracefully and made her way to stand beside him, drawing his covetous gaze. Leaning down, Jacob kissed Angélica's neck. The hunger inside him was growing fiercer. He wasn't sure he could wait until they reached the jungle. His body was that of a younger man now, his urges more insistent.

Angélica gave him a sidelong look, an inviting one, as she retrieved her phone and made a call.

"Victor. Yes, we're back in Mexico. Send the helicopter to us at Sian Ka'an immediately. We need to go to Chetumal right away." She paused, glancing up at Jacob again, parting her lips and licking them. It made him frantic inside. These were dangerous feelings—they robbed him of reason—and yet he couldn't find it within himself to mind very much. "You also need to shut down Villa Sara. It's been compromised. Move the treasures to the ruins. Is the Barrus family back at Cancún yet? Oh good. That's excellent."

"Ask if he's heard from Moretti," Jacob said, nuzzling her neck with his nose.

What a wonder it was to be young again, to live that stage of life with the benefit of the wisdom only gained with experience. He thought of the Spanish priests in the sixteenth century who had tortured his people for knowledge of where they'd hidden gold. If only they'd known that there was something so much more valuable than yellow metal.

The early Maya gods were just men and women. Men and women who had discovered the secret and used it. Again he wondered if there were other groves, other canyons, other places that concealed such a treasure. In the wastelands of Russia, perhaps? The oases of the Middle East? If so, no one knew, but that wasn't very surprising. Because it didn't take much imagination to realize that perpetual youth was worth killing for.

"Has Moretti called yet?" she asked.

Jacob could hear the voice on the other side— *"No."*

It was eight o'clock in Montana. If Moretti hadn't called to report his success, then he'd clearly failed. Anger began to churn inside Jacob's heart. Jonathon Roth had thwarted him *again*. He'd figured out that Moretti had been left behind, and he'd prepared for it. It was an inconvenience, an annoyance, especially since Agent Garcia had already been compromised. But Garcia wasn't Jacob's only resource in the FBI.

Was the CIA getting ready to launch a drone attack at Sian Ka'an that very moment? The possibility, however unlikely, was why Jacob had chosen the populated resort. The president of the United States would be squeamish about unleashing destruction in a friendly neighbor's territory, particularly since civilians would be killed. The drug cartels didn't even kill civilians, when avoidable, for fear of losing the tourism the foreigners provided. Jacob had no such compunction.

"Thank you, Victor. Meet us in Chetumal after you've secured the resort." She ended the call and put the phone in her pocket. Sweat had gathered in the hollow of her throat. The warm night air was pouring into the cabin.

Anger tasted like iron in Jacob's mouth as he gazed at Suki Roth.

After the end times, after hundreds of millions of people died, the world would be made anew. The jaguar priests would control the events of the day once more, just as the prophecy had foretold. *As a young jaguar in the forest. Among flocks of sheep. And none can deliver them.* Jacob himself was the fulfillment of that prophecy. After visiting Aztlán, he fit the words even better than he once did. He was younger now.

As he looked the daughter in the eye, he made a prophecy of his own. He would kill Jonathon Roth with his own hand and drink his blood as one of the ancient secret keepers of the Maya had done to an opposing war chief in Tikal.

"Are you ready to see the arena again so soon?" he asked her.

And watched with enjoyment as Suki flinched and gripped the armrests tightly.

EPILOGUE

Jaguar Temple

Calakmul Biosphere Reserve

December 27

Suki gripped the hand support on the four-wheel-drive Land Rover, the jarring bumps and dips making her joints ache and her stomach queasy. The jungle whipped past, the leaves slapping against the rooftop, the branches cracking against the sides. The constant up and down movement would have caused her dad a series of vomiting attacks.

Thinking about her father and brothers made her anxiety flare again. She missed them. She missed Brice and worried about what he was thinking. He didn't know the truth about anything, and now she wondered if he ever would.

Why had her dad insisted on going to Germany to find the stupid codex?

She repeated the Mayan words in her mind again, needing them. *Nake'ik. Nake'ik. Nake'ik.*

None of her surroundings looked familiar, but her body still remembered the humidity of the Jaguar Temple when they'd been brought there to play in the death game. And now she was going back.

If her dad had just left things alone, she'd still be in Bozeman. She'd be a normal high school teenager getting ready to graduate in a few months. She'd get to see Brice perform the role of a lifetime in *Gentleman's Guide*.

But as the vehicle jostled her violently, she realized her simplistic view of things wasn't true. She'd heard things. She'd known something bad was coming. *End times,* Calakmul had said. He seemed so sure it would happen too, and it had something to do with the Dresden Codex.

Another splash of muddy water on the windshield hindered her view. Theirs wasn't the only vehicle. One drove in front of it, two others behind. Jacob and Angélica were in the lead vehicle. Victor, the security guard from Cozumel, sat next to her, grimacing at the punishing road. They were taking no chances that she might slip away.

Others had joined them from the resort too—people she didn't recognize.

She recalled the warning Jacob had given her when they'd arrived by Pegasus jet the year before. The jungle was dangerous—howler monkeys, jaguars, snakes. There were no cities or towns in the reserve. No way to avoid getting lost and likely devoured. But Suki could summon and work the magic of the *kem äm*. Maybe she could find a way to escape with her mom. Find a way to get back to their family.

She didn't speak Spanish—well, a few words, but not much.

Suddenly, the Land Rover began to slow. Suki rubbed her chest, feeling the sweat-dampened fabric. They'd given her a change of clothes, a pair of hiking shorts and a button-down jungle shirt to wear over a tank top, but sweat still trickled down her ribs. She pushed her glasses higher up her nose.

The vehicles were all slowing as they entered the grounds of the temple. The canopy of trees still blotted out the sky, providing shade from the burning afternoon sun. They'd been driving for hours since the helicopter ride to Chetumal. She didn't know the geography well, but she thought they'd landed on the east coast of the Maya Riviera before taking the vehicles westward into the jungle. After that, all sense of direction had been obliterated by the terrain.

The vehicle she was in slowed to a stop. Victor held up his hand, his index finger pointing up in warning for her not to move.

"Stay here," he said curtly. "Do not get out. You try to run—I hurt you."

"Threat received," Suki said back. She pretended to cock a finger gun at him and shoot it.

Victor got out of the Land Rover and shut the door. He walked up to the lead vehicle, and through the smears on the windshield, Suki could see Jacob and Angélica getting out.

It was still a wonder to see how much they'd changed since leaving that canyon in southern Utah. Jacob looked like he was no more than twenty or twenty-one now. Although he hadn't appeared old before, he'd been at least ten years older. Angélica looked younger too, more like a college student than a graduate.

How was such magic even possible? Even though she'd seen and worked the *kem äm*, this felt different. It felt like more.

Jacob was clearly giving orders to Victor, pointing back to Suki's vehicle, and the big man nodded and started back. Suki noticed Jacob had his arm around Angélica. The vibe between them had altered in the canyon, or maybe before. She wasn't just his assistant anymore.

As Victor drew near, Suki saw one of the warrior dudes approach and start talking to Jacob. She recognized the man's armor and his ceremonial headdress. The sight made Suki's skin crawl. Someone in armor like that had threatened her brother's life last year.

Victor opened the door. "Out."

Suki unbuckled and then stepped into the humid air. The jungle was teeming with noise, mostly birds whistling and shrieking. The familiar pyramids and structures of the Jaguar Temple crowded around them, and servants wearing humble garb approached them with dishes of food and drinks. She'd eaten a feast at the resort the previous night, but she was hungry again after the long trip. Her stomach growled.

Victor put his hand on her shoulder and guided her away from the Land Rover. The other vehicles were discharging people too. In her mind, she pictured a squad of Navy SEALs coming to the Villa Sara resort in Cozumel and finding it devoid of life. The yacht and helicopter would be gone. The Mercedes vans driven away. There would be no clues left as to where everyone had gone.

"Where are we going?" Suki asked Victor, not enjoying the feeling of his hand pressing on her shoulder. She tried to shrug it off, but he gripped her more tightly. She winced.

"He wants you at the royal quarters," Victor said with a hint of anger in his voice. "This way."

They passed servants who offered food and *xocolatl*, but Victor waved them back with his other hand. A plumed warrior came up to them and said something to him in rapid Mayan.

Weirdly, Suki understood what he said.

"She escaped."

Victor looked at the warrior in surprise and confusion. *"How?"*

"No one knows. She disappeared this morning. The hunters have been searching for her in the jungle. There are no tracks to follow."

Victor's mouth tightened into a snarl of anger. *"Is Uacmitun telling him?"*

"Yes! He's very angry."

Victor shook his head, his grip on Suki's shoulder growing firmer. *"If she's not found, Uacmitun may get sacrificed for such a blunder."*

Could they be talking about Suki's mom? If she'd escaped, how had she managed it? A little throb of hope started in Suki's chest and began to expand.

Victor took her to the largest palace and led the way up the tight, thin stairs. She hadn't been brought here during her imprisonment last winter, so it was unfamiliar. Once inside, they were met by servants holding palm-leaf fans who were providing the man-made "air-conditioning" for the palace. What a sucky job they had.

Suki spied a monkey sneaking down the corridor, but it fled as soon as it noticed her and Victor marching that way. The palace was decorated with jade, obsidian, and gold. The stone walls had murals carved into them—scenes of the ancient Maya. But these carvings looked fresh, not ravaged by time. Suki kept gawking and staring at the costly treasures, but Victor urged her onward with a grunt.

They reached the main entry to a greater hall. It was illuminated by glowing spheres of *kem äm* magic, giving the appearance of natural daylight. Two thrones were set against the farther wall, both empty. The chamber was full of servants wearing the humble attire she'd seen before. They were all shorter than her, and some of the women were really old.

Suki started with surprise when she saw a little blond-haired girl she remembered from the previous year.

"Jane Louise!" Suki blurted, wrenching free of Victor and hurrying toward the girl, who met her and embraced her.

"Suki!" the little girl said with surprise.

She looked older now. She wore the same costumes as the other Maya servants but wasn't very tan. Although the jungle canopy blocked out most of the sun, Suki suspected she also hadn't been outside enough to be burned. Jane Louise hugged her close, squeezing hard.

Suki hugged her back tightly. Although she wasn't big on hugs, this was a special exception. "I thought you were dead," she finally said, pulling back.

Jane Louise's eyes looked haunted. "The rest of my family died," she whispered. "I miss my mee-maw."

Suki felt a lump in her throat and hugged the little girl again. Victor was speaking in Mayan to the elderly woman who seemed to be running the servants. As they conversed, Suki again had the strange sensation that she knew what they were talking about.

"*The master is going to test her. Give her one of the royal chambers. Assign her servants to meet her needs.*"

"*I obey,*" said the old woman with an aged voice.

"*The end times are near. Our days of glory are coming. The reaping has begun.*"

"*May it please the gods,*" murmured the crone.

Suki looked at Victor and the woman and felt a chill go down her back. The Calakmuls had been preparing for revenge since the conquistadors had come to the Yucatán five hundred years ago. They weren't likely to let anything hold them back. Again she thought of Brice, her brothers, and her father. As much as she sometimes thought her classmates were jerks, she didn't want all the kids to be murdered or killed by a disease.

"It's okay," Jane Louise whispered to her, patting Suki's arm. "It's okay."

Suki looked at the little girl in confusion. How was any of this okay?

"Have you seen my mom?" Suki whispered back. "Or did she escape?"

Jane Louise smiled, the fear in her eyes calming a little. "She's right over there," the girl answered, her voice barely audible, and pointed a thin finger.

Suki's brow wrinkled in confusion. Jane Louise was pointing past Victor and the old woman. Another female servant stood against the wall, holding a pitcher. She had wrinkled skin and hair the color of ashes, with thin black painted lines on her face and arms, which weren't tattoos but a decorative paint the people wore.

Suki blinked in surprise.

It *was* her mother. She could feel that knowledge tingling inside her, like the warnings she often got, except this feeling was positive. Hopeful.

But Sarina looked older than the crone talking to Victor, so Suki hadn't recognized her at all. Her heart leaped.

Mom!

She watched as her mother shook her head slowly, discreetly. A warning not to say a word.

AUTHOR'S NOTE

There is nothing so daunting as staring at a blank page. Thankfully, the pages don't stay blank for very long. After the Roths survived the death game, I knew a few things. Part of book two needed to happen in Germany where the actual Dresden Codex still resides. It also needed to happen in Bozeman, Montana, during the winter months. Life in snow country is its own experience, and I liked the Star Wars-esque switch from Tatooine to Hoth.

I've been to Germany before, so I knew something of the culture, the freeway system called the autobahn, and the delicious food. I knew there had to be a car chase and that Jacob Calakmul would come after the family in person instead of just using thugs. I continued to dive deep into the legends of the Maya and discovered nuggets that helped with this book as well as the finale.

Bozeman is a great city. I did a lot of research about it online but also decided to drive up there with my wife to case the town in person. There are subtle details you pick up when you actually visit a place in real life. I drove by the airport and the two high schools and even picked a certain neighborhood (and house!) for the Roth family to live in. The Beasley mansion is real too. Unfortunately, and I'm serious about this being a misfortune, there are presently no Chick-fil-A's in Bozeman, although there are a few in other cities. This is an injustice, which I hope will be remedied someday, so I decided to keep one of my kids' favorite fast-food places in this book in the hopes that Bozeman will get one.

I have also traveled back down to the Yucatán again and visited Calakmul and some of the other ancient ruins. Believe me when I say that it blew going to Chichén Itzá out of the water. I was able to visit the ruins, the ancient ball court, and climb several pyramids in the heart of the jungle. For my second trip, I took my father-in-law, Pete, with me, and we had an amazing time with our guide, Ezequiel from Helaman Tours. While most of the events of book two don't take place down there, you'll see more in book three.

Just as had happened while writing the first book, the plot for the third began to take shape while writing this book. My family also took a trip to the East Coast, where we visited New York City and Washington, DC. Many of our adventures and places we saw you will see in the third book.

Writing a new genre has really been a positive thing for me as an author. For fantasy books, I make so much up. Writing realistic fiction, like this series, has required a level of detail and accuracy I've never had to take on before. This is an alternate world, so to speak, and not just because I put a Chick-fil-A in Bozeman. But the impact of the era of the Maya still has repercussions today. A good book I'd recommend is *Fingerprints of the Gods* by Graham Hancock. There is so much we still have to learn about these people.

We'll learn what happens next to the Roth family in *Final Strike*, the final book of the Dresden Codex series.

ACKNOWLEDGMENTS

So many people had a hand in helping with this book. I have to give credit where credit is due and acknowledge my friend Robert who suggested the plot twist about Moretti after he read the first book. That also means I need to apologize to my friend Bill, who was the inspiration for the character, for making him out to be a bad guy. I loved that twist, and I'm so grateful to all my early readers who give their reactions to the books when they get to read the first draft.

I'm also continually grateful to my editorial team: Adrienne, Angela, Wanda, and Dan, who go through so much to find errors and inconsistencies and suggest ways to resolve them. For example, Jacob and Angélica originally went to Switzerland to pick up the Roths, and it was Wanda who calculated the flight times, time zones, and refueling stations and suggested we switch it to Nova Scotia instead, or it would have been impossible for the Pegasus jet to get to Bozeman on time. That's just one of many examples of how my team has saved me from myself once again.

I'd also like to extend thanks to several other content experts who helped me with this book. To Steve McKinty, who used to be the air traffic control supervisor at Sacramento International Airport, for his knowledge of transponders and aviation issues. My nephew, Jordan, who was the inspiration for the character Jordan Scott. He's even been tased in the butt, I'll have you know. I'm grateful to Dominik Stoltz, a librarian at the SLUB in Dresden, for taking the time to educate me about the physical characteristics of the Dresden Codex, how it was preserved, and where the blank pages are! To retired professor Victoria Bricker, one of the world's foremost experts on that codex, for her insights and making available some of her research to me, which ended up in the book. And to Casey Bertram, superintendent extraordinaire in Bozeman, for his input on high schools in that area.

I'm also very grateful to several individuals who took the time to read and review *Doomsday Match* before it came out and helped contribute to the successful launch of the book: Alessandra Torre, Melinda Leigh, and Steven Konkoly. Reading nice reviews is always a pleasure, but reading ones from your peers is electric. Many thanks!

ABOUT THE AUTHOR

Jeff Wheeler is the *Wall Street Journal* bestselling author of over thirty epic fantasy novels. *Doomsday Match* in the Dresden Codex series was the first thriller he's written since his early years as a budding author, but his many fans think his fantasy novels are thrillers in their own way. Jeff lives in the Rocky Mountains and is a husband, father of five, and devout member of his church. On trips to the jungles of Cozumel and the Yucatán Peninsula, he has explored Maya ruins and cenotes, leading him to dive even further into the history of ancient America and the Spanish conquistadors. There is more to the ball courts than meets the eye. Learn about Jeff's publishing journey in *Your First Million Words*, and visit his many worlds at www.jeff-wheeler.com.